Police Officer Barbara Babalino listened carefully as Frankie told her about going under cover.

"Let me give you a scenario," Frankie said. "What if you walk into a situation where they offer you coke? They know the man can't accept it. What are you going to do?"

"I'm not going to try it."

In a flash, so fast that she did not even see him do it, Frankie had his finger pointing at Barbara's forehead. His eyes flicked to the "coke" represented by an ashtray on the table.

"Try it!"

Barbara had gone a little hollow inside, but she reacted instinctively. She grabbed her purse and stood up, looking at Frankie.

"Hey," she said, "I came here to buy cocaine. And you're playing games. I'm leaving. You can pull the trigger if you want."

Frankie lowered the "gun."

"That's the right reaction," he said.

Another Fawcett Gold Medal Book
by Tom Philbin:

PRECINCT: SIBERIA

UNDER COVER

Tom Philbin

FAWCETT GOLD MEDAL • NEW YORK

A Fawcett Gold Medal Book
Published by Ballantine Books
Copyright © 1986 by Tom Philbin

Library of Congress Catalog Card Number: 86-90873

ISBN 0-449-12804-0

Manufactured in the United States of America

First Edition: June 1986

For Tommy, Anne and Mary

Acknowledgments

It is my feeling that the quality of a book is most intimately dependent on the quality of the research that goes into it. Here, I have been very fortunate, and I want to express my deep thanks to the following people: Jack Sturiano, PA, Suffolk County Medical Examiners Office; Frank Puello, Detective, NYPD; Frank Garrido, Detective. NYPD; John Carlton, Detective, Ret. NYPD.

CHAPTER 1

Cops in the Five Three called the Romano Avenue section of the precinct the Twilight Zone. Approximately two-and-a-half miles square, it was bounded by streets as savage as any in the country, even the world. Streets where homicide was commonplace (now 1.6 murders per week, highest in the city), unemployment rampant, a place where assault and rape and despair reigned supreme, a precinct generously deserving of its nickname, Fort Siberia, called that by cops who were sentenced rather than sent there.

But the Romano section was essentially as it had been for fifty years. On any day—but particularly on Sunday—you could walk down the street and get high on the scent of skilled Italian cooking; you could see old Italian men—and young men—clustered on corners talking because they loved to talk; you could hear the click of the old people's beloved boccie balls.

At night you could walk the streets in safety. A newspaper had even said you could drop your wallet and it would be returned to you before it hit the ground.

It was a place where girls were still shy and virginal, where kids respected their parents and grandparents, where the old ways, brought over from Italy and Sicily many years before, still thrived.

It was clean, it was safe, a great place to raise kids, a great place to live.

"You come off Third Avenue," a cop once said, "you

1

cross the street, and it's another world. I swear to Christ you expect to see Rod Serling standing there saying, 'Welcome to the Twilight Zone.' "

In the sixties, the blacks had tried to blockbust, and some found out the hard way why the section remained unchanged: It was not only, as the newspapers said in their profiles, "tradition." It was also that many of the men of La Cosa Nostra had their homes there, and none of them, though they went to church every Sunday, was Christian enough to let niggers into that world. Over a three-month period in the sixties four blacks were found dead in cellars in an adjacent precinct with their penises in their mouths. The blockbusters went off to conquer different lands.

The man walking at a leisurely pace down one of the blocks in the Romano section at around eight A.M. on Saturday, June 23, looked like he belonged. His name was Arthur Castelli. He was short, with heavy features and wavy salt-and-pepper hair. He wore a clean, pressed sports shirt and creased pants. He looked like he would be ready for the boccie courts in a few years.

Castelli was on his way to his brother John's house on Raffela Street, also in the Romano section.

Castelli was happy, and it showed. He was going to take John's kids, Anthony, six, and John Jr., seven, who were his godsons, to the Bronx Zoo, which wasn't too far away from Raffela Street.

Arthur was fifty-eight. He had never married. He had spent most of his life taking care of his mother and his two brothers, John and Mario. But Castelli was not whining. Life had blessed him. He had a thriving butcher shop, with an honest partner who would trade days off with him, and a girlfriend of long standing. He actually relished his role of eldest brother. The world had changed much since Arthur Castelli had been young, and he knew there was much wrong with it, but in his own little world he was happy.

He told himself he had never resented John's success. In fact, at the slightest provocation he would tell people: John is first vice president of the Mercantile Bank in

Manhattan. Smart. He has a CPA. "A Certified Public Accountant."

Castelli turned onto Raffela Street. John's house was another thing Arthur was proud of. John and his wife, Maria, were constantly expanding and improving it, and though it had started out as a flat, two-story affair like the others on the block, it had by now taken on a distinctive shape and was far and away the best-looking home in the area.

When he was young, Arthur worried about John: He was headstrong, brash, always in a hurry. But those qualities had worked well for him, though Arthur still had reservations about some of the things he got involved with, and some of the people.

Arthur let himself in through the gate of the small chain-link fence that surrounded the property, went up to the porch, and rang the bell. He could hear it ring inside.

No one answered. He rang again, and waited. After a minute or so he turned the front doorknob. The door opened.

"John," he called. "John?"

No answer. They had to be here, he thought. John's Corvette and Maria's station wagon were parked outside on the street. Then an icy thought gripped Arthur. Maybe they had gone to the hospital. Maybe . . .

He told himself to get hold of himself.

He walked down the short hall into the living room. It was empty, undisturbed, and so was the adjacent dining room.

He went out, continued down the hall, pushed open a bathroom door—empty—and went into the kitchen. Nothing. Just a table and chairs. There was nothing in the partially built sun room just beyond the kitchen.

He went up the stairs to the second floor. He checked the three rooms—John Jr.'s and Anthony's and the guest room. The beds were still made.

Arthur was puzzled and worried. What the heck was going on?

He went back downstairs and thought about what to

do, then went through the open hall door and downstairs to the basement.

It looked like a photograph or a painting, and for a fleeting, hoping-against-hope moment, he thought they were all asleep—John and Maria and the two boys.

And then he saw the blood and he was staggering upstairs, tears gushing from his eyes like he was five years old, and then he was outside the house, weaving down the path, and then his screams shattered the Saturday-morning quiet of Raffela Street, and beyond.

CHAPTER 2

While Arthur Castelli was making his grim discovery in the basement, Jose Delgado, a middle-aged Puerto Rican, was setting up at 174th Street for some fishing in the Harlem River, part of which flowed through Fort Siberia. The river wasn't much good for swimming anymore, unless you liked the idea of doing the breaststroke through waste from chemical plants and God knows what else, but you could still fish it. In the spring Delgado had taken good-sized striped bass and white perch from the murky waters, and now, in the summer, he was going for blues, savage fish that resembled small shark and made good eating. Delgado, who made his living in a sheet-metal factory, depended on his fishing to give him a little slack in his budget, which was very tight.

He located his beach chair close to the edge of a pier that jutted well out into the river. He baited his hook with a spearing—a small translucent green fish—and flipped the rod; the hook and line sang, and the hook plunked into the water.

Within two hours, he had two blues in his pail. Not huge—maybe three to four pounds each—but plenty of meat for himself, his wife, Camellia, and his boy, Jesus, who was now the only one of his six kids living at home.

Jose felt good, and he felt happy. At the factory he worked all week at a mindless task, and while he realized he was not the smartest man in the world, by Friday afternoon, after five days of repetitive tasks, he was

5

ready for the weekend. Indeed, the weekend sustained him. Occasional thoughts of sitting on his beach chair, waiting for a blue to hit the hook, gave him a jolt. It made his humdrum life worth living. Now, sitting on the chair with two in the pail, he could look forward to tonight and the rich smell of the blue frying in a big skillet filled with peppers and tomatoes and garlic. Who could dream that something like that could come from the Harlem River! Madre de Dios!

After another hour, he had a third blue in the pail, this one even bigger than the first two. At this rate, he'd have a freezerful of fish by evening.

It was around eleven o'clock that the thing came to the surface.

At first Delgado didn't notice it, because he was baiting a hook. Then he glanced across the water, preparatory to casting, and saw it. It raised the hair on his neck.

It was big and black and appeared to be furry, though just the top was showing, the rest being underwater. For a fleeting moment he thought it was a huge rat. But it was much too big for that.

Delgado dropped the fishing rod, walked fifteen feet up the pier, and looked at it.

He could not make out what it was, but two things were sure: It was covered with fur and there were ropes— two ropes about a foot apart—across the thing. It was definitely an animal of some sort.

He watched it for a moment. It was drifting toward shore, toward an old car that was half submerged. He watched it all the way, as it drifted toward shore, until— Madre de Dios!—almost as if it were alive—it floated through the doorless husk of the car and into it.

And there it stayed.

Delgado did not know quite what to do, but it had certainly taken the edge off fishing. He had to do something.

He packed up his gear, brought it to his car, which was parked near the pier, and stored it away. Then he drove to the first phone he could find and called the 53rd

Precinct, whose number he knew by heart. You lived in the 53rd Precinct, you knew the number by heart.

Delgado's call was transferred to a small office on the second floor of the dilapidated station house—located in Death Valley, vintage Fort Siberia—to Detective Third Grade Arnold Gertz, a mountain of a man who seemed to fill the office and who, it was said, could bench-press Rhode Island.

Last year, Arnold had become famous for his highly visible apprehension of two Hispanic drug addicts who stole goats to butcher and sell the meat from their modern store—a closet in an abandoned building. Around the station house the cops called it "The Grand Theft Goat Caper," but secretly some of them admired Arnold. His main investigatory technique had been to spend hundreds of hours waiting for the perps to return to the same pen they hit the first time. As a result of this success, Arnold was now viewed as semi-official lost-animal investigator, a "Mister Keen," said one cop, "tracer of lost Lassies." He had been able to find three dogs, two cats, and a half-grown alligator which, unfortunately, the ASPCA had confiscated from the owner.

Captain Warren G. Bledsoe, CO of the Five Three, silently encouraged Arnold—it was against his grain to vocally support or encourage anyone—to pursue lost animals. He thought of Arnold as a low-grade moron, but his animal escapades invariably found their way into the warm human-interest sections of the papers, and said stories helped keep the brass downtown from using Bledsoe's balls as a punching bag.

Delgado, who had only a slight Hispanic accent, described what he had seen.

"What do you think it is?" Arnold asked.

"Maybe," he said, "a bear?"

Arnold's brow furrowed. What would a bear be doing in the Harlem River? Maybe, he thought, it floated down from Bear Mountain. Were the rivers connected?

No. No, he wouldn't have. It was too far.

"Where is he now?" Arnold asked.

"In a car."

Maybe, Arnold thought immediately, he drove down. And then immediately cursed himself for being so stupid.

"What do you mean, a car?"

Delgado explained about it floating through the door-less opening.

"Oh," Arnold said.

Arnold thanked Delgado for calling and hung up. He thought about what to do. He had only been dealing with live animals, not dead ones.

He thought about it for a few more minutes, then called the Emergency Service Division and was told he was lucky.

"It's Saturday morning," the ESD man said. "They don't start climbing the bridges until around three. Ha-ha."

Arnold didn't think it was funny.

The ESD guy said they'd send someone.

CHAPTER 3

The old man's name was Charley Murphy, and he lived in Apartment 3-C in the left wing of the five-story gray brick building, number 2665, Bainbridge Avenue and 204th Street in the Bronx. Charley had lived there for forty-five years, much of the time with his two daughters, Cathy and Eileen, and with his wife, Marie. Cathy and Eileen had married seven and six years ago, respectively, and moved out and away. Marie had died four years earlier.

The neighborhood had changed a bit for the worse, and his daughters and relatives and friends had urged Charley to move. It was just a matter of time, they said, before it became like the 53rd Precinct, the notorious Fort Siberia, which was to the south, physically separated from the precinct Charley was in by Mosholu Parkway, which ran east and west. Charley was seventy-five and frail, a long way from the strapping young man who had stepped off the boat from County Mayo some sixty years earlier, and he would be easy prey for any of the predators who moved north.

But Charley did not want to move. It wasn't that bad, he told everyone. Oh, there was an occasional mugging, and sometimes there were burglaries, a rare homicide, but it was nowhere near like Fort Siberia.

"That Mosholu Parkway," Charley said, "is like a moat filled with alligators. They'll never really cross it."

But it wasn't logic or minimal crime statistics that

kept Charley Murphy in Apartment 3-C. It was something in his heart: He felt safe here at 2665 Bainbridge Avenue.

For forty-five years he had walked the same streets, climbed the same stairs, gone to the same church, the same stores.

He could walk his house blind; he remembered every color of paint that was applied to the walls; he knew that the crack in the girls' bedroom, which was repaired last year, would take about two years to open.

It was familiar; it was safe. It enveloped him and kept him from harm like a magical gas that nothing could penetrate. He had a history: He had never been hurt on these blocks.

But it went deeper than that. Though Charley perhaps could not have described it, the apartment and the halls and the buildings and the church and even the supermarket aisles and the subways resonated with the warm echoes of his life.

"C'mon, Charley," Marie would say to him on a warm spring day, "put the paper away and come in here. You'll catch your death of cold."

"Oh, Daddy, you're home! Do you know what happened today?"

"C'mon, Charley, let's get going. The movie starts at eight-thirty!"

"Oh, Daddy, I feel so sad leaving you today. But I love Joe. I have to go. It's not like the end of the world, right?"

"No," Charley had said. "It isn't." And then later, when Cathy was on some highway driving down south to Florida on her honeymoon, Charley Murphy had put his head on his wife's shoulder and cried like a baby. That day, when the first of his girls got married, was the end of the world.

No, Charley had thought when people asked him to leave. He would never leave. When I leave here, he told himself, I won't be walking.

And now, about the time Arnold Gertz was talking with Jose Delgado about the thing in the river, Charley Murphy was looking out a bedroom window into the broad red-painted courtyard, watching for the nigger, wondering if he would be next to be forced to leave his apartment.

Charley was smoking, and had been smoking for the last month—contrary to doctor's orders—when he first heard about what was going on.

First, the super, Mr. Wolciak, who had been at the building for twenty years, was replaced by a Puerto Rican named Gonzalez. And from that moment on things had started to change in the building.

Gonzalez let the garbage pile up in the alleys, he let the house get dirty, and no one could get any repairs done.

Charley had seen him a few times, and every time he did he was drunk. He was a short, muscular middle-aged man, and Charley got the feeling that if he tried to talk with him he would get nowhere.

A week later, Charley was returning from a local supermarket when he was surprised—shocked, really—to see that Ray O'Hara, who had been in the building at least thirty years, was moving.

"Ray, what's going on? You moving?"

"Yeah. I am."

"Why?"

"The nigger. A big nigger came around and said he'd torch the place if I didn't leave in a week."

"Did you go to the police."

"They can't do anything. They need corroboration."

"Oh."

"Mallon's leaving too."

Murphy thought of Mallon. He was a pretty big guy, though around sixty, and he had kids still living at home.

"You're sure?"

"He resisted. This black guy almost killed him right in front of his family."

Over the next few weeks, hardly a day went by when Murphy didn't see someone leaving. Longtime tenants. There was no way they were going to get a better deal than they had right here.

They knew it, too, Charley thought. He could see the expressions on their faces. They didn't want to leave.

They had been forced to. Then living in the building got worse. As each family was left, new people came in—blacks and Puerto Ricans who were loud and boisterous and stayed up till all hours of the morning.

Two months after the new super moved in, a notice was taped to the mailboxes on the first floor. It said that the new owner intended to "renovate the premises," and work was to begin in three months. Anyone wanting to move out now would be given moving expenses.

Charley checked with a lawyer he knew, and it was then that his eyes were fully opened as to what was going on.

In the first place, the new landlord had no right to put anyone out of a rent-controlled apartment.

In the second place, it sounded to the lawyer like a calculated campaign to drive tenants from the building so that they could indeed be renovated. Then they could be rerented, or perhaps turned into condominiums, at ten and fifteen times the rent—or more.

"They did the same thing in Manhattan," Murphy's lawyer friend said, "and drove a lot of people out of their homes."

Charley thought that when they came to him he would resist. He was frail, but he wasn't afraid. Or that afraid.

Then he heard about Mr. DeLoen, a man who lived in the opposite wing from him in Apartment 2-D. He was in his sixties, a construction worker all his life.

Charley heard that the big black guy had told DeLeon to be out in a week, and DeLeon had defied him.

One Friday night, while DeLeon was out, they broke into his apartment and stole things.

But DeLeon didn't scare easily. He put extra locks on the door, had a closed-circuit alarm system put in, and had sliding gates installed over the fire escape windows.

They got in by breaking through the wall of an adjacent empty apartment. They stole everything of value DeLeon had—TV, appliances, tools—and piled up all his clothing and personal things, like picture albums. They defecated and urinated on the pile.

DeLeon was enraged, and attacked the black guy, Ace, with a bat in the street outside the house.

Charley heard that Ace took the bat away from him and beat him so badly he landed in intensive care in St. Barnabas Hospital. Charley also heard that the black guy would have killed him if a couple of his friends hadn't pulled him off.

No matter what he had heard, Charley still resolved to stay. There was just no way they were going to throw him out of his apartment.

Finished with his cigarette, Charely was going to light another, but he caught himself. If he didn't stop smoking they wouldn't have to take the apartment from him; he wouldn't be here at all.

He went back into the living room, checking his watch as he did. It was nearly eleven, time for the one or two of the bewildering collection of medicines Dr. Katz had him on. Something for everything, Charley once thought, except to keep his sexual urge in check; time had more or less taken care of that.

The doorbell rang as he went into the bathroom, and, despite himself, Charley felt his stomach shift a little. If it was the black guy, now was the time to stand up to him.

But it could well be UPS, or the mailman, or Mrs. Torres, a lady from across the hall he had befriended, or . . .

He opened the door.

In his prime, Charley had been about five feet ten. Age had hammered him down a bit, but the black guy standing in front of him towered over him. He was wearing a tight-fitting white T-shirt with one of those little alligators on the left side. He had slablike muscles.

"How you doin', Murph," the black guy said. "I'm Ace. May I come in?"

He was smiling, but his eyes were black and mean.

This was it, Charley Murphy. Right then, right there. If he let him in the door he was dead. He would not be able to stand up to him.

But what was he to do? As a young man, he would have charged into him. But he was old, and feeble, and the cops couldn't help, and there was a terrible hollow empty fear inside him.

He opened the door and stepped back so Ace could walk by him, which he did.

Charley closed the door. Ace had walked right into the living room. Charley followed him.

Ace sat down in an armchair and put his feet up on a coffee table. Charley said nothing, but he felt an anger which he hid.

"I guess you heard, Murph," Ace said, "that this here building is being renovated. All the tenants are moving out."

Ace waited for Charley to answer. He didn't.

"Anyways, the new landlord, he realizes that the tenants who are leaving need moving expenses, so he wanted me to give you this."

Ace reached into his pocket with his right arm, the massive muscular development tensing. Charley did not want to think what a blow from that arm could do to him.

Ace pulled out a roll of bills.

"There's $350 there," he said. "All you got to do is sign this here paper."

Ace sprang gingerly from the chair and reached into his back pocket. He handed Charley a piece of folded-up paper. Charley opened it; his hands were shaking.

"Just sign on that line on the bottom," Ace said. "We'll fill in the rest."

One side of the paper was blank. Charley turned it over. The other side was blank except for a line at the bottom.

"There's nothing on this," Charley said.

"I said we'll fill it in," Ace said. He was not smiling.

"I can't move," Charley said. "I can't afford it. I just get my TA pension and Social Security."

"You'll be fine. Live with relatives."

Charley swallowed.

"I can't," he said. "I want to stay here."

Ace stepped up to him. "Listen, you old motherfucker. Either you sign the paper or I'll beat your old fucking brains out."

Charley was going to say please; he was going to . . .

he didn't know what. But Ace didn't care. Ace only cared about getting his signature on the piece of paper.

Ace handed him a pen. His hand shaking, Charley signed.

"You got a week," Ace said, folding up the paper. He put the money on the coffee table. "Have all your stuff out of here in a week."

"A week!"

"That's what the paper says," Ace said, the hint of a smile on his lips.

After Ace left, Charley sat down in an easy chair in the living room. He felt weakness and some discomfort in his chest, but that was nothing. A couple of pills would take care of that.

What bothered him was something else. The way he had been humiliated. The way the future looked. The way it had all ended.

Charley Murphy, seventy-five years old, felt like crying. And he did.

Chapter 4

Joe Lawless stood in the doorway of Barbara Babalino's small kitchen and watched her cook their breakfast. Her dark hair was still a little damp and curly from the shower they had taken together. Occasionally she would glance at him as she worked, and he would feel a hollow sensation in his stomach. It was ironic. He was a detective first grade in Fort Siberia, head of the homicide squad, and in his fifteen years on the job he had been able to acclimate himself to just about anything. But not her. And especially not this morning.

She moved scrambled eggs in a pan with a spatula. "Hungry?"

He nodded, but he was not. Should be, but wasn't.

"Why don't you sit down," she said. "You know I like to serve you."

Lawless went through a short hall into the living room, where there was a table by a pair of windows that looked out on a small backyard; a door to the left of the table led to the yard.

He had been more or less living with Barbara—though he kept his own apartment in the Pelham Bay section of the Bronx—for a little over a year, and it was only rarely now that he thought how perilously close Barbara had come to dying in this room. She had been trapped here by a psychopath, Richard Baumann, and had saved herself by pulling a light plug and throwing a heavy goblet through one of the windows, which were alarmed.

16

Then she had chased Baumann into Central Park and, in a terrifying encounter, had shot him dead.

Lawless had made a halfhearted attempt to get her to move. He disliked the apartment because it was equivalent to living in a cellar, off the beaten track. But the attempt was only halfhearted because he knew her well enough to know that she wouldn't move. Anyway, he thought, there was probably no place you could really hide as a cop; no place, really, anyone could hide anywhere.

He thought of that now as he sat down at the table and lit up a cigarette—a great appetizer. His mind drifted back eleven years to Karen, and their brief life together after they married, and then the ten years after that. He was hiding then, hiding in work and one-night stands, deep down hurt and scared, vowing never to take a chance again. When Karen had walked out the door she had taken, he thought, his heart with her.

And then Barbara had happened. He had thought of it much since he had met her at the Five Three, and he realized that she was probably one of the few women in the world who could have brought him back. She was open and persistent and loving, and she had tremendous guts. She would not give up on him, because she loved him, and it was through her that he had found his heart again.

Now it had come full circle. He was at that moment he had thought he would never come to again.

Actually, he thought, as Barbara came out of the kitchen with two plates in her hands—and his stomach did a little twist—he had been at the moment last night a number of times: when they were dancing, when they were making love, when they were just sitting on the couch sipping wine and holding hands and talking.

There had been ideal moments, and yet he, Joe Lawless, who had been through many situations that not one in a thousand people could have withstood, could not beat the fear in his stomach. And he knew as well as anyone the mechanics of fear, the way it worked: The more you avoided what you were afraid of, the bigger it got, until, maybe, you could never beat it.

Barbara put a steaming plate of ham and eggs in front of him. She did it slowly—on purpose. She was wearing a white terry-cloth robe, and, as she leaned over, Lawless was inches from and could not help but see her lovely, large breasts. Indeed, at Fort Siberia, she had the nickname "Towers of Babalino"—but no one dared utter it within earshot of Barbara.

"Can I get you anything else?" she said, slyly smiling, holding her position.

All Lawless could manage was a smile. He felt himself totally intimidated by everything.

"Oh," she said, straightening up. "I did forget the coffee."

She walked back to the kitchen, and, despite himself, Lawless watched her go. She glanced over her shoulder at him and smiled.

She came back with the coffee and poured some for both of them, then sat down opposite him.

He dinched his ciagarette and sipped the coffee. He scooped up a tiny portion of eggs with his fork and put it in his mouth.

Barbara looked at him. "Let's have it," she said. "What's the matter?"

Lawless looked at her. He was thirty-eight. If he didn't do it now, it could get away from him.

He put the fork on the plate and swallowed the eggs.

"Will you marry me?" he asked.

"Yes," Barbara said. And then tears formed in her eyes and started to roll down her cheeks.

Lawless got up and put his arms around her and led her to the couch. They sat down.

"What's the matter?" Lawless asked.

"I'm happy," Barbara said. "Italians always cry when they're happy. How do you feel?"

"Wonderful," Lawless said, "and scared."

Barbara wiped her eyes with a tissue. "It'll work, Joe. You know why? Because we care about each other. That's the bottom line of any realtionship, isn't it?"

"Yes."

"I care about you," she said, "more than I care about myself. Did you know that?"

Lawless nodded. "It's the same with me."

"Your first marriage," she said. "There you married a woman who—I have to be honest—didn't care enough about you. She wanted a cop hero, an image of something in her mind. She never saw you; she never even had a chance to want you."

"You're one smart lady," Lawless said.

"It's true," Barbara said. "I think I see you for what you are. That's why I love you."

They sat in silence a moment, just holding each other. Barbara looked up at him. "So, did you buy a ring?"

"Yeah," Lawless said. "Nonreturnable."

Barbara laughed. Lawless slipped the ring out of his pocket, where it had been a dead weight since he had arrived the previous evening, and Barbara put out her left hand. He slipped it on.

"I got your size while you were asleep," he said.

Barbara started to cry again. Her head was down to look at the ring, and a few tears dropped on the floor. Then she looked up, her eyes brimming.

She put her arms around Lawless's neck.

"I guess at one time in my life I thought it would never happen for me again. That when Jeff died I—"

"Well, it has happened," Lawless said. "For both of us."

Specific days of the week mean nothing to the vast majority of New York City cops, because most of them work on rotating tours. Sometimes eight to four, or four to twelve, or twelve to eight weekdays; sometimes any of those tours on weekends.

It so happened that both Barbara and Lawless had a weekend off together, so it was decided that they spend at least a good part of their Saturday at Barbara's house having what Barbara called a "controlled orgy."

The odds against their having a weekend off together were great, but so were the odds against Lawless getting through the day without being contacted on one squeal or another.

The Five Three did have the highest homicide rate in the city and had held that dubious distinction for four years. "If they ever made murder an Olympic event," one cop once said, "we'd field the best team in the nation. They get lots of practice."

Most of the killings were drug-related and what cops call "grounders"—cases where the perp is known and is collared quickly, or cases where the killer is not known and will never be known. These are grounders because making arrests is unimportant to the cops. They are cases of swine killing swine.

On such cases, Lawless could assign any of the men in his six-man squad. They would write up some five's on it, put it in the drawer, and that would more or less be it.

But some cases were not grounders, and on these Lawless had to leave whatever he was doing and go to the scene. It was this kind of squeal he hoped he wouldn't catch.

For most of the morning, he didn't think too much about bad killings. Once Barbara pulled the shades and took off her bathrobe he didn't think of much else except Barbara.

CHAPTER 5

George Benton, nicknamed "The Bent One" by his fellow cops, worked all the homicide squeals as Lawless's partner. In a precinct that teemed with unusual cops, "The Bent One" held his own.

A homicide cop, he was preoccupied with his own mortality and expected to be struck down at any time by "The Big C," a myocardial infarction, MS, peritonitis, an aneurysm, embolism, or any of a dozen other maladies.

He was out sick constantly, averaging about thirty-five days a year. He devoured medical books and had become fairly skilled at palpating his own body.

It was suggested that for Christmas the guys in the homicide squad give him a package containing all the equipment necessary to conduct a complete physical—including chest X-ray and sigmoidoscope—at the beginning of each day.

He was constantly looking for signs that he was on his way out. Probably the high point—or low point—of his obsession with his health had occurred about ten years earlier, when he was still married.

He lived in Queens at the time and was in the shower, soaping himself up, with one hand, his free fingers probing and palpating with the other.

The blood drained out of him when his fingers came across a hard lump right next to his anus. He felt it further. Very big and very hard—attached.

God, he had touched the Big Casino.

21

Yet, maybe not. Maybe it was just a boil forming. Or a sebaceous cyst. If it was red, then it couldn't be cancer. Right?

Maybe.

But how do you look at a lump next to your anus?

George figured a way. He got out of the shower, the water still going, and very carefully climbed up on the bathroom sink, then equally carefully positioned himself so that he could look through his legs at his ass in the mirror.

He did and saw life-giving redness. He was flooded with relief—thank God!—and it was just at that moment that his son, three-year-old George Jr., must have been looking through a space under the door, because he said, "What happened to your feet, Daddy?"

Benton had been treated for severe depression and anxiety at three institutions for periods of three, five, and nine months.

He lived alone in Queens, his wife having divorced him and moved to California. "She was always convinced," he once told Lawless, "that one day I was going to come home and do a Whitman."

"What's that?" Lawless had asked.

" 'Member that kid named Whitman in Texas in the sixties? He found a high spot on a Texas campus and made his last stand against the world."

"Or else," Benton once also said, "she was afraid I was going to eat my .38 in the house and dirty her wallpaper. Now that, ha-ha, was a distinct possibility."

Curiously, though, there was a side to Benton which operated with pure, cold, calm logic: the side of him that was a homicide investigator. Watching him function at a crime scene with such cool detachment, it was hard to imagine that the man had three medicine chests in his house, all completely filled.

It was Benton who caught the Castelli squeal.

He was in the homicide squad room, reading an article in the *Times* magazine section on AIDs among heterosexuals, when the call came through from a uniformed guy at the scene.

As soon as he got the details, he called Lawless at Barbara's number.

"I'm sorry to bother you, Joe, but we apparently have a bad one in the Romano section."

"Really?"

"Yeah. A man and woman and their two young kids."

"Is it buttoned up?"

"Yeah."

"Where is it?"

Benton gave Lawless the address.

"I'll see you there in about a half hour."

Lawless explained to Barbara what had happened and where he was going.

"I hate it," she said, "but I understand. We're cops, right?"

"You got it," Lawless said.

He kissed her good-bye and was gone.

Lawless took his own car to the scene.

He drove fast. This was the kind of case that would get the brass off the golf course on a Saturday, or away from their steaks in the backyard, or whatever, and the last thing he wanted at the scene was a lot of brass stampeding evidence and otherwise interfering with the investigation. Not that he would let them. It would be his case, and he would run it; but he didn't need the confrontation it would take to establish that.

He thought of Benton. There was no question that he was a little eccentric. But now was the time Lawless could appreciate him. Lawless did not have to ask if he called Forensic or the ME or if he would supervise keeping people out until he got there or if he was doing everything else to preserve the integrity of the scene and to get the investigation off on the right foot. Benton would do it all. Lawless appreciated Benton. It was sad that he had to go through life carrying so much heartache.

Chapter 6

When Lawless got to the scene, he was gratified to see that crime-scene tape had been strung up, uniformed cops were keeping a largish crowd of onlookers well back, and there was no evidence of brass in sight.

Seeing the house emphasized something Lawless had been thinking on the way up: He had never heard of a murder, except for the blacks in the sixties, that was related to the Romano section.

George Benton, dressed as usual in a suit and tie and smelling of an expensive after-shave, was on the porch.

"The brother of the male adult discovered them," Benton said as he and Lawless passed inside. "They're in the basement."

"Where's the brother?"

"Intensive care."

"Coronary?"

"Maybe."

They went into the house and to the basement door. There was no smell until they came to the door. Then he faintly smelled feces and urine, but not putrefaction. They couldn't have been dead long.

He and Benton donned vinyl gloves and went downstairs.

The man was the first one visible. Lawless guessed he was about thirty-five. He was lying on an expensive-looking velvet couch opposite the entrance to the basement. His hands were taped behind his back with duct tape, and there was tape over his mouth. He looked as if he had been watching TV and had fallen over on his side. His eyes were open.

A woman was lying across a high ottoman, her hands also taped behind her back and her mouth taped. Her shorts and panties had been pulled down to her knees; there was a smear of blood on her left buttock, and feces on her right. Lawless had seen the pattern before. She had been sodomized, he guessed, then the perp wiped himself on her buttock.

There was an entry wound of a small-diameter bullet in the back of her head, and very little blood. For a moment, Lawless thought it might be a pro job. It had that feel, for one thing. For another, pros favored .22 pistols, which you had to head-shoot with for a kill and which rarely left an exit wound. The main reason, though, was that bullets fired into the head from a .22 became ballistically useless.

He went back to the man's head and looked closely. There was considerable blood under and behind the head. It looked as if there was an exit wound there.

He went over to the kids. Both were lying on the couch, huddled together, their hands tied behind their backs and their mouths taped like the adults. Lawless guessed they were around six or seven. At first he thought it was a boy and a girl—one of the kids had longish hair—but then he saw it was two boys.

For just a moment, Lawless looked at them. He had been a homicide cop a long time and had seen things that would make a stone cry, and had not cried. He did not cry now, but the death of kids could still get through that protective wall to his feelings. He didn't understand why. He never looked closely at it. But it was fundamental and had to do with innocence, and loss.

A feeling of sadness whacked into him. He swallowed it, and it went wherever feelings go.

He got down on his haunches and looked at the kids. Apparently both had been killed the same way as the adults—one shot in the head each. He couldn't see any exit wounds, but he guessed they were there: There was considerable blood on the couch.

He stood up.

"Hey, Joe," Benton said. "I think the kids got killed before the adults."

"Yeah?"

"The kids are in full rigor. Feel this. Both adults are only partial."

Lawless went over and pressed on the jaw and upper arms of the man. They were rocklike, in full rigor. The feet were only partially hard.

He felt the woman. Same story. Jaw and upper extremities hard, feet only partially hard, everything else not in rigor.

He went over and pressed in the stomach of first one kid, then the other. Rock. Both kids had died, it would seem, before the parents.

Lawless knew what he thought, but he asked Benton, "What do you think?"

"The parents watched the kids die."

"I'd guess the woman died before the man, too," Lawless said.

"Yeah."

They had just started to search the cellar when Victor J. Onairuts, M.D., showed up.

Lawless was glad to see him. Of all the MEs he had ever worked with, he respected Vic Onairuts most. He was direct, honest, and the first to admit that "I ain't Quincy," that it was sometimes—most times—very difficult to find what had made a person die, and when, and why. The body didn't stop being a complicated machine just because it was inoperative.

"How you doing, Vic?" Lawless asked.

Onairuts's eyes, as blue as Paul Newman's, swept the room.

"Well until now," he said.

Lawless told Onairuts what he and Benton had determined. Onairuts made a preliminary examination—just visual—until the Forensic team, headed by Ray Meehan, a florid-faced Irishman, showed up and did their thing: shooting the scene and the bodies from every conceivable angle.

While Meehan and his partners searched the room with Lawless and Benton, Onairuts examined the bodies.

It didn't take him long—his most sophisticated procedure being to take temperatures—until he called Lawless over.

"I agree with you about the schedule of killings. The kids went first, I'd say sometime last night, then the adults. The woman was sodomized; I don't think she was vaginally raped. They were killed by a high-velocity weapon or weapons, not a .22. But I'd put this in the pro hit category, wouldn't you?"

"They're not beginners," Lawless said.

Onairuts bagged the heads and hands of the four victims, and they were removed from the basement one by one, after being put in body bags.

"When do you think you'll do the post?" Lawless asked.

"Monday or Tuesday."

"Okay."

"Any feelings about who might have done this?" Lawless asked.

"No," Onairuts said. "Not the Mafia, anyway. They wouldn't do this."

"I agree," Lawless said.

"One thing is for sure," Onairuts said. "Whoever did it is well down on the food chain."

After the bodies were removed, Lawless and Benton began their search of the house. They started in the living room. It was filled with fancy furniture and electronic gadgetry tied to the TV, but nothing suspicious.

They checked a couple of hall closets. They were filled with the usual stuff—linens, blankets, and the like—and a number of small appliances.

There was nothing suspicious-looking on or under the shelves.

Down the hall, they went into a bathroom which looked, Lawless thought, like one of those bathrooms you saw in the women's magazines: modernistic tub and toilet and sink and new tile in pastel colors and a recessed luminous ceiling. Lawless couldn't be sure, but the lavatory and tub and toilet handles, machined to look like fish, seemed to be gold-plated. Very expensive at the least.

The kitchen, down at the end of the hall, also looked like it belonged in a women's magazine. Everything was new: new cabinets, floor, ceiling, appliances.

"What do you think it's worth, George," Lawless asked, "ten thousand?"

"More like fifteen," Benton, who knew about such things, said.

Both men checked the sink. It was dry.

They pulled out the dishwasher tray. It was full of dishes. Onairuts would find, Lawless thought, what they had eaten.

They peered into closets, moved pots, pans, other things. Nada. Nothing suspicious.

There was a door leading to a sun porch.

It was under construction, in the process of being closed in. There were a few triple-insulated windows already in place, and the wall material had been stripped off to the studs.

"This guy had dough," Benton said. "We're talking thirty grand and we're not even upstairs. Plus the Corvette outside."

Lawless nodded.

They went upstairs, which was covered with wall to wall carpet, just as the downstairs had been.

They went into the master bedroom first.

Opulent was the word that came to Lawless's mind, and overdone. The bed was huge; it seemed to dominate the relatively small room with its high carved wood posts, satin bedspread, and the sheer plumpness of it.

This room, like the one downstairs, had the latest in electronic recreation gadgetry.

While Benton tossed the closets, Lawless went into a desk by a window.

He found some correspondence which clearly showed that the deceased male, John Castelli, was a vice president with the Mercantile Bank in Manhattan.

He found nothing on the wife and for the moment would assume she was a housewife.

There was also a guest room and two kids' rooms. Both kids' rooms had a TV and a VCR and a computer setup of some sort. Lawless and Benton exchanged glances but said nothing.

The guest room was also fully equipped with a TV and VCR.

"It's like Crazy Eddie's in this place," Benton said deadpan.

All the dressers in all the rooms and closets were searched. There didn't seem to be anything significant.

"Seen enough, George?" Lawless asked.

"Yeah."

They went downstairs, and then back down into the basement.

"Anything?" Lawless asked Meehan.

"Plenty," he said.

He showed Lawless a glassine pouch. In it were three bullets and four shell casings.

"Where were they?"

"It's like they had eyes," Meehan said. "All but one went down between the cushions and the couch body. The other one we found in a corner."

Lawless did not ask where the missing one was. It was likely in one of the victims.

But he did ask the caliber.

"Nine millimeter," Meehan said. "Automatic."

Two words came into Lawless' mind: Colombians and Dominicans. Both favored the fourteen-shot automatic 9mm.

In fact, it was probably more a Dominican than a Colombian weapon.

Lawless figured he had handled at least four squeals involving Dominicans and 9mms. One involved the Dominican version of the Irish beer racket. At the Irish beer racket people get drunk and go on the street and fight it out. That happened at the Dominican thing, except they fought with guns rather than fists. At that particular beer racket four had been killed, and the motive, it turned out, was a slight insult to the wife of one of the dead men.

They were a fire-breathing people, and moving up the ladder drug-wise, selling all kinds of dope and cocaine.

Meehan told Lawless that he probably would be finished by the next day, and would have something on his desk by Monday morning.

Lawless thanked him, and he and Benton left.

Outside, one of the brass, Deputy Inspector Macgruder, had arrived and was holding forth for the press, who had already arrived.

One of the reporters broke off from Macgruder and went over to Lawless. "How you doing, Officer? What's going on in there?"

"I have no idea," Lawless said, his piercing blue eyes flat.

He started down the path. As he went he still did not acknowledge Macgruder. But he remembered him. When Lawless had had his fight with the chief of Manhattan operations he had gone to Macgruder, who was assistant chief of detectives, for help. Macgruder had said he'd help. But when push had come to shove, he had walked the other way. And Lawless had gone to Fort Siberia.

Lawless was almost through the gate when he spotted it. Upside down in the grass.

He reached down and picked it up. It was a little red car, probably belonged to one of the kids. Lawless put it in his jacket pocket and went out through the gate.

CHAPTER 7

After he called the Emergency Service, Arnold drove over to the pier.

The animal was still there, but the car partially blocked it, and it was in shade. He couldn't tell what it was.

The ESD showed up a half hour after Arnold: a middle-aged, balding guy and a young, thin, dark-haired one. They looked at the animal, then went back to their van, donned boots, and got rope and rigging of some sort. Then they waded into the water.

The older guy slipped the rigging and rope around the back of the animal, which was submerged, and they floated it out without difficulty.

They pulled it next to the shoreline, slipped hooks through the ropes around the animal, and proceeded to haul it from the river.

Or tried to. They got it about halfway out, enough to reveal a rather pointed head and a tail, and then encountered resistance.

"If this has been in there more than a couple of weeks," the older guy said, "it's going to come out in pieces."

The thought revolted Arnold, but he tried to show nothing.

The animal did not come apart, and they were able to pull it all the way up on the shoreline. Then it became clear why they had the trouble.

The ropes around the back extended fully around the

body and were tied to concrete blocks. Arnold recognized them instantly because he had used the same kind to build a retaining wall in his backyard.

There were four of them. Each weighed forty pounds. The animal had been weighted down with 160 pounds of blocks. Someone, Arnold thought, had not expected the animal to rise. They were trying to hide it. They didn't understand about gangrene gas, which Arnold had first learned about in the Police Academy.

"Gas forms in the body," the instructor had said, "and it is capable of lifting tremendous weights. I had one body, in the trunk section of a car. It floated the whole trunk up."

The animal looked strange. Scary. Arnold said out loud what was on his mind: "It's throat is cut . . . and it doesn't have any eyes or ears."

The older ESD guy looked at him, his eyes glittering in his red, sweaty face.

"Those are delicacies," he said. "The crabs and fishies get 'em. If this thing is male it won't have any balls, either."

Arnold disliked his callous way, but he said nothing. Then: "What do you think it is?"

"A dog," the older guy said. "Look at the nails."

Arnold got down on his haunches and looked at the nails. They were flat, unpointed.

"I think it's a dog too," the young ESD guy said.

A dog, Arnold thought. Why would anyone want to get rid of the body of a dog?

"Hey," the older guy said, getting down on his haunches, "look at this."

He pointed with a gloved finger to the animal's snout. Arnold saw nothing for a moment, then he spotted it: The upper lip was punctured. He noticed other puncture marks on the face. The ESD guy slowly ran his hand over the fur, or hair, turning it back and revealing other puncture marks.

It looked as if someone had stabbed the dog, if it was a dog, over and over with an ice pick. But the older ESD guy had a different idea.

"These are teeth marks," he said. "Something has bitten the hell out of this dog."

"Oh," Arnold said. He stared at the dog.

"What do you want us to do with the remains?" the older guy said.

Arnold didn't know. This was a dead dog. What did you do with a dead dog? Take it to Bellevue to be autopsied? It was, he thought, a victim of something violent, but because it was a dog, no one would do anything.

Arnold looked at the swollen, punctured form, the eyes and ears—and maybe something else—missing.

He wanted to do something. At least find out why the dog died this way.

"We could take it to the ASPCA," he said.

"Okay," the older guy said. "Let's do it."

He and the younger guy cut the blocks from the dog. Arnold put the blocks in his car, and the ESD guys put the dog in a body bag, then into a van.

They headed down toward the ASPCA on East River Drive.

Arnold left work early, after taking care of the dog. As it happened, the ASPCA did not have refrigerated lockers and, anyway, were simply going to dispose of the dog. Arnold did not know where to put the dog, at least until it could be autopsied, because he definitely had decided to do that.

The older ESD guy surprised Arnold. He came to the rescue. He suggested that the dog be stored in Bellevue. Arnold wondered how it could be done—Bellevue is for people. But it was done.

"I see the guys in the morgue," the ESD guy said, "more than I see my family."

Arnold took the LIRR home, and on the way, watching the suburban countryside go by, he thought about the dog; he had not really thought about anything else since they had found it.

Forget the questions of who had done whatever was

done to the dog, or why. Arnold just hated the idea of seeing it dead.

He thought of his own dog, Misty. She was an Airedale terrier, a sort of oversized Benji that Arnold had gotten as a puppy for his twin boys, Aaron and Jude.

It was a gentle dog, and it could not be provoked, even when Arnold playfully snatched a bone from its dish. The most he got then was a careful stare by the dog. And that, Arnold knew, must be against every instinct she had.

The fact was that Arnold hated to see anything dead, even insects. He had never admitted this to anyone—especially fellow cops—except to Naomi, his wife.

Once when he was painting trim on the outside of his house he was continually bothered by a fat bumblebee. He got mad and took a couple of swipes at it, but missed. Then the paint took care of the bee: It foolishly landed on a freshly painted piece of fascia and immediately fell to the ground.

Arnold climbed down from the ladder and looked at the bee. It had paint on one of its wings and was trying desperately to fly, but couldn't.

Arnold wanted to help it fly. But how? He couldn't clean the wing off without damaging it.

Then he remembered something about Pepsi Cola being able to remove paint.

He had been drinking Diet Pepsi all day. He got a bottle—empty except for a few drops—and carefully herded the bee into it. Then he went back to painting.

Ten minutes later, he climbed down and peered inside the bottle. There was the bee, buzzing around. Most of the paint seemed to be off the wing.

He waited another five minutes, shook the bee out of the bottle, and held his breath.

It flew away. It made Arnold feel wonderful.

He had told the story to Naomi, and she didn't laugh. She had given him a long, slow kiss.

Arnold got home at a little before five. He opened the gate to the picket fence surrounding his house and let himself in. Naomi opened the house door and Misty charged out, per usual, as if Arnold were just returning from ten years as a POW in Vietnam.

Arnold picked Misty up in his massive arms. She was extremely excited, and this made him laugh. There had been days when he had gotten mad at her: when she would bark in the middle of the night at nothing, when she would get at the garbage, when she would leave unpleasant surprises on the kitchen floor.

But today was not one of those days.

CHAPTER 8

A week after Ace visited Charley Murphy, a man stood at the kitchen window of his apartment, 4-D, in the "middle building," as they called it, and watched the stream of Charley Murphy's belongings being taken out of the wing he lived in, across the courtyard, down the steps, and into a van.

The man looked like he had some serious disease, which he didn't. He was short, pale, very thin—125 pounds with his clothes on—and had a jutting Adam's apple, a heavily veined neck, and semibulbous wild glassy dark eyes.

The only thing healthy-looking on him was his hair. There was a great shock of it, black, and it was combed into a pompadour.

The man was dressed in checked shorts, combat boots, and a short-sleeved T-shirt which bore the legend "Get Lei'd Hawaiian Style."

Quite a package.

The man was not aware of the sounds in the living room behind him where his roommate was watching a game show on TV. He was totally absorbed by the scene below.

As he watched, things were going on inside him. Sad things, and angry things.

He was thirty-six and had been raised on the Lower East Side of Manhattan, a rough place where young men sometimes took advantage of old men. He did not like that, and when he was old enough, he got in the way.

36

They laughed at first, these young men, but then the small man acted, and acted again—and again—and they stopped.

He felt his eyes almost glistening. He was sad because there was nothing that he could do to help Charley Murphy.

He had to wait. That was what he had been instructed to do, and, as a police officer, he obeyed orders. But because of his personality, he found it particularly difficult.

He was Detective Third Grade Frank Piccolo, assigned with his partner—and physical opposite, Ed Edmunton— to the 53rd Precinct. Piccolo's last CO had wanted to have him institutionalized but didn't for two reasons: (1) It would have been difficult to do; and (2) Piccolo might not like it. So the CO had settled for Fort Siberia, which was a sort of crazy house.

Small wonder that Piccolo loved it.

"Action, man," he once told Edmunton, who had been assigned there for grass-eating—petty thievery that couldn't be proved—"I didn't join the cops to sit on my ass."

Now, though, there had been plenty of waiting, ever since he had first learned, two months earlier, that the very building he lived in with Edmunton had apparently been selected by a greedy landlord for gentrification. To wit: You drive out all the old rent-controlled and rent-stabilized tenants so you can rehab and rerent and make a killing. They had done it in Manhattan successfully, though some were caught and nailed good by the Manhattan DA, but greed is a smoke that clouds men's eyes, and they were going to try it again.

Against his better instincts, Piccolo had reported what he had discovered to Captain Bledsoe, the CO. Bledsoe, with typical fervor for justice and doing what is right and making a good case and having the brass stop squeezing his nuts and maybe making deputy so he could put this nigger- and spic-infested swamp hole behind him, contacted the Bronx district attorney. If a case was to be made, Bledsoe wanted to be part of it.

The district attorney, Anthony Spagnoli, was a man after Piccolo's own heart. He was large and heavyset, with dark rings under his eyes, and there was nothing wishy-washy about his attitude toward criminals: He hated them. "He doesn't favor the electric chair," someone once said about him, borrowing a line from comic Jay Lenno. "He favors electric bleachers."

He and Piccolo got along instantly, though Spagnoli was no fool; you didn't survive long in the New York political scene if you were a fool.

Spagnoli knew that he was dealing with, to put it mildly, an impatient man, and this was an important factor in their discussions.

"We've been aware of these swine for quite a while," he told Piccolo and Edmunton and Bledsoe. "They've emptied at least five buildings in Manhattan, and two in the Bronx."

"Do you know who's the kingpin?" Piccolo asked.

"He's a guy named Morris Fishman. He's clever and he's rich. It took us a long time to find out he owned these buildings. He's got layers and layers of interlocking corporations between him and the street."

"What do you want from us?" Piccolo asked.

"Well, first," Spagnoli said, "does anyone know you guys are cops?"

"No," Piccolo said. "I don't think so."

"Good," Spagnoli said. "Then the first thing I'd like you to do is clean out your apartment of anything that ties you to the job."

"Okay. Then what?"

"Then just sit tight. Wait until you're approached. We'll put a wire in your apartment. What I want to do is to get his chief headbreaker—that's a black guy named Ace—on tape, and then turn him. From him, we go to the next guy, Charles Bender. He's the middleman, reporting to Fishman. If we can turn Bender, then we can get to Fishman. We have good tools. I'll go for conspiracy. Each count carries seven to fifteen."

"Sounds good," Piccolo said. "So all we have to do is wait for Ace to show up."

"That's right," Spagnoli said.

"Do you want 'em assigned to your office?" Bledsoe asked.

"No, that won't be necessary. Just have 'em go about their business."

It was after Bledsoe left—he had an important appointment downtown which, translated, meant nine holes at the Briarwood Country Club in Riverdale—that Spagnoli poured out his concern.

"Look, Frank," he said. "I hate these scumbags just as bad as you do. But we got to do it by the book. If we don't, the case will come apart because Fishman has unlimited funds and platoons of high-priced shyster lawyers. And I know about your reputation of wanting to take the, uh, more direct route to get results quickly."

Indeed, Piccolo was unofficial holder of the all-time record for police brutality charges in the city of New York.

Piccolo shrugged, but Edmunton said, "Listen, Mr. Spagnoli, Frank has developed self-control. Great self-control. We'll do exactly what you want us to do, and we'll do it by the book."

"Yeah," Piccolo had said slyly. "Ain't no Clint Eastwoods here."

Edmunton had guffawed at that one. Spagnoli had even laughed.

But now it wasn't funny. Six weeks. Piccolo had spent six weeks watching these motherfuckers terrorize old people and had been able to do exactly nothing.

Now he blinked away what he was feeling as he watched the thin figure of Charley Murphy walking behind his belongings.

Something had to happen soon, Piccolo thought, or he was going to have to break his understanding with Spagnoli.

CHAPTER 9

By Saturday at around three o'clock, just a few hours after the bodies of the Castelli family were discovered, Lawless had a road check set on the streets near the house. As he had expected, and hoped, he had been assigned a half dozen extra detectives. Anytime the media was involved in a case, the brass rolled out the troops to solve it as quickly as possbile.

Everybody was prospering off this one. The media had brought out all the clichés, penned by people who cared as much about the family as the man in the moon.

Lawless knew he had to use the detectives as quickly and as well as he could. Because as soon as the story started to slide toward the back of the paper—if it did, and some didn't—the detectives would be quietly reassigned, and he would be left with just himself, Benton, and four other squad members who were constantly doing new business. His own time on the case also had to be limited.

Lawless and Benton were particularly concerned with people who had been driving in the area between the hours of eight and twelve. That was roughly the time he figured the Castellis had been done.

Perhaps someone had seen something.

He was quickly disabused of this notion. People who were stopped not only said they hadn't seen anything, but Lawless and some of the other detectives got the sense that they would always be mute. Like the newspapers said, the Romano Avenue section was a place of tradition.

They got the same reception from people who lived in houses in the area. Some didn't even open their doors, and no one on the block said they had seen anything. It was as if everyone was blind and deaf. A 9mm automatic wasn't a cap pistol; even if they had equipped it with a silencer, someone should have known something. It was just the kind of an area where everything out of the ordinary would be noticed.

Actually, Lawless doubted very much that a silencer had been used. Anyone who didn't care about the police retrieving spent shells would probably not be overly concerned about making noise.

No, someone probably saw or heard something—particularly since it was night and relatively quiet—but they just weren't talking.

At one point, Lawless encountered a heavyset muscular man who answered his question with a sneer. Lawless, a little tighter than usual after six hours of "I haven't seen anything," cracked:

"Someone should help us. It may not stop with the Castellis."

The man had slammed the door in his face.

Lawless called the hospital where the brother, Arthur Castelli, had been admitted. He was able to talk to an intern familiar with the case.

The intern told him that Castelli was no longer in ICU, and that he expected to be discharged in the morning. He had not suffered a heart attack.

Lawless pulled in the road check at around two in the morning. He arranged to have Benton install it again the next morning, and to hit further homes in the area.

Benton also said that he knew one of the capos in the area and that he would talk to him if Lawless wanted. Lawless said okay. Across the fifteen years of his life as a cop, he had seen too much to ever sit down with a wise guy, but to each his own, and they might get some information out of it.

It was too late to call Barbara, so Lawless just went home.

On the way, he recalled that she was now officially his fiancée. At that moment he was driving across Fordham Road, which was relatively quiet: Most of the businesses were closed, with corrugated iron doors covering them. A couple of people were out looking for what probably was a drug buy. There were two or three drunks. Even with the filth on the streets and the garish feeling the place imparted, today it almost seemed attractive.

CHAPTER 10

Lawless was at Morrisania Hospital the next morning at nine o'clock, an hour before Arthur Castelli was due to be discharged. He did not bring Benton for a specific reason. You usually got more from a witness if you made an interrogation seem like a conversation.

He used his tin to gain access to Castelli's room. The door was half open. He looked in, expecting to see Castelli getting dressed, ready to leave. He wasn't. He was sitting by the window in his pajamas, looking out.

Lawless wondered if he would be able to talk at all. He tapped on the door. "Mr. Castelli," he said. "I'm Detective Joe Lawless from the Fifty-third Precinct. May I come in?"

Castelli looked at him. He was sedated. He said nothing.

Lawless went in. He stood near Castelli and looked down. "How are you doing?" he asked.

Castelli looked up at him, shrugged, and started to cry. He put his head down, and the tears dropped onto the tile floor.

Lawless surprised himself. He did something Barbara would have done. He touched Castelli on the shoulder and kept his hand there until he stopped crying. Castelli wiped his eyes with a tissue.

"Do you have any idea," Lawless said softly, "who did this?"

"I told John," Castelli said. "I told him they were dangerous people. That he was fooling around with dangerous people. "But John . . . you know." He looked at Lawless as if Lawless had known the dead man all his life. "But John couldn't be told anything. You know. Ever since he was a little boy, Mama and Papa tried to tell him what to do—but no, not John, you could never tell John what to do."

His voice choked a little, trailed off. Lawless said nothing.

"John was so smart! What brains! An accountant. Went to college. Big schools. Not like me. I'm just a butcher. I never had John's brains. We were all so proud of him when he became a CPA. Settled down, married Maria. He . . ."

Castelli choked again.

"He had it all in front of him. But he always wanted more. John was never satisfied. John always wanted a loaf of bread under each arm. That's why he got involved with them. They got money. John told me he once saw a duffel bag full of money, a duffel bag like in the Army.

"But he wanted more from them. It was like a cancer inside him. Something that could never stop eating. He wanted more from them, and . . ."

Tears welled up in his eyes. The grief, it occurred to Lawless, had to be tremendous to get by the chemicals. Lawless's face showed nothing, but he had the feeling that Castelli was going to drop the perps in his lap.

"Why . . . why did they kill the babies? My mama . . . she's still alive. . . . They're her only grandchildren." His voice choked. He put his hands out, palms up. "How am I going to tell her? How am I going to . . . They're just little babies. They don't know nothing."

And then he was gone again, and Lawless waited for him to come back.

"Mr. Castelli, who was it that John was involved with?"

Castelli looked sharply at him, but said nothing. Lawless could almost smell his fear.

"I'm afraid," he said after a long while. "They might kill my family. They're not people. They're animals."

"I don't think they will," Lawless said. "But not

talking about them can't help. You don't know what they might do right now. What's on their minds. It's better to put them away."

Lawless saw more fear come into the man's eyes. Theoretically, what Castelli had said was true: You never knew who would be the next targets in something like this. But it was highly unlikely that Arthur Castelli or his family would be, and Lawless had to get whatever information he could out of him now.

Castelli still hesitated. Lawless looked at him, his eyes flat. Castelli inhaled sharply.

"Fu-Fuentes," he said. "The Fuentes brothers. I only heard John say it once, but I remember. Miguel and Enrique Fuentes."

"Dominicans?" Lawless asked.

Castelli nodded.

"Drugs?" Lawless said.

Castelli looked at him. Something passed across his face. "Will this be in the paper?" he said softly.

"Not from me," Lawless said.

"Maybe drugs," Castelli said. "They had a lot of money. They gave it to John. He put it in the bank for them."

Lawless nodded. John Castelli was washing the money for them. Perhaps he tried to rip them off.

"Why would they want to hurt him for that?"

There was a millisecond's hesitation.

"I don't know," Castelli said. "I just don't know."

Lawless sensed that Castelli was lying. It didn't make much sense, except it did. Somewhere in a pocket of Arthur Castelli's mind was an image of his brother, unsullied and pure. He didn't want to think of him as a thief. Maybe a long time from now, but not today.

Lawless had many more questions, but they were details, and he could have Benton check them out. He sensed that Castelli was through talking with him today, even though he might still mouth words.

"Thank you," Lawless said, "for speaking to me."

Castelli looked at him with lost eyes. "They had their wholes lives in front of them," he said.

CHAPTER 11

After he saw Castelli, Lawless went with Benton back to the scene. They went into a local restaurant which had an old world ambiance and a proprietor who eyed them suspiciously because they were not of the neighborhood.

Lawless ordered American. Benton ordered a glass of Perrier water to go with the six vitamins he would take.

They waited until they got their orders and the proprietor went away.

"I spoke with Guido Alacante," Benton said. "You know him, right?"

Indeed Lawless did. Alacante was a capo in the Benuto family. He nodded.

"He said he doesn't know anything except it wasn't a family job."

"Was he lying?"

"I don't know," Benton said. "These guys lie so much they don't know the difference between that and the truth, so their lies are very convincing. They're convinced that they're telling the truth."

Benton put all six pills in his mouth and swallowed them with a big gulp of Perrier.

"I'll say this," Benton said. "He did seem to know about it before I talked, and I couldn't detect any anger— you know, because these guys fouled the Romano Street nest."

Lawless sipped his coffee, lit a cigarette, and told him what he had learned from Castelli.

"That's great, Joe. You run 'em for a sheet?"

"Not yet. I'm going to do that in a little while. Why don't you check with INS."

"Okay."

"The killing made Page Two."

Benton nodded. "That should give us a few extra days with the detectives. I read it. They make John Castelli sound like St. Martin of Tours."

Lawless nodded. "Tomorrow we'll check out the bank. I'll meet you there at nine sharp. Okay?"

"Fine," Benton said.

Neither man said it, but they both knew that it was best to hit an institution as closemouthed as a bank in force. "You got to be like a mad dentist," a cop said once, "and pull it all out of them. Better two mad dentists."

A short while later they left the restaurant. Benton was sure that the proprietor thought he was a hophead.

They continued to work the streets, knocking on doors, but getting the same response: a wall of silence.

Still, Lawless decided to keep it up; he was going to work the road check that night. You never knew when you could get lucky, and he had the extra detectives. They weren't going to do him any good sitting around.

Around three on Sunday afternoon Lawless stopped for lunch: a slice of pizza and a container of coffee. Then he called Barbara from a corner phone booth.

"It's working out just the way we thought, right, Joe?"

"It's our first test."

"We'll pass," Barbara said. "Do you think you'll get over at all?"

"You're on nights next week, right?"

"Yes."

"I'm going to break away from this thing sometime tomorrow and I'll be over."

"Every time I think I'm engaged to you," Barbara said, "it does something to me."

"Likewise," Lawless said.

"Make sure you come," Barbara said.

If he noticed any ambiguity, Lawless let it go by.

"I'll be there," he said.

CHAPTER 12

At nine o'clock Monday morning, Lawless and Benton met at the entrance to the Mercantile Bank at 57th Street and the Avenue of the Americas.

Both men wore suits and ties and grim expressions.

A few minutes after they got into the bank, they were sitting in the walnut-paneled, heavily carpeted office of Reid Holman, president of the bank.

He looked like the classic banker: paunchy, pin-striped suit, flowing white hair. He had an imperious, patronizing lilt to the way he talked.

"We're all shocked and outraged at John's death," he said to Lawless and Benton, who were seated across a large oak desk from him, "and we'll be happy to cooperate in any way we can."

Lawless looked at him.

"That's good," Lawless said, "because we wouldn't want bad publicity to come to the bank. Having one of your employees and his family murdered is bad enough. But having him accused of financial misfeasance is something else."

Holman's face flushed slightly. "What do you mean?"

"We believe," Lawless said, "that Mr. Castelli was involved in a money-laundering scam for Dominican drug dealers."

"A what?" Holman said.

Lawless paused long enough to let Holman realize that he knew exactly what Lawless was talking about.

"He—Castelli—was depositing money in the bank that was drug money."

"John?" Holman said. "I can't believe that."

Lawless and Benton looked at him.

"Okay," Lawless said, and stood up. Benton stood up also.

"That's too bad," Lawless said. "We'll have to proceed down other avenues."

"What do you mean?" Holman said, also standing up.

"New York State Banking, Federal Deposit, FBI, whatever," Benton said.

Holman, who had been watching Lawless, had to flick his eyes to Benton. His face was mottled white and red. "I would, uh, like to keep this private."

"There's no guarantee of that," Lawless said.

"Well, can't we look into it here?"

There was, Lawless noted, not a scintilla of patronization in the voice.

Lawless looked at Benton, then at Holman. "You don't know anything about it?"

"No," Holman said, glancing down. "But one of the managers, I think, was starting to think there might be irregularities, but he didn't tie it to, uh, John."

"Okay," Lawless said. "Why don't you look into it and call me back by Thursday morning. Me or Detective Benton."

"All right, I'll do that."

"Good," Lawless said, and handed him a card with his number on it.

At a quarter after nine, Lawless and Benton left the bank.

They split up in the Bronx. Benton went back to the scene to knock on some doors, and Lawless went back to the station house to make a couple of calls.

Lawless made the calls from the Homicide squad room, a battered room with a big grimy window that had a view of a brick wall.

The first call was to BCI. Nothing had come in as far as either of the Fuentes brothers having a sheet.

"Call back this afternoon," the sergeant in charge said.

Lawless put his feet up on the battered green desk he was sitting at and thought about who to call next. Actually, he had only one name in mind. Frankie Pinto.

Pinto was a detective in Narcotics, which was difficult duty to begin with, but Frankie worked undercover, and had been working undercover for at least five years that Lawless knew of. There was simply no one better.

It was a job fraught with all kinds of peril.

When you made a knockoff, or bust buy, you could come upon more money at one time than you would make for the rest of your life. And all in nontraceable used bills that you could put in a plastic container and bury in your yard to use as you needed it.

Of course, if you did that you might be sorry. Because from time to time IAD or others would set you up. Then they would take away your tin and gun and you'd have to worry about how to stay a virgin in prison when you weren't worrying about being iced by someone you put there, or about how your wife and kids were surviving without possessions and food and clothing, and also without you, man, you.

But the greatest peril was the day-to-day dealings with drug dealers. That's what Frankie Pinto did all the time: He made drug buys and tried to stay alive doing it. When you walked into an apartment with three or four grand or more on you, you were a potential ripoff, which might include your being shot dead.

Or, they could find out you were the Man.

As a group, drug dealers were paranoid. They always suspected that anyone new coming in was the Man, and they would stay suspicious for a long time, and look for ways to trip you up.

Sometimes, they were told you were police by informants who would sell their own mothers for a dollar—or less.

Once they found out, you could be dead meat; down through the years, many undercovers had been killed— many more than the public ever imagined.

To survive at what Frankie Pinto did, Lawless knew,

you had to be something other than a street guy—you had to be a street animal, someone who could sense danger without really thinking about it.

"Once," Frankie told Lawless, "I went to a social club down on 110th and Lenox. I was getting in good with the dealers, working my way up to a half a key buy. But all day, I didn't know why, something was bothering me, and when I got to the social club—all the dealers were there—I got the feeling that they were going to kill me. I don't know why, I just did.

"Somehow, I was able to work my way out of there. And I found out later that they were. Not because I was the Man, but because I was suspected of having ripped off one of the bro's of one of the guys."

Frankie had been ripped off three times, he told Lawless. "Once I took a bad beating, but that's when I was inexperienced, man."

Lawless loved cops, and all, he thought, made their contribution. But deep in his heart he had a special place for the undercovers. They did their job day in and day out, and when a big bust went down it was not the UC who got the credit; it was the superior.

But the next day, it was not the superior who went back into the street. It was the undercover. If the NYPD had heroes, Lawless thought, the undercovers led the parade.

Lawless had not spoken with Frankie for about three months. He was in the DEA building over on West 57th, part of the joint NYPD-state-federal drug task force.

Lawless called him there and immediately recognized his voice.

"Frankie, Joe Lawless. How's life?"

Like most UCs, Frankie had a black sense of humor. It was, he had once said, "our way of coping with stress."

"Hey, mon. I don't think about life. I think about that, I couldn't work."

Lawless chuckled. "What have you been doing?"

"A gram of this, a gram of that. What have you been doing, Joe?"

"We caught that Castelli wipeout. We've been working on that."

"Sounds like a pro job," Frankie said. "Let me guess. That's why you callin'. Colombians?"

"No," Lawless said. "Dominicans. We even got a name. Fuentes. Brothers. Ever hear of them?"

There was silence. Lawless thought the line was dead. "Frank?"

"I'm here, Joe," he said. His voice was low. "I know 'em. They burned a UC about three months ago. He infiltrated. But they got him."

"I didn't hear about that."

"Yeah. Remember the 'vagrant' found shot on the East River Drive in the Seventies?"

"Oh, yeah," Lawless said.

"That was Johnny Padilla. Good cop. Experienced. But somehow they found out. We still don't know how."

"I'm sorry about that, Frankie."

"Yeah. I wasn't that close to him, except I was close to him. You know what I mean?"

"I surely do."

"How can I help?"

"What can you tell me about the Fuenteses?"

"A fair bit. You want to meet?"

Lawless arranged to meet with Pinto at four o'clock in Manhattan. In this way he could get to spend some time with Barbara, time that he badly needed. Just the thought of her gave him a little jolt of joy.

He was about to leave the squad room when he got a call. It was Ray Meehan from Forensic.

"We got those Castelli eight-by-tens, Joe. You want me to bring them up?"

"No," he said. "I'm going out. I'll pick them up."

"Why don't we meet by our peerless leader's office?"

"Fine."

A few minutes later, by Bledsoe's office, Meehan handed Lawless a fat manila envelope.

"I got seventy-five," Meehan said. "If you want blow-ups, just holler."

"I don't think I'll need them."

"We're still sifting through the other stuff. We're going to start to hit the other rooms this afternoon."

"Good, Ray. Thanks."

Lawless walked down the block and went into the garage that the Five Three maintained in an attempt to prevent their cars from being stolen.

He drove out on the street. Then he parked and began leafing through the eight-by-tens, which were in color.

They showed the Castellis from every conceivable angle, and there were a number of group shots taken with a wide-angle lens.

Lawless went through them twice. They gave him nothing new of an evidentiary nature, but he couldn't help thinking what a piece of work the shooter or shooters must be. Onairuts was right when he said they were well down on the food chain.

Lawless closed the envelope and laid it on the passenger seat. Then he was off to Barbara's.

CHAPTER 13

Before he got on the West Side Highway to Barbara's house he found a phone booth outside Fort Siberia that worked and called to say he was on his way.

"Bueno!" she said. "I'll be ready."

As he got in his car and headed onto the drive he realized that her being ready was why he had called. As tough a cop as she could be—and in the Baumann case he had seen just how tough—she was also a woman; and if he knew one thing about women—and he thought he probably knew very little except about the ones who commit homicides— it was that they liked to look their best to someone they loved, no matter what.

Or at least that's the way most women started out: looking good to their man. But in some places, particularly Fort Siberia, where poverty, crime, and just plain despair ground them down, they lost their youth and beauty and even femininity quickly. Most of the women in Siberia, he thought, were overweight and slovenly about the way they dressed, and many of them let the hair under their arms and on their legs grow out. They said the men liked that, but Lawless wondered.

He wouldn't, he thought, ever have any desire to find out if it was an asset.

When Barbara opened the door he could see she was dressed in what someone had once termed a stomach flipper—a tight white dress with deep cleavage. Her hair was up, and even standing in the doorway he could smell her perfume.

She opened the door wide and Lawless entered. She pushed the door closed behind him and then walked up to him, took his face in her hands, and gave him a long, slow kiss. He put his arms around her and he could feel her breasts. She had located her legs so one of his thighs pressed against her vagina.

She stepped away, took him by the hand, and led him to the bed. He noticed that the shades were drawn. There was only one lamp on, near the bed. She turned it off.

She undressed, stripping her dress over her head, then unhooking her brassiere. Her breasts wobbled free. She slipped off her panties. She did it slowly. He felt himself getting hard.

He stripped, first the jacket, shirt, pants, underwear. He was fully ready. But he wanted to prolong it. He wanted to do something to her.

He guided her so she lay gently back on the bed, her legs on the floor. He knelt in front of her and then spread her thighs wide. She knew what he was going to do. She sat up.

His head went down between her legs, and he could feel her breasts brushing against the top of his head.

He worked at her methodically, almost cruelly, sucking and gently chewing. He smelled a good smell, the smell of a woman.

She started to shudder. Her hands pulled his head into her. She contracted, inhaling sharply again and again. He worked at her.

Her breath was coming short—and so was his. He got up on the bed. She did the same. He mounted her, and then they controlled it the way experienced lovers can. Finally he just let himself pour ito her and her body arched up, shuddering almost violently.

Spent, they lay side by side.

"Hello," Barbara said.

Lawless laughed.

Later, semi-dressed, they sat on the couch drinking wine, listening to the stereo playing softly in the background.

She had let her hair down. She looked beautiful.

Lawless looked at her. "I don't think it ever gets any better than this," he said.

"God, I love you. You're so sexy, I want to go to work on you with a spoon."

"I never thought of myself as sexy," he said.

"Take it from me, you are."

The wine bottle was nearly empty.

"So what's going on now?" she asked.

"I'm going to see Frankie Pinto at four. We suspect some Dominicans of doing the Castellis. Frankie said they also killed a UC."

"Who are they?"

"Two brothers named Fuentes."

Barbara shrugged as if to say: I don't know them. "Then what?"

"I'm going to try to make it back here, if that's okay. I thought we'd get a bite."

"Good," Barbara said. Then: "By the way, what do you think the motive was for murdering the family?"

"It looks like Castelli was washing money. He got greedy some way and got caught."

"Drug money, right?"

"Yeah."

Barbara was silent for a moment. She had a fleeting distant image of her first husband, Jeff. Then it went away. "More wine?" she asked.

"I don't think so," Lawless said. "When I come back. But then you won't want any."

"You never know."

Lawless quaffed the last of the wine in his glass. "I better get going. Frankie is sometimes a tough man to catch, and I want to get him while I can."

"You better come back," she said.

"I will."

They kissed at the door.

"I'll see you later, baby."

Barbara looked at him. "Okay."

He was almost to the staircase going up when Barbara called to him.

"What about the package you brought in? You want it?"

"No. It's the Castelli eight-by-tens. I'll pick them up when I come back."

Lawless got caught in a traffic snarl on his way downtown and was twenty minutes late getting to Loughrey's, a bar near the DEA. When he did arrive, Frankie was nowhere in sight, and he thought he might have missed him.

But a few minutes after he arrived, the bartender came up to him.

"Are you Joe Lawless?"

"Yeah."

"There's a call for you."

"How'd you know it was me?"

"The caller said you looked like Steve McQueen."

It was Frankie. He told Lawless that he'd gotten hung up on some last-minute stuff and he wouldn't be able to make it for another hour at least—maybe more.

"I'll wait," Lawless said. "I know how famous you are for a disappearing act."

"You know me better than my wife," Pinto said.

Frankie called twice more, finally arriving at six-thirty. He looked exactly like what he was supposed to be: a fairly well-heeled coke dealer.

He was dressed in a white blazer, red pants, silk shirt open at the neck revealing chest hair, elevated shoes, and his neck was draped with gold chains. He was cocoa-colored, with an almost cherubic face and a flatish nose. He carried himself lightly on the balls of his feet, like a boxer, as well he might: He was on the PBA boxing team and also held a third-degree black belt in the Mantake school of karate. If you planned to take him out, someone had once said, you'd better really plan.

Frankie sat on the stool next to Lawless. "Sorry I'm late. You know how it is."

"That I do."

Frankie ordered a Perrier, and they went over to a table. They exchanged small talk about this cop or that, and then Lawless asked him about the Fuentes brothers.

"They run a heavyweight cocaine operation, and

they're growing. I wouldn't be surprised if they were in the top five by the end of the year. They've been in the States about four years."

"They have sheets?" Lawless asked.

"Not in the States. Both of them got sheets in Santo Domingo, where they're from. One of the guys in the squad talked with someone from the Judiciale down there, and he said they were suspects in a series of homicides, but that was about it.

"We do know that between 'em they've committed at least a dozen murders here."

"How'd you get a line on that?"

"An informant. We were doing good with him, learning a lot about a lot of people, and then we lost him."

"What happened?"

"He became a mule for a Cuban operation in Queens. He was taking in body packs. He got overconfident. He swallowed twenty-five condoms full of coke and a couple leaked."

"Where are they operating out of?"

"Manhattan North. They got dealers from 110th Street all the way to the Bridge."

"GW?"

"Uh-uh. 225th. It's Dominican country all the way up to there."

"I didn't know they went that far."

"They're ambitious, and no one is more ruthless or cold-blooded than the Fuentes brothers."

"What about their personal life?"

"There's Enrique the playboy, Miguel the serious one. Both are in their late twenties. They've been married a couple of times each, but they're not married now. They've got ex-wives and kids in Santo Domingo, but they've never been back, as far as we know. Just let 'em fuckin' go," Frankie added with a cynical smile, sipping the last of the Perrier.

"How am I going to get at them?"

"It's going to be hard," Frankie said. "What have you got now?"

Lawless explained what he had. Namely, the bullets and shells from the 9mm.

"You know where that gun is now, right, Joe?" Frankie said.

Lawless nodded.

Frankie laughed. "It's with the fishes," he said, "in a lake somewhere in fuckin' Oregon."

"Can they be squeezed?"

"Let me get a drink," Frankie said. "Another wine?"

"Sure."

Frankie got Lawless a glass of white wine and brought back a light beer. "Every now and then," he said, "I sin."

Lawless laughed. "You don't look like you sin too much."

"I'm a good boy most of the time."

Frankie paused and thought.

"I don't think they can be successfully squeezed. They're just too hard and smart. They got leaf bags full of money, too, and they'll have a carload of shyster lawyers on you before you know it."

"How about informants?"

"We can't get anyone to talk. Everyone's afraid of them. They'll clip your family and then go out and have a helluva good night on the town."

"You guys going to . . . What are you going to do about the undercover?"

"Oh," Frankie said. "Someday we'll get 'em for that. Or if we don't, maybe a drug deal."

"Where do they live?"

"Everywhere in Manhattan North. They keep moving around. They must have five apartments. We got some addresses, but there might be new ones in the last few months since we've been out of it."

"Can I put in a wire?"

"I doubt it. They're paranoid about wires."

"Tap?"

"We were going to put a pen register in a phone in a bar they go into a lot, but the feeling was to not risk discovery. Maybe you could put one in there. I don't know."

They were quiet for a few moments.

"I'm sorry I can't be more optimistic, Joe, but that's the way it is."

"I'd rather know what I'm up against."

"If anybody can bust these fuckers it's you; I know that."

"I'll just have to keep working at it. I got some help from downtown."

"How considerate," Frankie said, his smile showing very white teeth in his cocoa-colored face.

Lawless had an urge to stay with Frankie a bit longer, so he ordered another wine and got Frankie a beer. The meetings they had would, he know, be few and far between. Deep down, in a little place inside himself, he worried about Frankie Pinto and all the other Frankie Pintos he knew. Lawless knew that on any given day, street animal though he was, he could be blown away. He wanted to have a few laughs with Frankie now, a few drinks, tell him, by just being there, that he had his respect and affection.

Around eight-thirty, Lawless called Barbara. "I got involved with Frankie Pinto. I'm sorry, but I won't be able to make it tonight."

"Joe, I know you. Enjoy yourself. I'll see you tomorrow."

"Where have you been all my life?" Lawless, a little loosened by the wine, said.

He and Frankie stayed at the bar until around ten o'clock and then left. Lawless had a short ride home, but Frankie had to drive all the way to Shirley, out on the Island.

"I don't want you to be pulled over," Lawless said.

"Hey," Frankie said, "I'll blow the fucker away."

They both laughed hard.

At 57th Street, they stopped, shook hands warmly and said good-bye, and started to walk in opposite directions.

After a few strides, Lawless stopped and looked back. Frankie was boppin' along, and no more seemed like a New York City detective than the man in the moon.

Good luck, Frankie, Lawless thought. Good luck.

And then Frankie turned and looked back and waved. Lawless waved back. Street animal, he thought.

CHAPTER 14

Later, if she had sorted it out, Barbara would probably have said that it didn't start with the occurrence at the station, but it was certainly a factor.

It was one A.M., and she was at her desk on the first floor of the station house when they brought the junkies in for booking.

Even if she hadn't had a view of the booking desk, she could have smelled them. It had rained, and that made it worse, but you could smell a junkie even in the dead of winter.

Barbara got up from her desk and walked over. The junkies were all males. It was hard to tell their ages, even up close. All were pale, bearded, with shaggy hair, and wore makeshift dirty clothes. One had a large paper bag over his left hand.

One of the detectives who had made the collars was standing nearby.

"Where'd you bust these guys?" Barbara asked.

"A shooting gallery on Anthony, just off Tremont. They were up on the third floor. They're all far gone. We found one of them with a hypodermic sticking out of his neck. None of them have any veins left."

"What's that one doing with a paper bag over his hand?"

"It's swollen about five times normal. So's his forearm. It will probably have to come off."

Barbara stood there, trying to strike a disinterested

professional pose, but she was focused on the guy with the big hand. She looked hard. He had nice features, blue eyes, hair that had been blond when clean.

Once, she thought, maybe someone dreamed good things for him. And now, here he was, looking ten or fifteen years older than he was, his life a horror. He would likely be dead very shortly, and no one anywhere would mourn his passing.

She felt herself filling up with emotion. She turned and walked away.

She found privacy in the women's bathroom—usually only one female per night was on tour—and there she cried for the young man who was no longer young.

She willed the thoughts away, wiped her eyes, touched up her makeup, and went back to the desk. The junkies were gone.

She got home at around nine-thirty and went to bed. It took her little time to fall asleep—she felt very tired—but she slept fitfully, waking up a couple of times and thinking of the junkie, then telling herself to forget it. There was nothing she could do about it.

She got up around two o'clock, put shorts, shirt, and sandals on, had a couple of cups of coffee, and went into the living room. On the table was the envelope with the Castelli photos where Joe had left it the night before.

She sat down on the couch and opened the envelope.

Slowly, she leafed through the photos.

They did not shock her. She was a police officer. When you were a police offier, death was part of your job. In Fort Siberia, death was an almost daily part of your job.

Still, she lingered at the photos of the kids. Just little boys who play with toys and are dependent on Mommy and Daddy, and then some motherfucker comes in and shoots them in their heads filled with toys and hamburgers and cartoons.

Her eyes teared, and she put the photos back on the table. She got up and went over to the door and out into the backyard. It was a mostly concrete area, but it was flanked by two three-foot-wide strips of soil in which

she and Joe had planted tomatoes. Lately they had been
eating them until they were coming out of their ears.

It was only three o'clock in the afternoon and the sun
was out, but the yard was in shadow.

She thought of Jeff. She was so happy, so wildly
happy with Joe, but she knew that a part of her would
always love Jeff. He was her first love, and that was one
you never forgot.

Joe probably understood that. He understood it, and it
didn't bother him. He wanted her; he didn't want to own
her, which for sure she wouldn't have allowed anyway.
Ironically there was nothing macho about Joe. One of the
toughest people she had ever met in her life, and he
didn't seem so tough at all.

Jeff had hardly been tough.

Barbara sipped her drink. Something started to filter
into her mind from when she and Jeff were—what?
thirteen or so? She had known Jeff since he was seven.

They lived then in the tough part of Brighton Beach,
in Brooklyn, and one day there was this particularly
tough kid picking on Jeff outside school. He had Jeff
totally cowed until she finally stepped in and told him to
pick on someone his own size. The kid had responded
by telling "Barbara Big Tits" to shut up, and Barbara,
very casually, went up to him—she was simmering
inside—and hauled off and smashed him in the nose with
everything she had. The nose immediately started to
bleed profusely, and the fight in him flowed out with the
blood.

"You're lucky you're a girl," the bully had said to
save face. But everyone knew he was afraid of Barbara
and would never pick on Jeff again.

Later, when he and Barbara were walking home, Jeff
had started to cry.

"What are you crying for, Jeff," she asked.

"I wish I was strong like you," he said. "I should
have socked him."

"That's okay. I like you the way you are. You're a
poet, not a fighter."

Barbara went back into her apartment. She went into
the kitchen and refilled the wine glass, then went back

into the living room and sat down on the couch. She
sipped the drink.

He used to write long poems to her, poems about the
world and what was wrong with it. The poems used to
make Barbara feel warm all over, and she didn't care
that he wasn't tough. Not then.

They were married when he came home from the
Peace Corps, and they had plans to go to Appalachia
together, but it never happened. What happened was
that he had gone on drugs and it had started to come
apart for them and she had asked him to be strong. But
he couldn't be. He couldn't be even to save his life. The
drugs were there on the street, and he took them, and
one day he injected a speedball and was gone.

"Shit," she said softly.

She tried to turn off the thoughts, but they kept coming.

Alone in a roach-infested apartment, nineteen years
old and waiting for him, wondering where he was—out
hustling on the street to get some money to keep himself
going. And the more he got, the more he needed.

And she would wait and wait and wait, endlessly, but
he wouldn't come home, and she tried to think of something she could do, but there was nothing, except watch
him die.

Sometimes she got the same feeling of helplessness at
Fort Siberia. That no matter what you did you would
never make a bit of difference. That illegitimacy and
drug use would rise, that babies would be born with
AIDS, that people would live in fear and humiliation and
then die violent deaths.

There was one old dinosaur in the precinct, a guy
named Hutchens, who always wore a button that Barbara hated but he delighted in. He said it described
everything.

It said LIFE IS A BITCH. THEN YOU DIE.

She marveled at Lawless. He never seemed depressed
by anything. Nothing could beat him. "You try to make
a difference" was his abiding philosophy. "That's all you
can do."

She drained the last of the wine and went into the
kitchen to get a refill. She'd better watch it. She'd be

drunk before she was to go on tour. She wouldn't be able to do anything.

She took a long sip and put it down on the table in front of the couch.

Then she found herself in front of the closet. She opened the door, knelt down, and pulled out a small gray metal chest.

She brought it over to the bed and sat down.

She looked at it. In the chest were all the important papers of her life, including her will, which, she realized, she would have to change before she and Joe got married. And, of course, she would add another piece of paper: her second marriage certificate.

She had not opened the chest in a year or so, and it had been many years since she had gone deeply into it. The deeper the item, she thought, the longer ago the events around it occurred. It was her life, present to past, moving downward.

Now she opened the chest and took out all the top papers. On the bottom was an old photo album. She opened it up.

Once or twice she had thought about discarding it, almost as if she could throw out the pain with it, but she didn't. She knew she never would.

The reason was simple: It was all she had left of Jeff. That and the stone on his grave and the memories, and an occasional call to his father, who was the only surviving parent.

She leafed through the pages slowly. Some of the photos were very old, going back to when they were very young kids.

Was he handsome! She always thought he was the handsomest man she had ever met in her life. Oh, God, what drugs had done to him—turning her beautiful boy into a hollow-eyed, skinny monster.

Near the end of the book there was a picture of them that she thought was the oldest picture she had. They were dressed in winter clothes and were standing in front of a sled, and she remembered that she had loved him even then. He was so different from the other little boys. So gentle and caring. *Caring*. That was the most important thing. That's what she had always looked for in a man.

She could not remember what she had been thinking that long-ago day, but she had a vague idea: that some-day she would marry him and that they would live hap-pily ever after.

Tears filled her eyes.

Now, of course, she would live happily ever after. She had Joe Lawless. But what did Jeff have? Jeff had a plot of ground, and was a memory, sometimes, in the heads of some people.

"Oh, Jeff," she said out loud. "Why couldn't I help you? Why couldn't I make a difference in your life?"

The warm tears dripped on her legs, and she closed the book. After a while she stopped crying.

She looked at the book.

Who speaks for Jeff? she thought. Who speaks for the Jeffs of this world? Yes, she thought, Lawless was right. You had to make a difference.

But how?

CHAPTER 15

The older ESD guy was able to get the remains of the dog stored at the morgue through his friends there, but no one there would autopsy it. For one thing, there wasn't anyone there who knew how to autopsy an animal—"We only get the two-legged kind here," an assistant ME told him. For another, everyone was just too busy.

But Arnold got permission to have a vet of his own choosing come in and do the job. If he could.

He called Dr. Basil Manfredi, the vet who took care of his own dog, Misty, explained the situation, and Manfredi said he'd come.

Arnold knew he would, really. He had lower prices than most vets—"so people can afford to have the pets treated"—and he was active with a variety of groups who championed animal causes.

Three days after the animal was pulled from the Harlem River, Manfredi was able to get away from his own practice and do the autopsy or, as he called it, the necropsy.

There were cops, it was said, who could eat a seven-course meal while they watched an autopsy. Arnold was not one of them. Autopsies scared and almost sickened him, but he chose to be there while Manfredi did it; otherwise, he might miss something that would help the case.

When they wheeled the animal out on a gurney

Manfredi took one look and said, "It's a dog. A shepherd."

He looked further. "Female," he concluded.

As he worked, Manfredi dictated the various procedures into a recorder, just as a pathologist would.

At first, Arnold felt queasy and shaky, but then he got used to it to a degree.

But it was only a few minutes into the examination when Manfredi made an important discovery—not inside, but outside the dog.

"Look at this, Arnold," the doctor said, raising the rear leg. "It's got a registry number."

"A what?"

"There, tattooed under the leg. Those six little black numbers. That's an ADC number."

"What does it mean?"

Manfredi, not a man who smiled all that often, smiled. "It means that the owner registered the dog at the American Dog Club. It will have his or her name or address."

"Oh," Arnold said. "That's good. Very good." He was glad. But he wondered how the owner would react to the death of his dog. But he was a detective, wasn't he? It was part of his job.

The autopsy continued.

Dr. Manfredi amazed Arnold. He was coming out with words Arnold had never heard. He was so smart. It was hard to believe anyone could be so smart.

About ten minutes into the examination, Manfredi confirmed what the ESD guy had thought.

"I think this dog was in a fight with another animal. Look at this." Holding a pencil in his vinyl-gloved hand, he said, "There are puncture marks all over the body. Puncture marks are bite marks. And the throat laceration is rough, not clean, which is also characteristic of an animal bite."

"Any idea what kind of animal?" Arnold asked.

"Something very powerful. The puncture marks are very deep. And this dog weighs seventy pounds."

A few minutes later Manfredi made another discovery. "Her left front leg is broken," he said. "I think from a bite."

Twenty minutes later, Manfredi was done. At Arnold's request, the remains were put back in a locker.

Arnold and Manfredi went to a local luncheonette.

Manfredi ordered coffee. Arnold ordered a glass of water, which was about all his stomach could take.

"Do you have any idea," he asked Manfredi, "what killed the dog, or why?"

Manfredi shook his head. "No, but I will say this: I've never seen an animal chewed up worse. Still, she didn't die from that."

"What do you mean?"

Manfredi looked down at his coffee. When he looked up his light blue eyes were soft. "I know you love your own dog, Arnold, so . . . Anyway, this dog died of a heart attack."

"What?"

"That's right. The bite marks and lacerations and blood loss were only incidental. I would say that the dog died from sheer physical effort. It was fighting for its life, and its heart simply gave out."

"Was it old?"

Manfredi shook his head.

"No. Three, four years at the most. A young dog."

Arnold blinked. Now he didn't even feel like the water.

A few minutes later they were outside, and Arnold was glad. It was cool and pleasant and tended to calm the queasy feeling in his stomach.

He thanked Manfredi, then started walking. It occurred to him that it was only two o'clock, and he could still visit the American Dog Club. But he didn't feel like that. He just felt like being with Naomi and the kids and Misty. He went home.

CHAPTER 16

As he walked down Madison Avenue at around nine o'clock the next morning toward the building on 48th Street where the American Dog Club was located, Arnold was feeling a whole lot better than he had felt after leaving the morgue. He had gone home and done some heavy work with his weights, showered, had his favorite meal—pot roast and noodles (Naomi always had great timing)—played with the kids, spent the evening watching TV with Naomi, then made love.

Manfredi had told Arnold that the American Dog Club might not be so quick to give out the name and address of the dog's owner, so Arnold had dressed in what he thought of, without really thinking about it, as his battle uniform: an extremely tight-fitting T-shirt and pants which accented his massive, slablike muscles. At six foot three, 270 pounds, and with barely an ounce of fat on him, Arnold tended to intimidate people.

Sometimes he enjoyed intimidating people.

There was another reason for his battle dress: New York City itself. Arnold had been rasied in and around Freeport, Long Island, and the city's immense buildings had always scared him more than a little, and he had fantasied that the people inside the buildings were huge. They weren't, of course, but in his mind they always seemed to have an air of importance and bigness that made Arnold feel small.

As it happened, the ADC was very cooperative, and

not because Arnold was in battle dress. Once he showed his shield, the cooperation was immediate.

A Mr. Walters, a small, middle-aged man with thinning hair, who, Arnold thought, looked like a terrier, gave him the information.

"The dog's name is Miss Susie," Walters said, "and she was registered by Miss Daniela Keefe. Susie was registered on April 12, 1983. Miss Keefe lives at 2478 Jerome Avenue, Bronx, New York 10457."

Arnold wrote the information down as Walters gave it to him, then had Walters repeat it so he could get the last part of it. Arnold wasn't a fast writer.

"What happened to the dog?" Walters asked Arnold as they were walking to the door.

Arnold was going to tell him, but hesitated. "Oh," he lied, "she's lost. We're trying to help return her."

"Oh," Walters said.

On the way down on the elevator, Arnold tried to picture Jerome Avenue in his mind.

The El part was easy. It ran all along Jerome Avenue from two hundred and something street, down past Yankee Stadium at 161st Street and then went underground. Arnold had always thought it was painted a rust color, but recently he learned it was actually covered with rust.

He tried to think of an address on Jerome, and then he did: 2416. That was the number of Spinoza Brothers Hardware Store. He had picked up things for the house there a few times.

When he stepped off the elevator he checked the address of Miss Keefe again. 2478.

He closed his eyes and the area came into view. It was one of the private homes opposite the recreation house in St. James Park.

He opened his eyes; his brow furrowed. He didn't know anyone lived in those houses anymore. Most of them were so run-down that he just didn't think regular people lived there. Squatters, maybe, but not regular people.

On the street, he stopped and thought about what to do, but there was only one thing to do. Go and see Miss Keefe about Miss Susie.

CHAPTER 17

Arnold took the IRT uptown to the Fordham Road elevated station, then walked north to, where the house was.

He had remembered correctly. 2478 was one of a series of dilapidated houses flanked on one side by the massive Jerome Avenue post office and on the other by Sweeney's Bar. He had heard of Sweeney's. It had been stuck up at least three times since he'd been at the precinct.

Like the other homes, 2478 had a little yard in front, surrounded by a short chain-link fence. But unlike the other yards, which were overgrown with bushes and cluttered with garbage, the yard was in fairly good condition. The bushes were trimmed, there were flowers, and there was a little grass flanking the concrete walkway.

Arnold let himself in through the gate. His stomach was a little hollow. The gate had a rusted-out, almost unreadable sign: BEWARE OF DOG

As he walked up the path, Arnold sensed that someone was watching from behind one of the curtained windows that looked out over the porch. But he made believe he wasn't aware of it.

He rang the bell. Or tried to. It was broken. He tapped on the door, which had a glass insert, with his wedding-ring finger.

There was another, curtained interior door, and he

could see the shadow of someone come up to it. But the door did not open.

Arnold reached into his back pocket and took out his shield. He held it up against the glass. The interior door opened.

A woman who he guessed was in her early sixties came into the foyer. She had a lined face and white hair; she was sort of haphazardly dressed, with both a dress and slacks on. She opened the door and looked up at Arnold. She had soft gray eyes. "Yes?"

"I'm Detective Gertz from the Five Three, uh, Fifty-third Precinct. Did you lose a dog?"

"Oh, yes! Miss Susie. Did you find her?"

What Joe Lawless had told him once flashed into his mind: "Never tell anyone about the loss of someone they love until you're finished questioning them. Otherwise you can lose them to grief."

It wasn't a person, Arnold thought, but he had seen something in her eyes.

"No," he lied. "But I need to ask you some questions about her disappearance. May I come in?"

"Oh, yes, sure. I'll help in any way I can."

Arnold followed her into the house.

They went into a dim hallway, and Arnold caught the smell of dogs; from the back of the house, probably in the yard, he heard barking. Then it stopped.

He followed the woman into the living room, which was also dim. The only light came through the curtains and shades, which were pulled.

The room itself looked more like a store than a living room. It was so cluttered that there was only a relatively small space in the center of the room to stand in. It was filled with old, worn furniture and bric-a-brac of all kinds, but mostly statues and statuettes.

Each wall had at least three framed photographs, all of different kinds of dogs. And it took him a moment to realize that all of the statues and statuettes were also of dogs. Hundreds of them.

"Oh," Arnold said, suddenly remembering. "You're Daniela Keefe."

"Oh, yes," she said. Then: "Would you like to sit down? Would you like something?"

"I'll sit," Arnold said, "but I don't need anything. Thank you."

Arnold sat in a big battered overstuffed chair that looked like it could take his weight. Daniela Keefe sat in a chair opposite him.

"I'd like to know," Arnold said, "when was the last time you saw the dog. Uh, Miss Susie."

"Oh," she said, glancing at the clock on the mantelpiece. It will be eight days in three hours. Two o'clock."

"What happened?"

"I fed her," Miss Keefe said, "and then I walked her. I took her over to St. James Park, like I always do. I went into the park and then let her go. I do this all the time. She usually just romps around a bit, does her duty, and then comes back. But that day . . . that day she just didn't come back."

Arnold wrote "St. James" in the little notebook he had taken out.

"Uh, didn't you, uh, watch her?"

"Oh, yes. But I can't watch . . . I mean I couldn't see her all the time she was off the leash, but I never do."

"Why is that?"

"She always runs over the hill, and then I can't see her until she comes back."

"Where's the hill?"

"As you come into the park. The entrance near Kingsbridge Road."

"Oh," he said. "I know where it is. Kids sleigh-ride there in the winter."

"That's right."

"What did you do then? I mean after she didn't come back."

A troubled look passed across her face. She was reliving it.

"I went looking for her. There were so many dogs in the park, I thought maybe she had gone to play with them. She's very playful. But I . . ."

She paused a moment.

"But I couldn't find her. I started to ask people if they

had seen her. She's so easy to see, with her beautiful black coat of hair . . .''

Arnold blinked. He fought off the image of the dog being pulled out of the river.

''. . . and then I found a man who saw her. Or thought he did. It was all the way over on the side of the park, near Creston Avenue. He said he saw a big black dog chasing a squirrel. But she disappeared into some bushes near the entrance to the park and he didn't see her after that.''

''Did you get his name?''

''No. I don't know him. I went back to the park every day to see if she would come back, but I didn't see her or the man.''

She paused.

''I should have gotten the name of the man?''

''No,'' Arnold said. ''It's probably not important.''

He was going to ask her how the man was dressed, but he didn't want to. Then he realized he had to. He was a police officer.

''Do you remember what the man was wearing. In case I see him?''

''Oh, yes. He was wearing a suit and tie. Very clean-cut-looking man. Spanish. Black hair and all. I'd say he was about fifty-five.''

Arnold jotted down the description.

''If you see him again, call me, okay?'' Arnold said. He handed her a card.

''Do you have a photo of Susie I could borrow?'' he added.

''Hundreds.''

She went away and came back with a box that was full of photos of the dog and herself and other dogs.

She pored through them, and then took one out and handed it to Arnold. It showed the dog, in color, on its haunches, its tongue out.

''That was taken two months ago,'' she said.

It was hard to believe, Arnold thought, that the dog in the picture was the one taken from the river. He put the picture in his jacket pocket.

He couldn't think of anything else to ask her. It was time to tell her.

He looked at the carpet. It was old and worn. He glanced up and his eye caught an old photo on the mantelpiece. The photo of a man, small, in a gilded frame.

He looked at Daniela Keefe. Suddenly Arnold felt better. Because he knew he would not tell her now about Miss Susie, and he would never tell her.

"Well," he said, getting up, "I'll call you if I get any word. Could I have your number?"

She gave him her number, then said, "I think it's wonderful that the police are searching for her. I only contacted the ASPCA and an animal group downtown."

"Well," he said, "we sometimes work together."

She nodded. "Do you have a dog?"

"Oh, sure. Airedale terrier."

"That's a good breed," Daniela Keefe said. "Good for kids."

"I got kids."

"I would have guessed that," she said. And for the first time since he had come into the house, she smiled.

Once, he thought, she had been a pretty woman.

Arnold went down the walk. He knew he had made the right decision.

CHAPTER 18

Arnold went from Miss Keefe's house to the Jerome/ Kingsbridge side entrance of St. James Park.

The hill was right there, some fifty yards in from him, a swelling in the ground topped by an outcropping of rock.

Arnold had worked the park a number of times since coming to the Five Three, and had seen the hill often, but he never realized how high it was. From where he stood it seemed that the dog could have run over it and out of sight on the other side.

The park itself was a vast place made up of flat grassy areas crisscrossed by macadam paths generously spotted with trees. It was *busy*. There were clusters of blacks and Hispanics standing around, people walking their dogs, people riding bikes, kids walking along with big ghetto blasters, people running, playing grab-ass.

He decided to try to trace, as much as possible, the route that Miss Keefe's dog had taken.

As he walked into the park he could feel eyes on him, but he did not look back. He had found out the hard way that people, especially the people who lived in Fort Siberia, could think a simple glance was putting them down.

On the other hand, Arnold was afraid of many things in his life, but not physical confrontation, if it came to that. And it might. St. James Park, nicknamed St. James Pharmacy by the locals, was reputed to be the largest

78

"outdoor pharmacy" in the world. It was one of the main areas in the precinct, indeed the entire city, where small drug buys, usually nothing more than a gram, were made. But it was, of course, a world of ripoffs, and therefore violence. In the last three months there had been three killings in the park, a rape, and six assaults.

Arnold came to the top of the hill. Directly in front of him, at the base of the hill, was a vast complex of tennis courts, enclosed by high chain-link fences.

They were closed, and had been closed, he knew, for a year. The Parks Department simply got fatigued with replacing the constantly stolen equipment.

There were quite a few people inside. Twelve-foot-high chain-link fences were no problem to the kids of Fort Siberia.

Arnold went down the hill. To one cluster of kids he must have seemed like the Man, because they dispersed as he headed their way.

He stopped on the path, directly outside the fence. He could go left, around the courts, or right, which also led around them and were more toward the exit near which the unknown man had seen Miss Susie.

He headed right, then left when he came to the corner of the courts.

The path was taking him toward Creston Avenue, which ran parallel to Jerome Avenue; Creston ran from Morris Avenue on the southernmost corner to 193rd Street at the northern end. The park was separated from the street, as it was on the Jerome Avenue side, by a stone wall in which was embedded a spiked fence. Trees lined the wall.

Arnold continued to walk toward Creston, and he looked at the people quickly as he went, looking for a well-dressed Hispanic man.

He saw no one who resembled that man.

The park was as busy on this side as on the other. Kids, dogs, bicycles, ghetto blasters, all kinds of activity.

He took the picture from his breast pocket and approached a kid who was about ten. The kid looked at him suspiciously.

"Hey, kid, you ever see a dog like this?"

The kid looked at the picture. "No," he said. But his looking had attracted other kids.

Arnold asked the same question. The answer was the same.

He asked a few adults. One man who was walking a strange-looking dog gave him the most time, but he had never seen it.

Arnold's adrenaline spurted when a battered-looking Hispanic with dirty clothes said "*Sí*, I seen it."

"Where?" Arnold said.

"Everywhere."

At first, Arnold didn't understand. Then he did when the man said, "Choiman shepherd." The man knew the breed, not the dog.

Arnold stopped asking and looked out toward Creston Avenue. The far side of the street was lined with five-story buildings, some red, some gray brick. The people who lived in them would have a pretty good view of what was happening in the park, at least where trees weren't in the way.

He could leave the park one of two ways: To his left was a broad sweeping staircase, gray granite; to his right, some low steps. He walked toward the staircase, which let him out on 192nd Street.

There was only one way to find out if someone had been looking, he thought. Knock on doors. Go from door to door, showing the picture.

It was a big job. There had to be at least twenty apartment houses where some of the apartments had a view into the park, and all looked down onto the street.

He knew also that Captain Bledsoe would not give him any help. He only came around when it was time to take the credit, and over the last year Arnold had grown to dislike him.

Arnold wasn't even going to tell him what he was doing. He would wait as long as he could, then write a five on it.

He knew that some people would consider him crazy for trying to find out what had happened. But Arnold didn't feel that way. Since the dog had been discovered there had been an idea growing in his mind that some-

how the dog had been murdered. There were murderers
out there. Of a dog, but murderers nonetheless.

And there was a real victim here. In fact, there were
two victims. The dog was a victim, and so was Daniela
Keefe. Arnold knew that he could do nothing to bring
the dog back. But if he could find out what had happened and catch whoever it was that had harmed the
dog, he would feel better. And he was determined to do
just that.

CHAPTER 19

On Creston, Arnold saw that there were many open windows, with people, young and old, sitting at them. Maybe the people did this every day. Maybe he should just check them.

But no, that wasn't the way to do it. If the dog was seen, who's to say the person who saw it was by the window today.

He went into the red brick building on the corner of 192nd Street.

The smell—mostly from people using the area under the stairs and the first floor as bathrooms—was bad, but Arnold was used to it. And he was a cop. It was part of his job.

He decided to start on the top floor.

This was one of the smaller buildings. There were four doors per floor, and each seemed to have four or five locks. If a door had only one regular lock, you suspected that the apartment was abandoned.

He picked one of the apartments and knocked on the door when the bell didn't work. No answer. He knocked again and heard someone come to the door.

"Excuse me," he said through the door. "I'm Detective Gertz from the Fifty-third Precinct. I'm looking for a lost dog."

"He not here," came the female voice. "Gone to Ponce. Not here no more."

Arnold rang, then knocked on the next door. Movement behind the door. He made the announcement as before and heard the sound moving away from the door.

One door on the floor opened. A little Hispanic girl with big black eyes looked up at him.

"Hi," Arnold said, "I'm a detective looking for a dog. Is your mother here?"

The little girl shook her head. "Work," she said.

Oh." He reached into his breast pocket and showed the picture to the little girl. "Did you ever see a dog like this?"

The little girl shook her head.

"Thank you," Arnold said.

After trying each apartment, Arnold did his paperwork: He laboriously marked in a little notebook whether the person was in, not in, or maybe in.

On the fourth floor, Arnold thoght a moment before beginning. Maybe, he thought, he was using the wrong approach. Maybe he should say nothing, wait until the door was opened before he spoke.

He tried the first door. Surprisingly, the door bell rang. He said nothing, but the door opened fairly quickly.

Standing in the doorway was a short, muscular Puerto Rican who smelled strongly of alcohol. Arnold also got a strong whiff of garlic.

The man seemed to be about fifty-five. He was dressed in a filthy T-shirt and baggy pants.

"*Sí?*"

"I was wondering if you could help me," Arnold said. "I'm from the Fifty-third Precinct and—"

With surprising swiftness the door, which like the other doors was metal, slammed in Arnold's face with the speed and sound of a cannon shot.

Arnold's immediate reaction was to tear the door off its hinges, go inside, and hunt the man down. But he controlled himself. He was a professional, a police officer.

He had no luck on the rest of the floor. One of the apartments was empty. One door was opened by a very young Hispanic boy; Arnold made a note to report this to Welfare.

The other door was opened by a young woman who had red eyes and sniffled as they talked. She seemed wholly self-confident but knew nothing. Arnold knew she was on coke.

There was no answer at two of the apartments on the third floor. One was empty. At the next, he got a nice reception.

A well-dressed middle-aged Hispanic woman invited him into the apartment, which was clean; it didn't look like it belonged in Fort Siberia, but Arnold knew it did. There were many nicely kept apartments. The people who lived in them were forced by economics to live in Siberia, but they wouldn't let it beat them.

Unfortunately, neither the woman nor her husband recognized Miss Susie. The woman said she would say a little prayer that it was found.

Arnold struck out on the second and first floors. Then he went out into the street and down a flight of stairs to the super's apartment.

The super could hardly speak English. But he managed a no when Arnold showed him the picture.

When Arnold had started working the building it had been sunny out, but it had gotten cloudy and now it was starting to rain. He looked across the park. He couldn't see it, but somewhere behind the trees was Miss Keefe's house. She would be in that dim, bad-smelling place waiting for her dog.

Arnold went into the next house.

CHAPTER 20

Three days after he started canvassing the buildings, Arnold had worked his way about halfway down the block. He started at ten—he figured that was a respectable hour—and worked until there was no more light in the halls; only a few had bulbs that worked.

On the fourth day, Naomi took Jude to see the dentist. He had a couple of teeth that were coming in wrong and she was concerned about them. Her appointment was for ten. She suggested Arnold call her after twelve to find out what the dentist had said; she had a few things to do after the appointment.

After he completed his eleventh building, he walked down to a drugstore on Fordham Road and called her from one of the few pay phones that were operative in the entire precinct.

"The dentist said it's okay," she told him. "He'll watch the teeth for the next year or so. They should straighten out naturally, but if they don't he may have to pull one at the most."

"Oh, good," Arnold said. "That doesn't sound too bad."

"Dr. Manfredi called before I left for the dentist," Naomi said. "He wanted you to call. He said he was going to be in surgery for the morning but that you could call him between twelve and two—now."

"Oh, okay. Thanks. I'll call."

As he went through the process of getting Dr. Manfredi's number, Arnold wondered what he wanted. He had finished his autopsy, and he had seen Misty only three months earlier. She wasn't due for a visit for another month or two.

Dr. Manfredi answered the phone himself. "Oh, hi, Arnold," he said. "Thanks for calling back. I've been wondering about that shepherd. It's actually been bothering me that we can't determine exactly what happened."

Arnold was silent.

"But I think," the doctor said, "I know someone who can help."

"Who's that?"

"Captain Arthur J. Haggerty."

"Who?" Arnold said. But the name rang a bell.

"Captain Haggerty. He runs a school for dogs in the city and has a training facility upstate. But he's also an expert on animal bites. Years ago he got involved in dog-bite fatalities and expanded that into evaluating all kinds of animal bites."

"Is he in the Army or something?"

"No. 'Captain' is something he held over from the Army. He was head of the K-9 Corps in Europe in the fifties."

"Oh."

"Give him a call," Manfredi said. "See what he says."

"I will, Doctor," Arnold said. "And thanks."

"I'd like to know how it all turns out," Dr. Manfredi said.

"Oh, sure."

He should call Haggerty right away, Arnold thought. But he hesitated. If Haggerty agreed to help, who would pay him?

Arnold closed his eyes, thinking of asking Captain Bledsoe. If he couldn't go to Bledsoe, what could he do? Pay himself? He had no extra money.

Still, he had to try. He got Haggerty's number from Information and dialed it.

"Captain Haggerty's School for Dogs," a cheerful man answered. "May I help you?"

"I'd like to speak with Captain Haggerty," Arnold said.

"That's me."

"Oh," Arnold said. "Dr. Basil Manfredi suggested I call you. I'm a detective in the Five Three."

"Manfredi. Oh, yeah, the vet—I know him."

"That's right."

"How can I help?"

Arnold gave him the details of the case. A few times he had to go back and fill in. He was not good at telling a story. But he struggled through.

"I thought you might be able to tell us what attacked the dog," Arnold said.

When Haggerty spoke, he sounded much less cheerful than when he had answered the phone.

"Let me ask you a question. Are any of the animal's legs broken?"

"Yes. Front left. How did you know that?"

"I have some ideas. Where's the body?"

"Bellevue," Arnold said. "Uh, one thing—I don't think we can pay you on this. I don't think the Department would pay."

"That's okay," Haggerty said, his voice still low. "Some cases I charge for; some I don't. This one I don't."

"Thank you," Arnold said. "Uh, what do we do next?"

"I'd like to look at the animal."

"When?"

"How about right now?"

They arranged to meet at Haggerty's school, which was on East 91st Street, and go down to the morgue from there.

Arnold left for the school immediately after hanging up. He felt better now that he had an ally.

CHAPTER 21

A half hour later Arnold was walking up 91st Street toward First Avenue. Arnold expected to see a large building, but was surprised to see that the school was a converted store, just like others on the block. It had a plate-glass front window and a sign hanging outside: CAPTAIN HAGGERTY'S SCHOOL FOR DOGS.

Arnold went in. It was empty. There was a counter and behind it a door, but no one was in sight. The walls were covered with photos, certificates, and testimonial letters.

Arnold concentrated on the unusual-looking man in the photos. That, he thought, must be Haggerty.

And it was. Because the man in the pictures came through the door in the back.

He made Arnold feel small. Haggerty was just as tall, but he had broad shoulders, massive arms, an immense belly. Arnold guessed he weighed four hundred pounds. He was wearing a T-shirt and pants held up by suspenders. He was cue-ball bald, his head shaved. His face was unlined, and it was hard to tell just how old he was.

"May I help you?" Haggerty asked.

"I'm Gertz," Arnold said, flashing his tin. "From the Five Three."

"Oh, yeah," Haggerty said. "I just have to give a dog an attack session, then we can go downtown."

Arnold had no idea what Haggerty was talking about.

"An attack dog," Haggerty said. "It's time for his daily training session. After that we can go downtown."

He went back through the door, and a minute or so later a black guy emerged. He was holding a Doberman pinscher on a long leash, which he had bunched up short. Haggerty followed, some sort of protective device over his left arm.

Arnold stepped aside as they passed, then followed them out into the street.

Haggerty positioned himself a few yards opposite the man and dog and crouched.

He nodded to the black guy and yelled something Arnold didn't understand. The dog leaped across the concrete and hammered into the arm guard, biting ferociously.

Haggerty didn't budge an inch, but moved the guard quickly, yelling and agitating the dog at the same time.

The black guy pulled the dog back, and the procedure was repeated twice more.

Then Haggerty surprised Arnold: He went over and petted the dog.

"Okay," he said to Arnold. "I'll put this away and we'll take off."

They took Haggerty's van. It was only a short drive down to the morgue. On the way, they made small talk, and then Arnold realized where he had seen Haggerty.

"I've seen you in the movies, haven't I?"

"Yeah," Haggerty said. "I've been around. There's lots of roles for a romantic lead like me." He laughed.

They talked about Haggerty's film career for a bit, but as they neared the morgue, both men became quieter. Arnold didn't know how he'd react, now that the dog was no longer just a dog, which had been bad enough. Now it was Miss Susie, and Miss Keefe owned it.

As they entered the morgue, Arnold remembered something. "The autopsy report," he said. "I don't have that." God, what a detective he was.

"That's okay," Haggerty said. "I don't think I'll need it."

Arnold sensed that he didn't even need to see the body.

It took a few minutes to get down and into the morgue. An assistant ME saw Arnold as they were brought inside and came up to him. "We were trying to get you," he said. "We have to do something with the dog. We need the space."

"We'll be finished after today," Haggerty said.

A few minutes later the dog was wheeled out on a gurney and the sheet was removed.

Haggerty took a pair of rubber gloves from a pocket and slipped them on.

He first gripped one leg, then the other, and gently bent them.

Finished with the legs, he moved his face closer to the dog and looked at its lip, the laceration in the throat, and then slowly moved his hands over the dog's entire body, turning the hair back so he could observe the punctures better.

His examination only took a few minutes.

"I've seen enough," Haggerty said. Arnold looked at him. Haggerty had blue eyes. Arnold saw something very sad and angry in them.

They exited the building and walked down the block toward where Haggerty had parked his van.

"I think," Haggerty said, "no, I know—it was killed by another dog."

"What kind? Do you know why?"

"I don't know the why, but the kind is the American Staffordshire terrier."

"What?"

"Commonly known as the pit bull terrier."

"What's that?"

"It's a war machine on legs," Haggerty said. "The toughest dog alive. Not pound for pound—alive."

"I don't think I know it."

"You've probably seen it. They weigh from thirty-five to sixty pounds and come in all colors. They have a kind of wrinkly face, but their most dramatic feature is their jaws. For their body size it's massive—they look like they have golf balls in their mouths. They have tremendous biting power, the strongest of any breed."

Arnold remembered something. "Oh," he said. "I

remember. About six months ago a kid broke into a yard
and there was a dog on a leash. Two dogs. One got loose
and bit the kid in the leg. Neighbors tried to beat it off
with sticks but couldn't. A uniformed guy had to shoot it
dead.''

"That's it," Haggerty said, stopping and puffing, sweat
beading his bald dome. "The most dramatic example I
ever heard of—this was documented—was a pit bull
who got hold of a steer by the neck. The farmer tried to
beat it off but couldn't. Finally he used a chain saw to
cut the dog in half—and it still held on."

"Oh my God," Arnold said.

They started to walk again in silence.

"It was the broken leg," Haggerty said, "that made
me almost sure it was a pit bull. That's how some of
them fight. They're called 'leggers.' They go for the
legs, knock the other pit down, then go for the throat."

"Why," Arnold said after a while, "would Miss . . .
the shepherd be fighting a pit bull?"

"I don't know," Haggerty said. "Usually pit bulls
only fight pit bulls."

"Yes," Arnold said. "I saw something about that on
'20/20.' They're like, uh, formal fights."

"They call them 'conventions,' " Haggerty said. "A
plywood ring is set up somewhere, and then the dogs go
at it. Putting a shepherd in with a pit bull is first-degree
murder."

"The shepherd's a lot bigger, isn't it?

"Yeah," Haggerty said. "The pit bull's smaller, but
he could beat it with ease. He could beat a Doberman—
any dog alive. You have to understand, Arnold, that pit
bulls have been bred and trained to fight. They have
great endurance, a tremendously high pain threshold,
and they're dead game."

"What's that?"

"They fight to the death . . . usually. Some dogs do
give up, don't come up to the imaginary line—called
scratch—in the center of the ring."

"How long are the fights?"

"Two, three hours," Haggerty said. "You got to have
a strong heart to watch one. I've seen them on film. The

thing is, the dogs are quiet while they fight—they're tearing each other apart—quietly.''

"It's unbelievable," Arnold said.

"Yeah," Haggerty said. "And cruel. The guys who fight the dogs will tell you that few of them die in the ring, and that's true. But after the fight the mortality rate soars—dogs die from loss of blood, dehydration, heart attacks. That shepherd must have been brave—it took a hell of a beating before it died, but it didn't have a chance."

Arnold felt anger surging inside him.

"What kind of people do this?"

Haggerty stopped again. He looked at Arnold, his blue eyes hard.

"Subhumanoid cocksuckers," he said. "Good old boys with egos the size of BBs who want to prove how tough they are. But it's the dog that gets in the ring, not them. You know what happens to a pit bull that loses and has the misfortune to live?"

Arnold almost didn't want to hear.

"They're like lepers. Nobody wants 'em. You can't give 'em away. Some owners just shoot them."

"It's so sad," Arnold said.

"That it is," Haggerty said. "And illegal—in all fifty states."

They got to the van. Haggerty swabbed his brow with a handkerchief.

"Why," Haggerty said, "would they want to hide the dog's body? I figure they're having fights. But I don't understand why they're going to so much trouble to make sure a dog isn't found."

"Yeah," Arnold said.

"There must be something bigger going on," Haggerty said. "More at stake."

"I'm checking out the area where the shepherd was last seen. Maybe someone saw something that could lead us to whatever it is."

"Right," Haggerty said. "Meanwhile, I think I'll put some lines out. Maybe we can learn something, though the boys who fight these dogs are really paranoid."

They got into the van.

"Where can I drop you?"

"Back at the store will be okay. Then I'm going back to the area."

"That's okay," Haggerty said. "I'll run you all the way."

CHAPTER 22

Four days after Charley Murphy left his apartment, Frank Piccolo and Ed Edmunton sat in their living room and watched TV. Or at least Edmunton did. Piccolo was thinking about a fight he had seen the night before. Two lightweights. It had reminded of him of when he was a kid and wanted to be a boxer. He remembered his coach saying to him, "Frankie, you got the best instincts I ever seen in a boxer. But unfortunately there are rules on how you fight, so you'd be at a disadvantage."

And he had laughed.

The coach had been right, Piccolo thought, but he had said something else: He didn't have the ability either. It was one of the major setbacks of his life, and he never really forgot it.

Then he thought of something he had not thought of in a long time—how he had wanted to be a zookeeper. Reptiles. He liked them above any of the other animals and felt most at home with them.

Well, he didn't become that, either. But he had been able to get a few pets, and he took great care of them. They were in perfect health.

Every now and then he would think of Ace. And his deal with Spagnoli, the DA. He didn't want to blow it by taking action on his own. But there was a terrible frustration in him.

"I feel fuckin' nine months pregnant," he told Edmunton. "I got to deliver."

"We got to wait it out, Frankie," Edmunton said. "You're a great detective, and with self-control you'll be even greater."

Piccolo had seen Ace today. Going into the left-wing building. From his vantage point, he had thought, watching the top of Ace's head disappear into the building: I could put one in him that would come out his balls!

Piccolo had, in fact, seen Ace go in all the wings. But he was unpredictable. There was no telling when he would show up.

There were three sharp raps on the door, and Piccolo sprang from his chair like he was pulled up by a wire. Edmunton got up, turned the TV sound way down, and tiptoed rapidly to the closet. He took out a .38, which he slipped into the pocket of his baggy short pants, and passed a Nagra recorder, no bigger than a pack of cigarettes, to Piccolo, who turned it on and slipped it in his short pants.

The knock came again, more insistent than before.

Piccolo went to the door, put his hands together as if praying, and looked skyward. Please, God, he thought.

"Who's there?" he said in a squeaky voice that was in harmony with his size.

"Landlord."

Piccolo laboriously opened the dead-bolt lock, then a door lock. He opened the door a crack, chain still on, peeked out with wide eyes, then opened it all the way.

Piccolo was tremendously excited, but his face showed nothing but concern and fear.

Ace looked at him with mean black eyes, and he looked over Piccolo's shoulder—an easy task—at Edmunton, who also showed concern and fear.

"The landlord want me to talk with you," Ace said, stepping through the doorway unbidden so Piccolo had to open the door to let him in.

"I don't understand," Piccolo said, closing the door.

Ace looked down at him. "Sure you do. This place being renovated, and all the tenants got to get out. Everything's being torn out."

"I got a lease," Piccolo said as Ace strolled into the living room. "It's got a year to go."

"The fucking landlord own the fucking building," Ace said, turning to face Piccolo. "He say what happens, no piece of paper."

"I don't see other people leaving," Piccolo said.

"They fucking leaving," Ace said, his voice loud. "Twenty apartments are empty. I know. I gave 'em fucking notice. And they'll all be empty soon, including yours."

Piccolo furrowed his brow. "I can't move," he said. "What would I do with my pets?"

Piccolo's pets were arrayed in glass cases around the living room. Ace had been looking at them. "Wha' the fuck are they?"

Piccolo stepped quickly over to one case. "This is a python," he said, pointing to a large olive-colored snake with brownish rings.

He stepped to a nearby case. "This is a boa, which I'm sure you're familiar with. And this is a monitor," he said, stepping over near a two-foot-long lizard with a brownish color and white underbelly.

"And this," he said, pointing to a smaller lizard that was purplish and very ugly, "is my pride and joy. It's a tokay gecko," he said, his eyes glittering a little as he looked at Ace.

Ace was momentarily transfixed.

"Did you know," Piccolo continued, "that it is the only natural enemy of the roach? I let it out at night— that's why there are no roaches in the apartment. And that it has a tremendous biting power. If it bites you the only way you can get it released is by surgery."

Ace's eyes refocused.

"Wha' the fuck you talkin' 'bout? You and your boy-friend and these fuckers got to be gone in a week."

Piccolo looked at him, the saddest man in the world. "What do I do with my pets? What do I do?" he asked, rubbing his hands together.

"We give you moving expense," Ace said. "Five hundred dollars." Ace took out a thick wad of bills. He peeled off $500 and offered it to Piccolo. "All you got to do," he said, "is sign this here paper."

"What paper?"

"This here one," Ace said. He pulled a sheet of folded-up paper from his pocket and handed it to Piccolo.

Piccolo took it. He turned it over. "This paper's blank," he said, "except for a line where I sign."

"We'll fill it in," Ace said.

Piccolo stared at the paper. He looked plaintively up at Ace. "I can't sign this."

Ace, who was perhaps six feet from Piccolo, stepped forward.

"You better motherfuckin' sign," he said. "Both you and your boyfriend."

Piccolo's hands shook. "Are you threatening us?" he said.

"You bet your motherfuckin' ass. I'll do a number on both of you you won't motherfuckin' forget."

"Give me a pen," Piccolo said. Massive things were happening inside him. It was like he was on a drug, his mind clicking off and on. But he and Edmunton signed the paper.

Ace threw the money on the table.

"Is that all the money we're getting?" Piccolo said. "Five hundred dollars?"

"One week, I say. I'll be back to see."

Piccolo's head was down, and stayed down until Ace had left. Then he raised it. His face was contorted in rage, the whites of the eyeballs almost red, like he had just awakened from a sleep. Which, in a way, he had.

He took the Nagra out of his pocket and placed it carefully on the coffee table.

Then his body started to tense. He turned and scuttled into the bedroom in a Groucho Marx–like walk. Edmunton followed.

He watched as Piccolo leaped on the bed, buried his head in a pillow, and then screamed. He screamed for two minutes.

When he finally took the pillow away, his face was the color of a tomato and tears streaked it.

Edmunton sat down on the bed and looked at him. "Hey, Frank," he said. "You did great. What self-control! You've come a long way. Wow!"

Piccolo nodded. "My time will come," he said.

*　　*　　*

The next day, Piccolo and Edmunton brought the tape from their encounter with Ace to District Attorney Spagnoli at his office in the Bronx County Court House, a large gray block building on 161st Street and the Concourse. As they walked up one of the broad sets of sweeping stairs which led to massive entrance doors, Piccolo was quiet. Edmunton had known him long enough to know that something was on his mind. He was bothered by something.

They went to Spagnoli's office, then to one of the conference rooms on the third floor. Present were Spagnoli, Piccolo, Edmunton, an assistant district attorney, and Dave Whittaker, the chief of the DA's investigations unit. Bledsoe was not there, for a simple reason: Piccolo had not contacted him.

They listened to the tape, and Spagnoli was delighted. The recording was very clear, and as the threatening voice of Ace was heard, one could almost see Spagnoli adding up the years on the variety of charges Ace would be facing.

"We should be able to turn him easily with this," Spagnoli said. "Congratulations on a fine job." He looked at Piccolo, then at Edmunton, and back again. The investigations chief and the assistant DA nodded.

Piccolo looked as if someone in the room had just shit in their pants.

"In other words," he said to Spagnoli, "you're ready to make the collar."

"Yeah," Spagnoli said. "Anything wrong with that?" He had sensed Piccolo's displeasure.

"Who makes the bust?" Piccolo asked.

"Oh," Spagnoli said, "I see. It doesn't matter. If you want it, that's okay. Right, Dave?"

Spagnoli looked at Dave Whittaker, his chief of investigations.

"No problem," he said.

"Understand," Piccolo said. "I don't give a fuck about credit in this if it comes to that. I just want to make the bust. I want to see this fuck's expression when I collar him."

Spagnoli nodded. He was quiet. For the moment, he had become acutely aware of the fire-breathing qualities of the little man standing opposite him.

"Of course," he said. "Our deal still goes. You don't hurt him, and it's our job to turn him. We have to do it or, like I said, that platoon of shyster lawyers Fishman has will allow this guy to walk."

"Don't worry about that," Piccolo said. "The only way this guy is going to get hurt is if he dies of a coronary."

And Piccolo smiled his gap-toothed smile. The others in the room tittered, a little nervously.

CHAPTER 23

It was relatively quiet for the homicide squad at Fort Siberia in the days before Ace was to show up again to make sure Piccolo and Edmunton had vacated the apartment. An Albanian drug dealer had shot two Hispanic twin brothers named Cruz to death in St. James Park, and there was one potential homicide. A Cuban guy who was about to perform cunnilingus on his attractive young wife noticed bite marks in the area which were not his. He burned her down there with a frying pan and then used the same pan to put her in intensive care. Piccolo and Edmunton were unsure if she was going to make it.

Other than that, it was routine. Digging in and investigating the many uncleared homicides in the precinct.

Piccolo was antsy all week, and so, for a change, was Edmunton. They did so want the thing to go down smoothly.

To that end, they stayed away from their apartment as much as they could. The last thing they wanted was a confrontation with Ace that was unplanned.

On Monday, two days before Ace was to show up, Piccolo had an idea that could result in an additional charge being lodged against Ace: B&E—make him force his way in. He didn't tell anyone about it except Edmunton. He didn't want any interference.

Monday afternoon he was called into Bledsoe's office. Bledsoe wanted to know why he hadn't been apprised until that afternoon—by the DA—of what was going on with the case.

Piccolo said he assumed Edmunton had told him. Taking his lead from that, Edmunton said he thought Piccolo had.

Bledsoe didn't press it. In the first place, Piccolo and Edmunton were experienced cops and would likely make the collar, which would lead to bigger and better things later, and ultimately reflect well on him. And who knew? Maybe he would be transferred out of this rat's nest.

In the second place, Piccolo worried Bledsoe. He was like Lawless. Unpredictable. They were both stupid about one thing: putting their ass on the line. Either man, he thought, was capable of bizarre behavior, maybe even so far as trying to hurt Bledsoe.

He didn't exactly know what he meant by "hurt." But they were just characters it was better not to screw with.

It was dead summer, and most of July had been so hot that it was an effort just sitting in the shade.

But the Wednesday Ace was to show up a cold front came in from New Jersey and blew the steam away, and it was obvious by dawn that it was going to be one of those cool, fall-like days that reminded you that summer didn't last forever.

Piccolo and Edmunton, both on a four-to-midnight the night before, were nevertheless up before dawn, each man with his own thoughts as they had coffee and then watched the orange sun slowly rise over the Bronx.

Edmunton felt good, very good, just to be here with Frank Piccolo. Other people, he well knew, regarded Piccolo as nuts, but not Edmunton. To him, Piccolo was the essence of what a good cop should be: ballsy and loyal and smart. Frank Piccolo was all that, and much more to Ed Edmunton. Edmunton's own ten-year career on the job had been chaotic, and the last year, before they shipped him to Siberia to die or throw in his papers, was very, very bad indeed. His wife had left him with the kids, he had been knocked down a grade for drinking, and then there had been the grass-eating. He didn't know why he had done it—taking relatively small gratuities such as meals and ball-game tickets to look the other way on gambling, he just had.

And then, when he went to Siberia, he quickly learned that his reputation as a dirty cop had preceded him. At another precinct it probably wouldn't have meant anything. But Siberia was like a prison camp, where some of the cops walked around feeling like dog shit, and if they could look down even a little on someone else they would.

For weeks, Edmunton just sort of drifted on his own in this precinct comprising psychos, drunks, other grass-eaters, a few meat-eaters, old guys, and guys who had just angered the brass. He was a misfit among misfits.

It hurt him bad, but he told no one.

And then one day Frank Piccolo came up, introduced himself, and invited him for a drink.

"There's a slot open in the homicide squad," he said. "I thought you might be interested."

"You know who I am?" Edmunton had asked.

"Yeah," he said. "I know you. I know a guy in the Four Two. He said you're a good cop."

Edmunton nodded.

"Yeah," Piccolo said. "I know who you are. I know they accused you of grass-eating. Well, la de fuckin' da. Everybody eats grass. I don't see that as bad. As long as you aren't a meat-eater, that's fine."

"What about the squad leader? Lawless, right?"

"Joe? No problem. The first day you come on the squad is the first day he ever heard of you. You're a blank page."

In the relatively short time they had been at the Five Three, Piccolo and Edmunton had been through a lot, because life and death there is in condensed form. One year in Siberia is like a career in another precinct. And his feelings about this little gap-toothed man who sat next to him watching the sun come up were simple: He would die for him. And the feeling, he knew, was mutual.

Frank Piccolo was feeling good too. He had the same kind of feeling he had had when he was in Nam in 1970. It was his first time. Waiting expectantly for the dawn to come, and with it, all his GI buddies knew, the attack by the Cong.

That day had worked out well. The firefight had been all theirs, and no one had been killed. Of course, there had been other days . . . but he didn't want to think of them now.

It was the day a cop worked for—the day the collar was made. All your work for this one moment: "You're under arrest."

But it went beyond that. It was the sheer excitement of it all. He heard a cop put it this way: "You get addicted to your own adrenaline." Yeah, that was the feeling he would get. That and . . . helping people, especially old people, people who had all the odds against them. All his life he had enjoyed reading stories about people who were sick or warped or damaged in some way—the Elephant Man, the writer who typed with his toes; and he had tremendous admiration for the Japanese gymnast in the 1976 Olympics who had won a gold medal on the rings while performing his stunts with what turned out to be a broken leg.

Someone had once asked him if he didn't get afraid of the situations that he got involved in. He had answered, truthfully, that he did, but he didn't really say that he was only a little afraid.

Today he hoped, first, that Ace showed up. He wanted that very badly.

But it would also be good if he came armed. That was the ideal. He probably wouldn't have more than a blade on him, but Piccolo could hope.

The day seemed endless, and then, around two o'clock, his heart vaulted with joy: There were three sharp raps on the door.

"Open de fuckin' door," came the deep-voiced command.

Piccolo, sitting on a couch, sprang from it as if a cattle prod had been applied to his ass. Edmunton stood.

Piccolo actually rubbed his hands together as he went to the door.

He opened it but kept the chain on.

"You supposed to be gone today," Ace said.

"I told you," Piccolo said in a squeaky, plaintive voice, "my pets. What will I do with my pets? Please . . ."

"You movin' today," Ace said.

Piccolo shook his head.

Ace backed up a few feet. Piccolo backed off the door. C'mon, motherfucker, he thought.

Ace kicked at the door with one of his massively muscled legs. The chain lock was ripped from the door molding, and the lock clattered across the floor. The door flew open and banged against the wall.

Piccolo backed up, Edmunton behind him.

Ace entered. "You a wise-ass motherfucker," he said, and reached into his pocket. He came out with a gravity knife and flipped it open.

"You can't break in here," Piccolo screeched. "And now you're threatening me with a knife."

"Get your shit out of here," Ace said. "Now. Or I'll make you hamburger and feed your pets to the cats."

Piccolo was going to continue it, but Ace's reference to the cats made things inside his head short-circuit.

He backed over to an upholstered chair where his gun was in a holster draped out of sight on the far side.

Ace advanced toward him, and Piccolo brought the gun up. Ace stopped as if he were suddenly turned to stone.

Edmunton was laughing. Piccolo was not. Neither was Ace. Ace's eyes were wide.

Piccolo dropped into the Weaver stance, a kind of combat shooter's position which worked well for rapid fire of larger handguns. He was a holding a stainless steel .44 Magnum, the world's largest and most powerful handgun, capable of stopping a charging elephant.

Words sprang to Piccolo's lips, but he was conscious of the Nagra going in his pocket.

"You're under arrest. Read him his rights."

Edmunton came up, showed Ace his tin, and started to read the rights. Ace looked at him, then back at Piccolo when he heard and saw him cock the .44.

"Hey, hey, what you doin'?"

"Nothing," Piccolo said, "as long as you do nothing.

But if you do anything, I pull the trigger and the bullet won't stop till it reaches Hoboken.''

Instinctively, Ace threw up his hands.

Finished reading the rights, Edmunton ordered Ace to lie on his stomach on the floor. Ace did without a word. Roughly, Edmunton cuffed his hands behind his back, then pulled him up.

Piccolo uncocked the gun, got the holster on the chair, and put it on over his T-shirt, this one saying "BEATLEFEST 1985.''

A half hour later, Ace was delivered to the district attorney's office. It was Saturday, and Spagnoli was not there. An aide told Edmunton and Piccolo that he had to go out of town on a speaking engagement, but that he would be back Sunday night, and then the interrogation could begin.

Piccolo left his number. "Tell him to call me," he said. "He should also book this guy under B and E, assault, criminal trespass, and a variety of other things.''

"Okay," the aide said. "We'll call you.''

CHAPTER 24

The Tuesday after the Castellis were killed, Dr. Anoruits autopsied them with Joe Lawless witnessing it.

There was nothing really new.

Each had been shot once in the head, and it was highly likely that the children were killed up to an hour before their parents. Acid phosphotase tests confirmed that the woman had been brutally sodomized. It could not be determined if the man or woman had died first, though the theory propounded at the crime scene was logical: The kids were killed with their parents watching, the woman sodomized and killed, then the man, John Castelli, shot.

Onairuts put their deaths at between ten P.M. and twelve midnight on Friday, June 22.

Ballistics tests were also confirmed on Monday. They had been shot with a 9mm pistol.

Onairuts had not been able to determine how close they had been shot from, but it didn't seem to matter.

The wake was held in a Romano section funeral parlor and the funeral mass at St. Carmel's Church. Burial was at St. Raymond's Cemetery.

As a matter of course, Benton showed up at the burial ceremony, and the people who had gone there were photographed from afar by Lacy, a homicide squad member, using a 400mm lens on a 35mm camera. Later, the pictures would be examined for knowns, or anyone who seemed out of place in any way. Lawless didn't expect anything from it. He was almost convinced, now, that the Fuentes brothers were the perps. Getting to them would be another story.

On Wednesday afternoon, Benton got to see one of the assistant managers at the bank. It was amazing what the threat of a little public scandal could do. The manager, a young man named Roberts, said that there were two accounts that John Castelli had insisted he and only he oversee, a rum company named La Puelo Rum Company, Inc., and the Westside Coffee Importers, Inc. They were quite substantial accounts.

"Do you have the figures?" Benton had asked. His mind was traveling the RICO statute path: The government could seize the assets of anyone who it believed was involved in what seemed to be a "pattern of racketeering."

"I do," Roberts said, "but I don't know what sense it makes."

"Why don't you let us decide that?" Benton said.

"It's just that both accounts were closed yesterday."

"What?"

"Yes. All the money was withdrawn."

"By who?"

"Miguel Fuentes."

Benton was silent for a moment. He knew his blood pressure had just vaulted. He didn't want to blow the top of his head off.

"Why didn't you contact us?"

"I don't know," Roberts said. He was rattled.

"Where was it transferred?"

"Swiss International investments."

In other words, Benton thought, gone.

By Friday, the story had slipped to the back pages of the newspapers, and it was not mentioned on radio or TV.

The detectives started to slip away too. They went back to their own precincts, and by Saturday morning there were only three detectives left knocking on doors in addition to Lawless and Benton, when they weren't doing other things. And the extra detectives were set to be reassigned Monday.

Lawless didn't think they'd do any good. No one in the neighborhood, he was convinced, was going to be telling them anything. It was just the pattern of the responses, the grain, if you will. They weren't even trying to be helpful. It was a stone wall all the way.

The word must have gone out from the Benuto family not to cooperate. Or at least they had not given the okay to cooperate. It amounted to the same thing.

Under ordinary circumstances, the Mafia wouldn't have stood for what had gone down. It was regarded as a fouling of their nest.

He had caught a squeal once when the Mafia clipped a common thief for stealing proceeds form a local poor box.

Lawless guessed the reason for their noninvolvement: fear. The Colombians and Dominicans, unlike the Mafia, had no rules at all. You might get your family killed. Lawless could understand their reluctance.

Lawless had not gotten to spend any real time with Barbara all week. But he was determined to do so Saturday, which she had off.

They planned to have deli food, and Lawless headed down to her apartment at around six o'clock, taking the subway.

As the train rattled along, it occurred to Lawless that, in fact, he had only seen Barbara once, for a grand total of around five minutes, during the entire week.

He had walked slowly up to her desk the night before, where she was busy working on something, and when she had seen him standing there her face had brightened, then pouted.

"Why," she said, taking his hand, "do we meet in such public places?"

"Because," he said. "I'm a fool."

Lawless told her about the case, the lack of progress, and his growing feeling that on this one, as bad as the perps were, they would probably end up just going through the motions.

Barbara had listened to it all, and had said absolutely nothing. Then he had left.

He realized now for the first time that something had been troubling Barbara. It was nothing she had said, nothing dramatic, just the way she looked at him and smiled. Maybe it was the smile. Not a plastic smile—she didn't do that ever—but one that was . . . what was the word? Rueful. That was it. Sorry about what he was telling her, but more. She seemed sad about something that went beyond the Castelli case.

Then again, he thought, as the train pulled into the 72nd Street station, maybe it was all in his head. Work fifteen, sixteen hours a day and lots of things can get in your head that don't belong there.

CHAPTER 25

Barbara brought out the cold cuts a few minutes after Lawless arrived. They sat down at opposite sides of the table by the windows.

Lawless ate with relish. All week he had been subsisting on coffee, pizza, and donuts, and when he sank his teeth into the pastrami sandwich he had made for himself it was delicious, as was the cold light beer he used to wash it down.

He was halfway through the sandwich when he noticed that Barbara was just toying with her salad: taking mini bites, chewing slowly.

"Not hungry?" Lawless asked.

"Not too," she said. "But please, you enjoy yourself."

Lawless did, digging back into the sandwich, shoveling in forkfuls of macaroni, potato salad, and cole slaw, interrupted by an occasional bite of a crisp sour pickle.

"Any progress on the case today?" she asked after a while.

"No," Lawless said. "Status quo."

Barbara said nothing for a while. Then: "So these guys just keep peddling their stuff. People keep dying. They go on, living high on the hog."

"They'll make a mistake," Lawless said. "One day they always do. Then we'll get 'em."

"You don't get everybody, do you, Joe?"

Lawless shook his head.

He took a long swig of beer, washing down the last of

the sandwich. He put the can on the table and looked at Barbara.

"Is this leading somewhere, honey?" he said.

"I have an idea to get those brothers."

Lawless looked at her. He sipped at the beer. "What's that?"

"Put in an undercover."

"They tried that," Lawless said. "The Fuenteses burned him." And he told her the story of Johnny Padilla, the good cop who was the vagrant found on the East River Drive.

"That makes it even better," she said, looking at Lawless, her eyes intense.

"Why?"

"They'd never suspect another UC this quick. Never."

"Maybe," Lawless said. "But maybe they'd be very afraid. Maybe what they're supposed to be like, they won't be like. I don't know."

Lawless drained the last of his beer. His eyes were on the tablecloth.

"What about," Barbara said, as if Lawless had not spoken, "putting in a woman? These guys are so macho they'd probably never suspect a woman."

Lawless's eyes flicked up. "Like who?"

Barbara looked at him. "Me."

"You?" Lawless said. His stomach had tightened a little. "Why?"

"I'm a police officer, but you have to admit I don't look like a police officer when I'm dressed. Do I?"

"No, I guess not." Lawless did not like the discussion at all.

"Well, then, why not?"

"Hey, Barbara. You have to be experienced at undercover. No disrespect intended, but it's not a job for a beginner. The cops who buy drugs are experienced—and tough and tremendously street smart. And resourceful."

"Last year, around this time," she said evenly, "I was alone in this very room, unarmed, with a psychopath who had killed his stepdaughter and was about to kill me. I had no chance. But I'm still here, and, not to sound egotistical, that says something about my resourcefulness.''

Lawless was quiet. He lit a cigarette. His stomach was a little hollow.

"Why would you want to do this?" he said.

"I got to thinking," she said after a moment or two of hesitation, "about things. I haven't really done enough against these dopers. You got to do something significant."

"Does it," Lawless said very quietly, "have something to do with Jeff?"

Barbara who had been looking out the window, turned her head toward Lawless.

"Yes," she said. "It does. I was thinking about him. Thinking that maybe, just maybe, if there had been a cop somewhere who had done just a little bit more, he wouldn't have died. Maybe the H that killed him would never have gotten to his arm. Maybe a miracle could have happened. Maybe he'd still be alive instead of . . . while you and I live happily ever after."

"It's a guilt trip, Barbara," Lawless said. "A guilt trip. You're just feeling guilty about being alive and happy while Jeff . . . Jeff's life is over; yours just beginning. You got to take a risk, punish somebody, punish yourself—and me."

"Maybe there is some guilt. But still," she said, "you can't deny it. Maybe it would work; maybe it would put these bastards off the street and save some kid's life somewhere and maybe keep the dreams of some parent or some young girl somewhere alive and . . ."

Her eyes filled with tears. Lawless wanted to go to her. But to do so would approve what she was saying.

"I love you, baby," he said. "But I can't let you do it. It's a police decision. My evaluation is that you're not qualified to go in under cover."

"Who are you," Barbara said intensely, "to stop me?"

Lawless's face went hard. "It's my case," he said. "I'm the fucking guy whose squeal it is."

They looked at each other. The obscenity was like a slap in the face. He had never cursed in front of her.

"And," he said, "you're my fiancée. I don't want to lose you. I got dreams too, baby."

The last statement was said low, filled with emotion. But Barbara could not listen. She knew what she had to do.

"I'm going to do this thing," she said, "one way or another, with or without your help."

Lawless looked at her. His eyes were filled with pain. He stood up, dinched his cigarette in an ashtray, and walked out the door.

CHAPTER 26

After Lawless left, Barbara cleaned the table in a mechanical way. Then she got herself a beer and sat down on the couch. It was her fourth beer of the evening.

She knew she had hurt Joe. He had come back a long way from Karen and the years after. Ten years was a long time to swallow your impulse to love, and she knew that for Joe, one of the bravest people she had ever met in her life, there would never be a braver act than letting himself fall in love again.

She took a long slug of beer.

Now he didn't want to lose it. Her.

Still, who spoke for Jeff, and all the Jeffs of the world?

No, maybe it wasn't as grandiose as that. It was just her, remembering her Jeff and doing one thing to settle a score for him and maybe help someone else.

Joe was wrong about her ability to do it. No question. She could do it. She just knew it. There had been so many things in her life she had been able to do that surprised people.

Yes, Joe was wrong. But she hated to hurt him and wondered what it would do to their relationship. There was a part of him that was so hard inside that it almost scared her. She didn't want to have him go into that.

Her thoughts drifted, a montage of Jeff and Joe and . . . She put the beer can on the table in front of her and was soon asleep.

When she awoke it was dark, around eleven.

She went into the kitchen and started to make herself a cup of coffee.

Joe was probably in his bedroom now, lying in bed in the darkness, staring up at the ceiling. Hurting. Worrying about her. Worrying about their relationship.

She had sat down on the couch and had taken her first sip of coffee when the thought occurred to her. She went out of the living room and into the kitchen and dialed the number on the wall phone.

"Joe," she said.

"Hi."

"Can you come over, please?"

"I'll be there in about forty-five minutes."

It seemed a long time to Barbara, but he was there in forty minutes. She kissed him lightly on the mouth.

"I've been thinking about this undercover thing," she said when they were settled on the couch. "I'm not going to do it."

"Why not?"

"You matter more to me," she said, "than a memory, or anything else. Much more."

Lawless gulped and swallowed. He looked at her. His eyes were incredibly soft.

"I was thinking about it too," he said, "and maybe you should do it."

"What?"

"Yeah," he said. "I know you. You're deep-feeling, and as long as you live, this thing will haunt you. I don't want that, Barbara. I want you to put it behind you."

They said nothing. He was right, she thought. Dead right.

"You're sure?" she said.

"Absolutely. But I'm still worried about the Fuenteses, the whole scene."

She said nothing.

"Do you want to do it?"

"Yes."

Lawless nodded. "Okay, but before you do, I'd like you to talk to somebody I know. Frankie Pinto. He's been a UC for a long time, been working the streets for years. Let him tell me if you can go under. Okay?"

"Fair enough." Barbara said. "I feel better about that."

Lawless lit a cigarette and inhaled deeply. He looked at her.

"You're some piece of work," he said.

Barbara took the cigarette from his mouth and put it in an ashtray. She turned out the light.

"Shut up," she said.

CHAPTER 27

They pulled the remaining three detectives from Lawless on Monday, and then it was just him and the squad members. He found himself thinking a lot—probably too much—about Barbara going undercover, but there it was. It was really too late to turn back now.

On Tuesday he called Frankie Pinto. Pinto didn't like it.

"Hey, Joe," he said. "This is your fiancée. I don't want to make a wrong move. It's a burden."

"I know, Frankie," Lawless said. "But to me you're the only show in town."

Reluctantly, Frankie agreed to take a look at Barbara, talk with her, get a feel for just how she would fare in the drug set, particularly with two *maracones* like the Fuentes brothers.

That night, Lawless had dinner at Barbara's house, and he told her that Frankie had agreed to meet with her.

"It's exciting," she said.

"Yes," Lawless said. "It is."

She laughed.

The next day, Barbara called Frankie at the DEA about nine o'clock. He wasn't in. She was told to call again at eleven o'clock, and did.

"Hello."

"Frankie Pinto?"

"Yeah."

"I'm Barbara Babalino. Joe Lawless talked to you about me."

"Right." He had a slight Spanish accent.

"When can you see me?"

They made an appointment for the next day.

At one-thirty the following day, Barbara Babalino went to the fourteenth floor of the DEA building, and a sign told her to go to the twelfth floor. She did, and the receptionist, a large black woman ensconced behind a plate-glass window, called down to Frankie.

"He'll be up to escort you," the woman said.

While she waited, Barbara looked at the pictures on the walls. There was a picture of the President, the attorney general, and a face she didn't recognize. They all smiled beatifically at her.

Within two minutes, a small, cocoa-colored, rather nice-looking Hispanic turned the corner. He was dressed, Barbara thought, like a pimp or a coke dealer. He had on red satin pants, an aqua shirt, white jacket, patent-leather shoes, and innumerable chains hung from his neck.

"Barbara," he said, approaching her. "I'm Frankie Pinto." He smiled, his perfect teeth very white against his skin.

"Glad to meet you," she said.

She followed him to an elevator.

"So you're going to marry Joe, huh?" Frankie said as they waited for the elevator.

"Yes."

"That's good."

"I know," Barbara said.

"Where'd you grow up, Barbara?"

"Brooklyn."

"You know drugs?"

She nodded.

"All the terms?"

"A lot."

"You know green tape, yellow tape, red tape, Three Five Seven, Not Responsible, Double Skoal, Cherry Coke?"

"No," Barbara said.

Frankie looked at her. "They're the brand names. Local cocaine. It's just important to know how they're sold—different brands on different streets."

Barbara nodded. "That's the way they're sold in Fort Siberia," she said. "Different areas sell different brands. Eye of the Tiger . . . White Death . . . Devil's Dust . . . like that."

"How come you're dressed the way you're dressed?"

Barbara had dressed in as sexy a way as she could and had really swabbed on the makeup.

"I sensed it was the way to dress. Like a dealer."

"But why?"

"I just sensed it."

The elevator came, and they went down two floors. Frankie led her through two doors into a small room that contained a few metal chairs and a metal table. The walls were white and scuffed.

"Have a seat," he said.

Barbara sat down on one side of the table, Frankie on the other.

"You know what the Fuenteses look like?"

"No."

Frankie went to the pocket inside his jacket and took out two photos. He placed them on the table in front of Barbara.

"That's Miguel on the left," he said, "and Enrique—Ricky—on the right."

The photos, obvious blowups of surveillance shots, were of good quality, but you didn't need that to tell the differences between the brothers.

Enrique was almost white, with straight hair and fine features, handsome. Miguel was black, with short, kinky hair and heavy Negroid features. He wore sunglasses.

Dress was different too. Ricky was dressed like a playboy, Miguel conservative in suit and tie.

"They don't even look like brothers," Barbara said.

"They are," Frankie said. "Ricky's the playboy, Miguel the serious one. But both are dangerous. Joe tell you about Johnny Padilla?"

Barbara nodded.

"He was one of the sharpest undercovers I ever knew. . . ."

He let his voice trail off. Barbara saw something in his eyes that quickly went away.

"Ricky," Frankie said. "He likes ladies. What you going to do if he wants to, uh, forgive me, screw you?"

"I wouldn't let him."

"How you going to stop him?"

"I'll tell him I do business. I'm a coke dealer, right? Sex has nothing to do with that."

"What if he insists?"

"I'll take a walk."

Frankie paused a moment. His eyes flicked away, then swung back.

"Let me give you a situation," he said. "You meet the Fuentes brothers. Of course, you wouldn't just meet them—we'd have to find somebody to introduce you. You're introduced as a small-time dealer looking to eventually buy weight.

"You go in there for your first buy. Say it's a banged-up apartment on 116th Street. You sit down at a table like this to do your business. It's just you, Ricky, and Miguel, okay?"

Barbara looked at him.

"Of course you got a gun in your purse, okay?"

Barbara nodded. She was tense.

"So right away Miguel says to you, 'Who the fuck are you? Where the fuck did you come from, bitch?' "

Frankie's voice shook with hostility.

"And you say, 'So-and-so introduced me. Randy. Don't you remember?' "

" 'Who the fuck is Randy?' " Frankie screamed. Barbara was taken aback. " 'Who the fuck is he? He's a two-bit scumbag. Who else do you know? Where in the fuck did you come from!'

"And then," Frankie said, "he takes out his 9mm and lays it on the table, his hand on it.

" 'C'mon.' Now he's getting hysterical. 'Who the motherfuck are you?'

"Now it looks like he's going to shoot you, right? But then he says, 'Wait a fuckin' minute. I know. I know.

Do you know Slim? You know, Slim with the fuckin' Afro and the gold tooth, tall skinny bro? Lives on 111th. You know him?'

"What would you say?" Frankie asked.

Barbara answered without a moment's hesitation. "I'd say, 'No, I don't know him.' "

Frankie looked at her. "That's good," he said, "because there would be no Slim."

They were silent a moment. Frankie looked at her.

"That's the first rule of undercover," he said. "Never lie about something you don't know to be true, or can be checked. You're tested all the time, and Dominicans—particularly the Fuenteses—don't spend much time wondering if you're the Man. They'll either blow you away or take a hike. But the undercover is over. They're even more dangerous than the Colombians. The Colombians think first before they whack you out."

And, unexpectedly, Frankie laughed.

"Real thinkers," he said, laughing a little harder. "Ain't that rich?"

Barbara couldn't help but laugh too.

"Let me give you another scenario," he said. "What if you walk into the situation where they offer you coke. They know the Man can't accept it. What are you going to do?"

"I'm not going to try it."

"What if," Frankie said, "one of the Fuenteses goes like this."

In a flash, so fast that she did not see him do it, Frankie had his finger pointing at Barbara's forehead. His eyes flicked to the coke, represented by an ashtray on the table. "Try it, huh?"

Barbara had gone a little hollow inside, but she reacted instinctively. She grasped her purse and stood up.

She looked at Frankie.

"Hey, I came here to buy cocaine. And you're playing games. I'm leaving. You can pull the trigger if you want."

And with that, she headed toward the door.

Frankie lowered the "gun."

"That's the right reaction. You're here to do business. Nothing else. It's all business. Nothing interferes with business.

"I'm sorry," he said.

"That's okay," Barbara said. "I know what you're doing." She sat back down.

"I could sit here for days and make up all kinds of situations, but the key is: You got to be able to think on your feet. And think like a dealer. That's the bottom line."

He paused. He looked at her.

"I think that a woman going in there is a good idea. I think you could catch them asleep, even though Miguel is super-paranoid."

Frankie paused.

"Maybe."

He said nothing for what seemed like a long time. Then he looked at Barbara.

"Joe asked me to see if you're qualified to go undercover. I'm going to tell him I sense you are."

Barbara's reaction was mixed. She was happy and strangely sad at the same time.

"I'll tell you something else, though," Frankie said. "I'm not right all the time. I put one lady out there who was overconfident. I didn't see that. It ended badly."

"I'm not overconfident."

"It happens," Frankie said, "that we got a chance to get you to meet the Fuenteses. A possibility. It would happen quickly, if it does. A matter of days. There'd be some training, but you'd go under quick. Is this okay?"

"Yes."

"It would be a change in lifestyle. Seeing Joe regular would not be in the cards."

"It wouldn't be forever," Barbara said.

"Another question," Frankie said. "Can you kill someone quick, without thinking about it?"

"I have," Barbara said. And she explained about Baumann.

"That's good," Frankie said. "You can't be a priest in this job."

They paused.

"How come you want to go undercover?" Frankie asked.

"I have an old score to settle. How about you?"

"Probably the same thing. Someone I knew . . . it happened a long time ago, but I guess I never forgot it."

Barbara nodded.

"You got to be powerfully motivated in this job," Frankie said. "Or permanently out to lunch."

And he smiled broadly, his teeth white against his dark skin.

CHAPTER 28

The day she met Frankie Pinto, Barbara was on a four-to-twelve. She took a break, in uniform, about ten o'clock to have a cup of coffee with Joe. They sat in a booth in the back of one of the few clean restaurants in Fort Siberia.

She told him what had occurred with Frankie Pinto. Lawless's face hardly ever reacted to anything, even to Barbara, even now. But his eyes showed what he felt: resignation.

"I can still call it off," she said. "In fact, there's no guarantee I'll even get a chance to go under. Frankie said it's a possibility, that's all."

"No, it's okay," he said, lighting a cigarette. "If it happens, it happens."

"How's the case going?"

"Not well," Lawless said. "But you never know. Maybe we'll get lucky."

Lawless inhaled deeply. Barbara reached across the table and took his free hand in hers. "I'll be all right; believe me."

Lawless looked at her.

CHAPTER 29

A week later, Barbara Babalino got a call at home from Frankie Pinto.

"We got a way in. Can you meet me soon?"

"Name it."

"In two hours," Frankie said. And he named a bar on West 57th near the DEA building.

"I'm going to have someone with me," he said.

"Who?"

"Andy Fenwick, assistant chief of the DEA."

Frankie had called Barbara at about three o'clock. She arrived at the bar about five.

For a moment, she had trouble spotting Frankie, even though, as she came to realize, she had looked directly into his eyes when she first looked around the bar. He was sitting at a booth with a well-dressed, dark-haired man who looked to be about forty-five.

As she walked toward the booth she realized why she hadn't recognized him. His hair, which had been in a sort of Afro when she first met him, was combed flat, and he wore a conservative suit. Today he looked like a cop.

The two men rose as she approached, and she found herself glad to see Frankie. There was something solid and real about him that she liked.

He introduced her to Fenwick. Fenwick ordered drinks for them all.

They exchanged small talk—what precinct she had been in before the Five Three, how Lawless was, etc. After about five minutes Fenwick got into it.

"I'm here," he said, "because I wanted to meet you and explain what we have.

"What we have," he continued, "is a three-time loser named Jimmy Pollo who was caught upstate with half a key of coke in his car. If he goes to trial and is convicted, he'll die in prison.

"Jimmy wants to deal, and so do we. He knows the Fuenteses. In fact, a few years ago they screwed him out of a lot of territory that was his. He looks on this as not only an opportunity to deal with us but to get even with them."

"What will you be giving him?"

"He'll walk. Plus some bucks."

"What would he do?"

"Give you a good introduction to the Fuenteses. We know that Ricky frequents a disco called the Crazyhouse in Manhattan. What we figured was for you and Pollo to go there Saturday night and accidentally run into Ricky."

"That's only a few days from now."

"That's right," Fenwick said.

"Let me ask you a question," Barbara said. "Would the Fuenteses have any idea Pollo was arrested? They might expect him to be in jail."

Frankie shook his head. "No. Pollo was caught accidentally. Some state narcs were sitting on a wire. We found out and arrested Pollo fast. No one found out anything."

Barbara said nothing.

"We explained everything to him," Fenwick said, "and he said okay. But he says once he introduces you, he's gone. No way does he want to be associated with you."

"Does he know I'm a cop?"

"We didn't tell him," Fenwick said, "but it's reasonable to assume he'd figure you're that, or an informant of some sort."

"Why do we have to move so fast?" Barbara asked.

"You never want to give a guy like Pollo a chance to

think things over. He may change his mind," Frankie said.

Barbara nodded.

"Over the next few days we can go over some things," Frankie said, "and we'll introduce you to Pollo. He's going to introduce you as a small-time dealer."

"We're going to try to get them on drugs?"

Fenwick shook his head. "No. Get them to make an open admission on the Castelli homicides. They're paranoid about being set up about drugs. But we hope they have their guard down about the Castelli hits."

"What about my background and so forth?"

"We can put that together fast," Fenwick said. "We do it all the time."

"What about Joe? Does he figure in this?"

"He'll certainly be involved," Fenwick said, "but your chief contact will be Frankie."

"I talked with Joe about it," Frankie said. "He thought this way would be best."

Barbara thought: That's what makes Joe such a good cop. He knows this is Frankie's kind of game, and it would be better for him to run it.

They had another round of drinks, and the talk drifted away from Barbara going undercover.

A depression started to settle over her. Somehow, she knew she wouldn't be seeing Joe for a long time. She could, of course, back out. Now. But she knew she wouldn't. If she did, she would still have the same yearning, the same guilt, tomorrow as she did today. Lawless was right. It was something she had to do.

CHAPTER 30

On Saturday, Barbara was, as Frankie Pinto said, "to go into the set." Which meant she only had a few nights left with Joe.

She was particularly disappointed, then, when Lawless called early Tuesday evening and said that he couldn't make it. An old lady had been raped and beaten to death up in the Fordham Road section. He would be going all night and probably Wednesday night too.

"Oh, that's okay," she had said as chirpily as she could. "I'll see you soon."

"I certainly hope so," he said. "I love you, baby."

"Me too."

As she lay in bed in the darkness that night, she felt very attuned to the sounds: the beeping of horns, the gurgling of pipes, the faint sounds of radios and TVs, the opening and closing of doors.

These are the sounds of loneliness, she thought. They reminded her of when she was a very young girl and had gone away to camp one summer. She must have been about seven.

It was all right during the day, but the night was a different story. The sounds were different—the drone of a faraway plane, the whisper of the wind, other kids making sleeping noises—but she felt the same way. Lonely. She missed her mommy and daddy very badly, and she had cried the first few nights she was there.

Now she missed Joe. It was different, and yet it was

the same. Loneliness never changed, no matter how old you got to be.

All her life, she realized, she had been lonely at one time or another. She remembered reading Thomas Wolfe when she was in high school: "What man knows his brother? Who has looked into his father's heart? Who is not forever a stranger and alone?"

Then she had thought Wolfe was right. But he was wrong. It was true that you could never know anyone completely, but you could know them well enough so they weren't strangers, so that their love could banish the loneliness and you were not a stranger and alone forever, but just for moments.

She touched the ring that Joe had given her and closed her eyes. She could feel his love pulsing through the darkness. He was not there, yet he was there. Softly, peacefully, she fell asleep.

Chapter 31

The next morning at about nine o'clock, Barbara met Frankie Pinto in front of a building on Wexford Terrace in Jamaica, Queens, where her new apartment was to be.

It was a large cream-colored modern building with an overhang, a turnaround for cars and a parking garage. It said to Barbara that the people who lived there had money.

They went though glass doors. Directly to the left of the entrance was a counter behind which sat a young security guard monitoring a bank of TV receivers. Frankie stopped.

The guard smiled. "How are you doing, Mr. Aguello?"

"Fine, Roy. This is Ms. Russo."

Barbara smiled. She had tinted her hair red and was wearing tight clothes.

The security guard smiled and nodded. His face was bland.

"She'll be staying in my place awhile, and we'd like to keep it a secret. Anyone ever asks about her, don't say anything."

"No problem, Mr. Aguello."

"Good," Frankie said, and slipped a folded-up bill to Roy, who immediately slipped it into his shirt pocket.

They went to the bank of elevators.

"What's my first name?" Barbara said.

"That's easy," Frankie said. "Barbara."

They got off at the sixth floor and walked down the hall to the left. They stopped at one of the apartments at the end of the hall, and Frankie opened the door.

Inside, he took her on a tour.

It was a bit like hers, only bigger. There was a foyer, a kitchen to the left, a living room, but then a hall to the right which led to a bedroom and bathroom.

The apartment said money too. The furniture and appointments were modernistic, and there were sliding glass doors off the living room which led to a small balcony with a good view.

"On a clear night," Frankie said, "you can see the lights of the city. The rest of the time"—he smiled—"you can see Queens."

They went into the kitchen, where Frankie made a pot of coffee. Then they went back into the living room. Frankie sat on a Breuer chair that partially faced the sliding glass doors. He turned his face toward the doors for a moment or two. Then he turned back to Barbara.

"The main thing about undercover work," he said, "is to believe you are who you're supposed to be. Live it. Depending on the situation, some undercovers can go home at night. By day they're drug dealers, by night ordinary people. But some can't. You have to decide how you can do it best. I mean, you may think you can meet Joe every now and then and still keep this belief inside you. That's fine, as long as you believe it. At the very least, though, I would suggest you not go near your own apartment while on assignment. Okay? One of the Fuenteses might follow."

Barbara nodded.

Frankie got off the chair and started to walk back and forth across the polished wood floor.

"If you can believe you're a dealer, you'll be on your way to handling your greatest threat—their finding out you're the Man. Like I said before, they will test you. Particularly Miguel Fuentes. He's as paranoid as they come.

"You got to be concerned about other things, too—things drug dealers worry about. Mainly, about being ripped off.

"Also, there will be a little concern about this Jimmy Pollo. I assure you," he said, smiling, "this dude ain't the cream of society. He's an opportunist. He's not your usual informant, but he's trying to save his own self. You're expendable if he sees it that way.

"Any questions?"

"I'm sure I'll have some," Barbara said, "but not right now."

"The first thing I'd like to do," he said, "is to ask you some more questions. You imagine I'm, say, Miguel Fuentes, okay?"

"Okay!"

"Cops bother you much?" Frankie said, smiling.

"How do you mean?"

"Where you live."

"No," she said. "They don't even know I exist."

"What precinct you in?"

Barbara didn't know the precinct, but she thought they were in the Nine Four.

"Nine Four."

Frankie had been smiling. The smile faded.

"That's wrong, Barbara," he said. "That's what a cop says. Nine Four. Five Three. Six Two, One Ten. A drug dealer—a civilian—doesn't talk the way. He says, 'Fifty-third Precinct, Ninety-fourth Precinct, One Hundred tenth Precinct.' He would have made you as the Man instantly."

"Shit," Barbara said.

"It's okay. It's why we're training you.

"Okay," he went on. "I'm the dealer again. Where do you live?"

Barbara was about to say the street and the cross street. But that's what a cop would say. She said, "Wexford Terrace, in Jamaica."

"Good," Frankie said. "You're getting it."

He proceeded to go through a whole series of questions designed to prune all police jargon from Barbara's answers.

"You didn't make a single mistake," he said. "Now let's move into the mere, uh, subtle things. Like the way you stand and look. Body language."

"What do you mean?"

"The other day," Frankie said, "when you came into the bar, you did what most cops do. You looked around. Big dark searchlights in your head probing the bar. Looking for what? Looking for crime. It's as natural for a cop to do as breathing. And it's something the Fuenteses will spot in a second."

"What are you supposed to do?"

"You can look, but don't look *hard*. If it's a look around a place that lasts more than a couple of seconds it's too long. Look as long as a civilian would look. Maybe a little longer. You're a drug dealer. You're looking out for the Man too."

"Okay," Barbara said.

"Another thing. When you stand, don't fold your arms in front of you, or behind you. That's the way cops stand. A dealer may not pick up on it, that is, say to himself, 'Hey, that's the way cops stand,' but this guy lives on the street, this will tickle his unconscious. He'll focus on you."

They worked on Barbara's body language for a half hour, then they sat down in the kitchen and had coffee.

Frankie said, "The thing that dealers understand about the Man is that the Man wants to make the deal. The Man's got to make the deal to make an arrest. That's where you don't want to be anxious. You want the deal, but don't be too anxious."

"Can you give me an example?"

"Sure," Frankie said. "Let's say you arrange with the Fuenteses for, say, a key buy. So you go in there and one of them says to you, 'Hey, baby, we come up a little short. A couple ounces. You want that, huh?'

"What would your answer be?"

"I'd tell them to wait until they get the full key."

"That's right; that's exactly what you should say."

Frankie sipped his coffee.

"Another thing. Try not to have the exact amount of money for the buy. You come up a little short. "Hey, bro, I'm light fifty bucks on this—is that okay?' You know why?" Frankie continued. "Because the Man, he always has the exact amount of money for the buy."

Barbara laughed.

Frankie finished the cup of coffee and poured himself some more.

"More?" he said.

"No thanks."

"Another thing," he said. "Don't have the money all in one place. Have some of it in your purse, some in your pocket, some in your bra. The Man always has his money in one place. And in case you get ripped off, maybe they won't get it all."

"That's comforting," Barbara said dryly. Frankie laughed.

"How many times have you been ripped off?" Barbara asked.

"Three times. Once I got beaten—I mean I had to take a beating or blow my cover."

After they had finished the coffee, Frankie said, "That's about it."

"Shouldn't I learn more?"

"There's no way I can teach you everything you got to know. The thing to do is to just think about being a drug dealer, not a police officer. All you need to know will come out of that."

"Are we going to get together tomorrow?"

"Oh, sure," Frankie said. "Tomorrow we meet Jimmy Pollo."

Frankie smiled.

CHAPTER 32

Frankie Pinto picked Barbara up the next morning at her apartment and they drove upstate to meet Jimmy Pollo, who was in a rooming house in Ossining, not too far from the prison.

It was a pleasant, sunny day, and they made the drive in just under an hour.

The rooming house was in a run-down section of the city, made up of faded two- and three-story wood homes that reminded Barbara of swaybacked horses. None had been touched by a paintbrush in a long, long time.

Like most of Ossining, the area was hilly, and Barbara was puffing by the time they reached the two-story gray job that Jimmy Pollo was staying in.

None of the bells worked, so they climbed a flight of stairs to Number 3 on the second floor.

Frankie knocked softly.

"Yeah?"

"It's Frankie."

The door opened, and a man Barbara guessed to be about fifty or so stood in the doorway. A sour smell came out of the room behind him.

The man was tall, thin, and bald. He had a puffy face and shifty eyes. He looked like he had not smiled in ten years.

Frankie greeted him as if he were a long-lost cousin from Santo Domingo. "Hey, Jimmy! How are you? Lookin' good. This is Barbara!"

Jimmy nodded at Barbara and opened the door so the two cops could pass inside.

The room was worn and faded and peeling, but you could see Jimmy had spent time in the penitentiary: The bed was made, the thin gray blanket pulled taut, and things were generally neat and in place.

"Have a seat," Jimmy said.

Barbara and Frankie sat down on two broken-down fold-up wooden chairs, and Jimmy sat on the bed.

"We got it all figured," Frankie said, "so the operation can go smoothly and be over quickly as far as you're concered."

Barbara watched Jimmy watching Frankie. His eyes were like a snake's.

"What we think is best," Frankie went on, "is to introduce Barbara to Ricky at a place where he's relaxing. Less suspicion."

Jimmy nodded. "Is Miguel going to wherever . . . ?"

"I don't think so," Frankie said. "But the place is a disco in the city. Ricky's been going there quite often. Every weekend.

"What we were thinking was to have you accidentally meet Barbara at the disco, then the both of you run into Enrique."

"Who is she supposed to be?" Jimmy said.

"An old business associate. Did a little of this, a little of that. Now she's dealing coke. She's got bread and wants to go multi-ounce. If he doesn't suggest him and Miguel, then maybe you can."

Jimmy Pollo was quiet for a while. Then: "If they find out she's connected to the Man, they'll hunt me down."

"She'll do all right."

"Yeah," Jimmy Pollo said.

"Why don't you tell her about yourself? She's supposed to be an old business associate, right? Maybe you knew her father, huh?"

"Yeah."

Jimmy Pollo told Barbara about himself. He was in fact, forty-eight. He had spent a third of his life in various prisons. He had been married twice, had six kids he didn't see anymore. He had been dealing various types of shit for twenty years.

And, Barbara thought, he had that sniffly, watery look of a user.

"How'd you get to know the Fuenteses?" Barbara asked.

"When they first came up from Santo Domingo a few years ago, I hired them as mules. Then I was busted, and when I got out they had taken everything. If I tried to take it back I'd have to either kill them or get killed."

"So you haven't seen them since before you went into prison?"

"Since before my last bit, right."

"Don't you think they might think you've got a grudge against them?"

"I don't think so. They probably figure if I didn't do somethin' by now I ain't goin' to do anything."

"Okay," Frankie said. "We want to move. Saturday. Tomorrow."

Pollo frowned. "That's no notice at all."

"After Saturday," Frankie said, "you're out of it. You'll be on the street free with a lot of bucks in your pocket."

"When do I get the dough?"

"It'll be delivered here Sunday. By the way, you got clothes for Saturday?"

"No."

Frankie peeled three hundreds off a thick roll and handed them to Pollo. "Deck yourself out," he said. "Have some fun."

Barbara looked carefully at Jimmy Pollo.

Joe called Barbara Thursday night at her home. "Christ," he said. "I can't make it tonight, either."

"I'll be gone into the set Saturday, baby. I got to see you before then."

"Me too. I don't care if Jack the Ripper shows up. I'll see you tomorrow night."

"Good night, baby," Barbara said.

CHAPTER 33

Barbara left Frankie about four o'clock on Friday—after he had picked up a wallet full of phony ID for her in the name Barbara Russo—and went home. Joe was to show up at six o'clock.

At five after six, Barbara started to panic a little, and at ten after she started to pace the living room, a glass of wine in hand. This would be their last night together for a long time. She would talk to him on the phone, and maybe they could steal a visit together, but there were no guarantees.

She felt the relief surge through her when the bell rang three times, his signal.

She restrained herself, though she felt like staying in his arms forever. She didn't want him to know how much she would miss him.

They sat down at the table and ate Chinese food, though neither was particularly hungry.

They talked about the operation a bit. Lawless wanted to know about Jimmy Pollo, and asked her if she was satisfied with her sessions with Frankie Pinto. She said she was.

"You're going to try to get in tomorrow night?"

"Yeah," Barbara said. "At the Crazyhouse disco. You know it?"

"I've heard of it."

They made arrangements on how Lawless could be

138

contacted, at home or at the station. If he was on the street he would try to leave a number.

"But this is Frankie Pinto's kind of game," he said. "Lean on him for advice. Okay?"

"Okay."

When the meal was finished, Barbara realized the discussion of the case was finished. She sensed that Lawless didn't want to talk about it anymore.

But she made sure.

"Any other questions or discussion on this?"

"No," Lawless said, "that's it. You're ready. You got good backup. That's it."

They had more wine, they danced, they discussed everything but the case, and through it all it occurred to her that she had never seen Lawless in a such a good mood. She had a ghoulish thought at one point, that if things went wrong he would have this night with her locked in his mind like a videotape that he could play when he needed to.

But that thought vanished. He just loved her, that was all. She was facing danger, and he wanted this time with her.

Later they made love, and then she fell asleep in his arms.

She didn't know what time it was, but she awoke sometime during the night and opened her eyes. His face was toward her, his eyes open, just looking at her, and when he saw she was awake he kissed her softly on the lips and pulled her head next to his heart.

CHAPTER 34

The next day Barbara moved into the apartment. She brought only one suitcase, filled with underwear, cosmetics, and the like, but nothing to tie her to her job or her real life. Walking through the door of the Queens apartment she felt like she had never had a life before this.

The DEA had stocked the medicine chest, pantry, and refrigerator. Some of the stuff was partially used. They had thought of everything.

It was mid-July now, and the day had been gray and rainy and muggy. She wouldn't be able to see New York by night; she couldn't even see Queens by day.

The mere act of moving in had depressed her, and she was tempted a number of times to call Joe. But that would only drag him down too. She had asked for this. She should try not to be Barbara Babalino, but a small-time coke dealer who wanted to go bigger.

She was wrong about not seeing New York. By nine that night the haze and rain had lifted like a curtain, and she could see the lit-up skyline of Manhattan quite well.

During the day, she had spent much of the time psyching herself, doing a kind of mental yoga to convince herself that she was a coke dealer, not a cop.

She reached an important conclusion: As a coke dealer, she didn't have a thing to wear. Her own taste in clothes ran to very simple, high-quality garments. She had always believed that the clothes should harmonize with the person, not stand out by themselves.

But a dope dealer, she thought, wouldn't be that way. She got the feeling from talking with Frankie that Dominican coke dealers liked to wear their money. In that respect, she thought, they were no different from any dealer—or pimp. And the two female dealers she had seen had been the same way: They liked to show the kind of bread they had.

She went into a local shop and bought red pumps and an expensive, white-spangled low-cut dress. She hated the dress, but when she put it on she liked it because it helped her to accept the role she was trying to slip into.

At six, Frankie called. She was glad to hear from him. Very glad.

"Stick it to him, Barbara," he said.

"We will," Barbara said. "Thanks for calling."

"Talk to you."

She started getting ready at about seven-thirty, and by eight-thirty was putting on her makeup. She swabbed it on, accenting her eyes to an almost possumlike degree, using the reddest lipstick she could find, and liberally using green mascara.

There was a full-length mirror on the back of the bedroom door. She looked the role, she thought. She could be dealing coke—or herself.

She had her doubts whether Jimmy Pollo would show. But at around nine o'clock the intercom buzzed.

"Mr. Pollo is here," the guard said.

"Send him up." Barbara was excited.

The Jimmy Pollo who stood in the doorway a few minutes later was not the same one she had seen in the sour-smelling room in the dilapidated rooming house.

He had used the three hundred dollars well. He was dressed loudly, and had dyed his graying hair black. There were a number of rings on his fingers.

But the changes were more than cosmetic or haberdasheral. He seemed much calmer, cooler than he had in the room, particularly since he was taking a big risk.

As she watched him pass into the living room, Barbara felt a little spurt of fear. She recalled what Frankie had said and what she knew: It was a viciously double-dealing world.

Then, when she saw him in better light in the living room, she understood, and relaxed: He had taken a hit of something.

Then again, maybe that wasn't a good thing.

"You okay, Jimmy?" she asked.

"No sweat. I'm cool."

"Do me a favor," she said. "Don't take anything else until this is over."

Jimmy Pollo nodded.

"Let's go," she said.

A couple of minutes later they were on the streets, and a couple of minutes after that they were in the cab the doorman had called.

The cab made a right turn, then went up the block on its way to Grand Central Parkway, and the city, the Crazyhouse, and Enrique Fuentes—hopefully.

Lawless, sitting in a borrowed car far down the block, watched the cab.

There was nothing he could do now. He had just wanted to see her.

Then the cab turned out of sight.

It was a long time since Lawless had formally believed in any kind of God. But now, at this moment, he closed his eyes and an old Irish saying came back to him from his childhood:

May God hold you in the palm of his hand.

He opened his eyes. There was only the darkness on the street. He started up his car and headed for home.

CHAPTER 35

Once, when she was at John Jay College, Barbara had taken a course in civil complaints and had learned more than she had ever wanted to know about noise, or, as the instructor had called it, "unwanted sound."

Unwanted sound. That's the term that struck her as she and Jimmy Pollo entered the Crazyhouse. The driving disco beat must have been up at around 120 decibels, close to the painful range, and it occurred to her that a lot of people would suffer permanent hearing loss tonight—including her.

The place, basically one big room, was pretty well crowded with dancing couples, about half black and Hispanic, the other half white. Colored lights played over them, and on a ramp that hung near the ceiling, men and women clad only in bikinis rocked to the music inside cages.

You could cut the smell of marijuana with a knife.

She was in, Barbara thought, the set. This was the beginning.

She looked around the room, but suppressed the urge to give it a hard cop sweep. She had to control that.

She could feel and see eyes on her. That was okay. She was used to that. Men had been giving her the once-over since she was twelve.

"You wanna drink?" Jimmy Pollo said above the noise.

"Sure."

They went around the dance floor to a bar against one wall in a corner. Jimmy ordered a Jack Daniel's, Barbara a Bloody Mary. They sipped the drinks.

Barbara's eyes played over the dancers. She had only seen that one photo of Enrique Fuentes and thought she might not recognize him if she did see him.

Jimmy Pollo, she knew, was eyeing the throng on the dance floor too.

"I don't see him," Pollo said after a while.

"Neither do I," Barbara said.

She was about halfway through her drink when, in her peripheral vision, she saw someone coming toward her.

At the last moment, she turned lazily and looked. It was not Fuentes. It was a Hispanic—Dominican, Puerto Rican—she couldn't tell. She made him for about twenty-five. About her size, dressed in tight-fitting pants, shirt open at the collar, gold chains dangling.

"You wanna dance?" he asked.

"Why not?" Barbara said. "See you later, Jimmy."

Barbara hadn't discoed in a long time; her love affair with it had ended when John Travolta stopped doing it. But she remembered how, she was in pretty good shape, and if she was going to do this thing, it had to be all the way.

She gyrated to the music, her partner keeping in perfect time. She drove herself into the dance; but it wasn't just a dance: She was driving herself deeper into the set, so deep that she wouldn't remember who she was or where she came from, until that moment when she had to.

The music pumped. Barbara pumped and drove with it. Occasionally, she could hear someone yell, "Do it, baby!"

She kept it up, kept it up, driving, feeling herself getting deeper and deeper into it. She thought of Joe, and thought him away. There was only here, now, this guy, this place, the Fuenteses and her.

The music stopped.

Her partner came up to her. "Hey, baby," he said. "You some dancer. You want to have a drink?"

"I'm waiting for somebody."

"Maybe later?"

She smiled. "It's my boyfriend."

He shrugged and went away.

She threaded her way through the crowd on the dance floor and back to the bar.

Her stomach tightened.

Enrique Fuentes was standing next to Jimmy Pollo. Just like that. Her eyes were on him only a moment, then off; he was looking at her.

She had a quick impression: very expensively dressed in an all-white outfit. Small, handsome. He undressed her as she walked toward them.

She came up to them. "Hey, I'm getting too old for this stuff," she said to Jimmy.

"You kidding?" Jimmy said. "You did great. We watched you."

Jimmy turned to Fuentes. "Barbara, I'd like you to meet an old friend of mine, Ricky Fuentes."

Barbara turned and looked at him.

Glittery black eyes, strong sweet cologne.

"Glad to meet you," she said.

Ricky Fuentes' eyes were on her cleavage. He slowly raised them and looked at her. "You dance good," he said. He had a very slight accent.

"Thank you," Barbara said. She suppressed a feeling of annoyance at the arrogance that oozed from him.

"This is like old home week," said Jimmy Pollo, who looked like he had taken another hit. "First I meet Barbara, then Ricky."

"You from around here?" Ricky said.

"Queens," Barbara said, "but before that I spent some time on the Coast."

Jimmy Pollo laughed. "But not like me, huh?" He was referring to prison time.

Ricky Fuentes smiled slightly; Barbara smiled also.

The music, which had been off for about five minutes, started again. Fuentes looked at Barbara, raising his eyebrows in an invitation to dance.

Barbara nodded. Fuentes took off his jacket and handed it to Jimmy Pollo as if he were a clothes tree.

As they walked onto the dance floor, it occurred to

Barbara that they were both dressed in white. And it also occurred to her that what she was about to do right now was against every fiber of her being: use her body to accomplish what she wanted to accomplish. Since she had been a little girl she had always acted like a whole person, composed of body, mind, and soul, and demanded that she be treated as such. Using your body to get ahead was a trick guaranteed to keep a woman at the level where only her flesh mattered.

Still, it was no time for philosophizing, no time for regrets, no time for anything except accomplishing her goal: getting an admission on the Castelli killings. And she knew goddamn well that it was likely she could worm her way into Fuentes' good graces, and not arouse suspicion, by using her body. He'd be too interested in looking at her to think about what she was.

As a dancer, Enrique Fuentes was an absolute whirlwind of energy, and not shy in the least. At various times during the record he fixed her with a simmering stare and thrust his crotch toward her.

Barbara responded, dancing harder than she had ever danced in her life, and doing a few bumps and grinds of her own. After a while they had a small crowd around them, and people started to clap rapidly in time with the music. Barbara kept telling herself over and over again: You turn me on, you turn me on, you turn me on . . .

When they were finished, the crowd gave them a little round of applause.

They walked toward where Jimmy Pollo was.

"You're the best dancer I've ever seen," Barbara said.

Fuentes looked at her and nodded.

"That was great," Jimmy said. "What a pair!"

Fuentes bought the next round of drinks, paying for them with a hundred-dollar bill, peeled off from what looked like a roll of hundreds about an inch thick.

They sipped the drinks. Fuentes looked at Barbara. "Jimmy tells me you do a little dealing."

Barbara flashed her eyes toward Pollo.

Fuentes caught it, as he was supposed to. He smiled.

He had perfect teeth, very white. "It's all right," he said. "I deal a little myself."

He smiled, and Jimmy laughed hard.

"What's so funny?" Barbara asked.

Jimmy looked at Fuentes. "Actually," he said, "it's not so little."

"You wholesale?" she asked Fuentes.

"That's all we do."

"Oh," Barbara said, impressed.

Jimmy was still holding Fuentes' jacket. Fuentes took it from him and put it on. "Let's get a drink somewhere else," he said.

"Oh," Jimmy said. "I can't. I'm supposed to meet somebody."

Fuentes didn't look unhappy. "How about you?"

"Sure," Barbara said. "That'd be okay. Nice seeing you again, Jimmy."

"Yeah," Fuentes said to him. "You need something, give me a call." He handed Pollo a card.

There was the slightest hitch of hesitation, then Jimmy took it.

If he noticed, Fuentes said nothing.

"I'll see you around, Jimmy," Barbara said, looking into his eyes carefully. Was there something there that spelled danger for her? She didn't think so.

Fuentes and Barbara waited by a garage.

"How long you been in town?"

"A few weeks."

"Jimmy said you were in Hollywood."

"Yeah," Barbara said. "I spent a couple of years there." In fact, she had vacationed in Los Angeles two years earlier and had a friend who had tried to hook on in the movie business. She knew some things.

"What were you doing?"

"At first I was trying to get in the movies. But I drifted away."

"You a user?"

"No," Barbara said. "Very occasionally, not anymore."

A sleek white current-year Corvette emerged from the parking garage and Fuentes stepped toward it.

The attendant got out and Fuentes hit his palm with what looked like a five.

"Nice car," Barbara said.

"I got three like it in different colors. Cars are my hobby."

And killing, Barbara thought.

Fuentes got in and Barbara let herself in. Her dress hiked up a bit, showing thigh, but she made no attempt to pull it down.

She thought they were going to go to a bar in mid-Manhattan. Instead, Fuentes, who handled the car very skillfully and drove fast and aggressively, went cross-town, and they were soon tooling up the West Side Highway.

"Where we going?" she asked.

"Uptown Manhattan."

Barbara said nothing.

"You looking to make a buy?"

"Yeah."

"How much?"

"Ultimately a key."

Fuentes was quiet.

"How much for that?"

"Forty thousand."

"Whew," Barbara said. "That's a lot of bucks."

"What were you looking to spend?"

"When I do, around thirty-two thousand."

"No. This is the purest. From Brazil. We cut it here. You can hit it two, maybe three times."

"I'd be looking to get it on a regular basis."

"What would you want now?"

"Start with an ounce. How much?"

"Nineteen hundred."

"Too much."

"It doesn't matter, the weight. Still pure, seventy percent. You can stick it up your nose, you'll know right away."

"That doesn't tell me nothing."

Fuentes was silent. Maybe, Barbara thought, she had

blown it. But her instinct said she hadn't. She had to follow what Frankie told her: 'The Man, he will settle. The drug dealer will not. He will haggle.'

Or she, Barbara thought.

Frankie exited the West Side Highway up near Dyckman Street.

She had been up there a couple of times during her school days when her high school team played Immaculate Conception. The neighborhood seemed to have gone downhill, though there were still some good buildings.

Frankie parked near a hydrant. Barbara got out. He didn't lock the car.

This guy didn't need to, she thought.

As they walked down the block, a few of the people looked at Fuentes. They knew him, and she got the feeling that he was being shown a lot of respect. He was a big man around here.

They went into the La Hoy, one of those Spanish-Chinese restaurants, and she marveled at his arrogance. He didn't ask her if she wanted to go; he just took her. Or, more precisely, she followed him.

The place was pretty crowded, and some of the diners, in booths that lined the place and white-tablecloth-covered tables arrayed down the middle, looked up and smiled. A couple waved. It was easy to see that this was Fuentes country.

As she followed him toward the back of the place, the maître d' came out. He was Chinese and all smiles.

"How you, Ricky?" he said. "Your brother in back."

Barbara felt a little twist in her stomach. So this is why she was being brought here. To talk with the brother, Miguel. Probably for him to pass judgment on her.

This was where she was going to be at her best, where she was going to have to bring all of Frankie's training to bear.

They went though a doorway adjacent to the kitchen.

A man was eating alone at a table covered with a white tablecloth. There were a lot of plates on it. The man was black and wore dark sunglasses, and even in the dim light Barbara could make out who it was. It was

Miguel. Somehow, she would have been surprised if there had been someone eating with him.

They went up to the table. Miguel was dressed in the same kind of suit as in the surveillance photograph. He was eating pork chops and some kind of yellow rice. He looked up at Barbara and Ricky, then went back to his meal.

Ricky sat down in a chair opposite Miguel and told Barbara to do the same.

"Hey, bro," he said. "This is Barbara. Friend of Jimmy Pollo. She wants to do some business. I told her we may be able to help her."

"What are you dealing?" Miguel said, continuing to eat.

"Just grams. But I want to go multi-ounce."

"How long you been dealing?"

"Three years or so."

"Where?"

"Hollywood."

"I see," Miguel said. "What are you looking for right now?"

"Just an ounce. But it promises to get much bigger."

Miguel Fuentes dabbed his mouth. His plate was empty.

"What are you looking to spend?"

"You tell me," Barbara said.

Miguel looked at her, points of light glinting off the glasses. A quick image: those kids, bullets in their heads, only seven, but dead, of Jeff, . . . She wrenched herself back, suppressing the anger.

"Two grand."

"That's too much."

"How much?"

"Fifteen hundred."

"Too low."

"Make an offer."

"Nineteen."

"Seventeen," Barbara said.

"I can't go to that."

"I can't go any higher."

"This is seventy-percent pure. You can hit it two, maybe three times."

"Thank you, Miguel," she said. "I got a budget."

Barbara turned to Enrique. She had an expression on her face which she hoped said: He's giving me the same old crap.

"Could you take me back downtown?"

She felt Miguel's eyes on her. Please, she thought. Please.

"Sure, baby. Why don't we get a couple of drinks here, then go back."

"Okay."

They got up to go.

Miguel spoke. "I'll think about it. You got a place where you can be reached?"

Barbara handed him her card, which just had her name, address, and number. He took it, looked at it, and looked at her. She got a crawly sensation.

A couple of hours later, Barbara started to complain about a stomachache. An hour after this Enrique Fuentes was dropping her off in front of her apartment in Queens.

She sensed that Ricky was deeply disappointed, even pissed. Good.

Later, as she lay in bed, Barbara found herself thinking about Miguel Fuentes. Eating.

Why should he be alive eating pork chops and Jeff and those children dead? She needed to push the image away. It was not the kind of thing that was going to help her now.

CHAPTER 36

Barbara awakened about ten o'clock the next morning. It was a cool bright day and she had her breakfast—a cup of coffeee—on the terrace.

She started to think about Joe, but she cut the thoughts off. Try to think only of the Fuenteses, she told herself, and your role as a coke dealer.

She sipped the coffee and looked out over Queens. It was clear, and she could almost see the skyline of Manhattan.

Frankie had said that Miguel Fuentes was very paranoid, but he didn't seem that bad. With Jimmy Pollo's intro, she had gotten right in. It had taken all of a couple of hours.

Enrique Fuentes was not so paranoid either. He had been ready to accept her right away for what she was supposed to be.

Maybe, she thought, it was because I'm a woman. Their macho image of women was such that they couldn't imagine a woman would be an undercover police officer.

Or maybe it was that they wouldn't expect someone else to try to get in so short a time after another was burned.

Whatever the reason, it had been much easier than she had expected.

There was something about that, though, that bothered her a little. By all accounts, Johnny Padilla had been a very smart cop—but they had burned him. And the Fuenteses hadn't gotten to the position they were in with muscle alone—they had to be smart.

She recalled what Frankie had said about the girl he had trained who was overconfident.

Barbara had another cup of coffee and was putting the cup and saucer in the sink for washing when she heard the ringing. At first, she didn't know what it was, then realized it was the front doorbell. She had never heard it. Jimmy Pollo hadn't rung it when he had come up yesterday.

Who could it be? Probably the super or someone else from the building. Anyone else would have been announced.

She opened the door. It was Enrique and Miguel Fuentes. Her insides lurched, but she automatically smiled.

"Hey," she said. "How are you? What a surprise."

"Yeah," Ricky said as the two passed into the apartment. "We were in the area and thought we'd drop in."

"Good," she said. And thought: Was there anything incriminating in the apartment? Her ring? No. That was hidden.

She led them into the living room, and it was easy to see that they were checking her out.

"Nice place," Ricky said. "Very nice."

"Hey," Miguel said. "Where's the bathroom?"

"That way," Barbara said. "Go ahead. Don't mind my stuff on the sink."

"Would you like some coffee?" she asked Ricky.

He shook his head and sat down on the couch. Barbara sat down in a chair opposite him.

"Nice place," he said again. His eyes bored into her. There was nothing of the playboy about him now.

Barbara briefly thought of where her gun was. In her purse. But if they tried something she wouldn't be able to get to it.

"On a clear night," she said, "I can see New York. You live in the city?"

Ricky nodded.

They said nothing, and Barbara got the definite sense that she was in danger. But what could she do about it? Nothing. She would just have to play it out.

Miguel came back into the room and sat down on the couch. She couldn't see his eyes well, despite the brightness in the room. But his head was motionless, his face toward her.

"I was thinking about your offer. I'll go to seventeen, but that's the bottom."

Barbara nodded. Okay, she thought, what's next? "Fine," she said. "When can we can make the buy?"

"How about right now?" Miguel said. He and his brother were watching her.

"You got the stuff with you?"

"You got the money?"

"Yeah."

"Go get it."

Barbara left the room. The money—she had brought in two thousand—was in the bathroom, in a talcum tin; the gun was in the bedroom. Going for a gun would be a mistake.

As she turned into the bathroom her peripheral vision caught someone watching her from the end of the hall. She couldn't tell which of them it was.

She counted out seventeen hundred. She was surprised her hands weren't shaking. She had an idea. She glanced in the mirror. No one was in the doorway.

She took a chance. She put fifty dollars back and went into the living room.

She put the money on the table. It occurred to her it could be a ripoff, but discounted that. They were too big for that. This was penny ante.

"I only got sixteen fifty," she said. "I can make up the difference on the next buy."

Miguel said nothing. He took out a tin and placed it on the table. Barbara opened it up—her hands still steady—and smelled it.

"Try it," Miguel said.

This was the purpose of their visit. A test. Frankie's test. Only now it was for real.

"I don't use it," she said.

"Try it," Miguel said.

"My people will check it out."

Miguel reached into his coat pocket and took out a 9mm automatic. "Try it," he said.

"Fuck you," Barbara hissed. "Fuck you both. Get the fuck out of here or pull the trigger. I want to make a buy, you wanna play games. You think I'm the Man you shouldn't of come here."

Barbara reached down and took her money back. They looked at her.

There was a moment. A suspended moment. Barbara thought of nothing except: Fuck you.

Fuentes lowered the gun, then put it away. "Okay," he said.

"We got to be careful," Ricky said. He was smiling.

Barbara made no move with the money. She looked as if she were debating with herself.

She put the money on the table. Ricky took it. She left the tin where it was.

They got up and walked silently to the door. She let them open it themselves.

"We see you later," Ricky said before she closed the door behind them.

"Don't hurry," Barbara said.

A few minutes after they left, Barbara, sitting on the couch, started to shake. And it was only with the greatest effort that she resisted calling Joe.

CHAPTER 37

Arnold Gertz had gone through all but two of the buildings on Creston Avenue when Captain Haggerty showed up unexpectedly. Arnold was just about to go into the next-to-the-last building, around noon of a hot and muggy day, when he saw him coming up the block from Fordham Road, and quickly.

He waved to Arnold. Arnold waved back and started down to meet him.

They shook hands.

"I'm glad I found you," Haggerty said. "I think I may have something." He mopped his brow, which was beaded with perspiration. "Let's get out of this heat."

A few minutes later they were at a table in an air-conditioned restaurant on Fordham off Creston. Haggerty sipped on a jumbo Coke; Arnold sipped on a water. It occurred to him that that was about all his stomach could take whenever he heard from Haggerty.

"I made some calls," Haggerty said, "to see if I could find a similar circumstance—a nonfighter killed by a pit bull."

Haggerty took a long drink on the Coke.

"Just this morning," he said, "I talked with a trainer I know in Baton Rouge, Louisiana. He enlightened me. He said that there's a new kind of convention. . . ."

Arnold furrowed his brow.

"Dog fight," Haggerty said, "a kind of dog fight that got its start in Louisiana, which is the most liberal state in the nation about these fights. It's called the 'mixed convention.' In it the pit bull is matched against dogs which haven't been trained to fight, but the odds are evened a little. For example, they might put two shepherds in with a pit bull, or two rottweilers. . . .''

"What's that?"

"A huge, tough, mean dog."

Haggerty paused. He took another long gulp of soda.

"The trainer—his name is Perkins—even heard of pit bulls matched against three terriers."

"How cruel that is," Arnold said, "for all the dogs."

Haggerty paused. He said the words very slowly: "Subhumanoid cocksuckers."

"Don't the police try to stop them?" Arnold asked.

Haggerty laughed bitterly. "Some of the police *fight* dogs down there. It's all considered great fun, part of Southern honor or some crap."

Honor. Arnold could not put honor together with the sight of the dog taken from the Harlem River.

"The thing is," Haggerty said, "that one of these conventions may be coming here."

"What do you mean?"

"Perkins said he heard of ones in Cincinnati, Columbus, Los Angeles, and that the next big one is going to be in New York City."

"Does he know when?"

"No. Just that it's going to be like the others, a big one. It's on a scale with a Roman orgy. They'll have dogs coming in from all over the country if it follows the pattern of the other conventions."

"Could he find out when and where it will be?"

"I don't think so," Haggerty said. "He pieced together this information I'm telling you with the greatest difficulty; a lot of it came from a conversation he overheard. A pit bull fighter is not ordinarily going to talk to him."

"Maybe the death of Miss Susie means it was held already."

"I doubt it," Haggerty said. "If it was held, then I don't think the people running it would care about the dog being found."

"We have to find out what's going on," Arnold said.

"Believe it," Haggerty said. "Or I have the feeling that a lot of innocent dogs are going to lose their lives."

CHAPTER 38

It took Arnold to the middle of the next day to go through the final two buildings.

Four or five people remembered seeing a big black German shepherd running around the park near Creston, but nobody could remember what day it was or what happened to it.

Arnold had a fantasy, as he knocked on the very last door in the very last building, that the answer would be behind it.

It turned out to be a young woman openly suckling an infant. She knew nada.

Arnold went into the park. He found a bench in a shady spot and sat down, leaning his back against one of the concrete frames. He took out the notebook he had been using to mark who was in and who wasn't—or who wouldn't answer the door.

Laboriously, he went through it, and when he was finished, he found that some seventy-two people had not opened doors for one reason or another.

On the one hand he felt good about it—he still had some hope—but on the other he felt bad; he was very tired.

He started to go through the buildings again.

It took him another two days, and by the time he had rechecked all those who originally had not answered, he had contacted almost half of them. The rest he would just have to forget about.

He had come up empty.

In a way, he was glad it was over. Naomi was starting to get a little antsy. By the time he had been getting home at night over the last couple of weeks the twins were asleep, the dog was asleep, and she was half asleep. Besides, she disliked the idea of Arnold, as big as he was and as unafraid as he was of physical confrontation, roaming around Fort Siberia late at night. It was at night that the real predators of the precinct came out of their caves.

Still, he felt sad. He had to find out what had happened to Miss Susie. If he didn't do something, if Haggerty didn't do something, then more animals would die.

He got up from the bench and walked out of shadow into the bright, muggy day. He could see the buildings he had just gone through.

He walked toward them, and as he did he noticed the people sitting in the open windows.

Most of them were older, but there were young kids and young mothers, too. He wondered why so many people looked out the windows in Fort Siberia.

His eyes tracked along the buildings where the open windows were, and he vaguely remembered some of the people sitting at them. They had come to their doors and he had shown them the picture of Miss Susie and there had been no ID.

In the middle of a red-brick building there was an open window on the second floor with an old lady sitting in it. He remembered her from when he first started to check the apartments. He did not remember her answering the door. No, she definitely had not answered the door. He remembered more. Every time he had looked at those windows, he had noticed her sitting there.

Arnold went out of the park at the 191st Street entrance to Creston, crossed the street, and walked up to the building the woman was in.

"Hello," he said, smiling up.

The woman looked down and said nothing.

"I'm Detective Gertz," he said. "I wonder if I could talk with you a minute."

"Why?" The woman said. She had a brogue.

"We're looking for a dog. Somebody who might have seen a dog."

Arnold expected the woman to say, 'I haven't seen a dog,' but she didn't.

"I'm in Apartment 2J," she said.

Arnold let himself in through the entry doors, which did not have a lock, then climbed the stairs to the second floor. As he did, he checked his book. He had knocked on her door. He had her marked as a "no answer."

The door was open a crack when he got to the top of the stairs. The woman was peering through it. Her eyes were blue behind glasses, and they were alert.

"You got yer credentials?" she said.

Arnold showed her his shield. She opened the door. Arnold went inside.

The apartment was typical of the apartments of older people. Old furniture, old rugs, old photos. On the walls were paintings of Jesus Christ, Mary, and the saints. On top of a bookcase and on some shelves were statues of religious figures.

The woman led him into the living room, where the open window was. She walked slowly.

Arnold said, "Thank you for letting me in, Mrs. . . ."

"I'm Mary O'Rourke," she said, her brogue even more evident than before. "Around here you let in the wrong person and . . ."

Arnold knew.

"How can I help you?"

Arnold took the picture of Miss Susie out of his shirt pocket.

"We're trying to find out what happened to this dog," he said. "She disappeared."

Mrs. O'Rourke took the picture and squinted at it. Then she brought it over to the window, where the light was better, raised her glasses, and looked at it.

"I seen it," she said.

Arnold felt something grip him. "What? Where?"

"In the park. About two weeks ago. Big beautiful black dog. It was running after something, a squirrel, then it came out the entrance down there and the Perez boy took it away.''

Arnold could feel his heart pounding.

"What do you mean?" he said.

"The Perez boy—" Mrs. O'Rourke abruptly stopped.

"What's the matter?" Arnold asked.

"I don't want to get in trouble. I live alone here. And that Perez boy. I talked to his mother a few times. She's a nice lady. She's had trouble with him. I understand he's mean. He, uh, might hurt me. I live alone here."

"No, he won't," Arnold said. "Any information you give will be between me and you."

She looked at him and blinked.

"That day," she said, "I saw the Perez boy park his white van across the street. The dog came out of the park, and couldn't get the squirrel. He trotted past the van and then started back toward the entrance. But when he got to the van I saw the Perez boy start petting him, and then he put something around his neck and sort of helped him jump into the van. He closed the doors and drove away."

Arnold felt a surge of anger.

"Where does he live?" Arnold asked.

"Two houses down," Mrs. O'Rourke said. "2432. His mother's the super."

Arnold jotted the address down in his notebook.

"Please," Mrs. O'Rourke said, "make sure he doesn't find out it was me that told you this."

"He won't find out. Don't worry."

Mrs. O'Rourke smiled. "Do you have time for a cup of coffee or tea?" she asked.

Arnold did not. He wanted to pursue the lead right away. "Sure," he said.

Arnold spent fifteen minutes with Mrs. O'Rourke. She told him about the kids she had, and her deceased husband. She was very interested in his family. Arnold got a sense of how lonely she was. He started to understand why she, and so many other people, spent so much time at the windows.

When he got on the street, Arnold went immediately

to the phone down on Fordham—passing by 2432 in the process—and called Arthur Haggerty.

He got his answering service and told him to call him at the station or at home—he left his number—he had some important news about the investigation.

Then, though it was muggy, he walked down to the station house.

As he did, he could feel the nervousness swelling in his stomach.

This was a great lead on the case, and he didn't want to mess it up. He knew he could do a lot of good, or some bad people would do a lot of bad.

CHAPTER 39

Back at the station house, the first thing Arnold did was check Perez out. He put his name in BCI and the Motor Vehicle Bureau.

Haggerty called him back at around three o'clock.

Arnold told him what he had gotten.

"That's great, Arnold," Haggerty said. "What are you going to do next?"

"I don't know yet," Arnold said. "I have to figure it out."

"We could follow him," Haggerty said.

"Yeah," Arnold said. "That's one possibility. We'll see. I'll call you when I know what I'm going to do."

"If you need my help, just call," Haggerty said.

"Okay," Arnold said. "I will."

At around four o'clock, Arnold was going to the men's room on the first floor when he saw Captain Bledsoe leaving for the day. Bledsoe saw him, but he didn't even say hello. That was the way he was.

Now, Arnold thought, would be the time to confide in him. But he had no idea what Bledsoe would do. He still might think that Arnold was making a big deal out of nothing.

At around four-thirty, the report came back on twenty-one-year-old Luis Perez.

He had a yellow sheet "as long as your arm"—he had arrests for B&E, assault, burglary, and grand theft, though he had been convicted only once. He had served two of a five-to-seven-year sentence for armed robbery. He was on parole.

That night, Arnold discussed the case very carefully with Naomi. She worried about him so, and he didn't want to give her the impression that he was going to be in great danger.

As usual, Naomi only did one thing for Arnold: She told him he could do it, whatever it was. She just believed in him, and that was that.

He didn't get much sleep during the night, because he hadn't made up his mind what to do, and when he went to the station the next day, he was still in the dark.

He had an idea to call Joe Lawless, and did that with disappointing results. Lawless was working three separate homicide squeals, including the killing of the family in the Romano section, and would not be available in time. Arnold had to make a decision soon.

Oh, how he ached to be smart; then things would be clear and easy. But he knew he would have to go with what he had.

At ten-thirty the report came in from the MVB in Albany: Luis Perez owned a 1985 black Trans Am, license plate BAD 768, and he was a scofflaw: He owed on three tickets, two for speeding, one for going through a light.

At around noon, Arnold made his decision. Right or wrong, he made it. But he would need help.

Ideally, he would have liked to take Joe Lawless with him, but that was out of the question. The only guy available was a skinny young cop named Stewart, who had just recently made plainclothes. He would ask him. Stewart liked Arnold. He had arrived at Fort Siberia fresh from the Police Academy, and Arnold had given him some tips on how to survive on the streets.

Arnold explained the situation, and his plan, to Stewart in the middle of the afternoon, and Stewart agreed to help.

Arnold was glad. He didn't want to approach Perez alone, even though he merely wanted to "talk" with him. It wasn't technically a bust, but what Sam Turner, the morning roll call sergeant, said still seemed to apply.

As he once put it, "Trying to make a one-man collar is as fast a way to the bone orchard as I know."

Late in the afternoon, Arnold called Naomi. He tried to be as nonchalant as possible, simply telling her that he had to work late. Bledsoe wanted him for something. Since he didn't know the something, he couldn't trip himself up if she asked some questions.

He and Stewart had supper together at a kosher deli just outside Fort Siberia in the Five Two, then went back to the station house to get ready.

Arnold thought it best that they wear bulletproof vests. He had received one as a gift from the church group he was in. Stewart didn't have one, but he borrowed one from a guy who had his build, and the armor fit pretty well. If he wore a loose shirt no one could tell he was wearing it.

At eight-thirty, with darkness descending, they left the station using Arnold's car, a 1978 Ford LTD.

It was getting a little cooler, after another very hot day. Arnold hoped it would continue to get cool. Sitting in a hot car with soft body armor on would be hard on them.

They drove around the area once before they parked, checking to see if either the white van or black Trans Am was parked. Neither was, so they parked up the block, next to a fire hydrant. Arnold sat in the back, Stewart in the passenger seat. At least for a while they would look like two guys waiting for the driver to show up.

The street was in full swing. Ghetto blasters playing rap music mixed with Spanish music, women with baby carriages, kids running in and out of cars and across the street, some guys working on a jacked-up old Chevy down the block, and to the right, in the park, God knew what.

Stewart, Arnold saw, was nervous. Arnold was not. All his life people had hurt him with words: his father telling him he couldn't do this or that, his mother fretting about his grades, kids poking fun at him, other cops making sly remarks. He didn't even try to answer anyone, because he knew he couldn't; he would just get tied up in his own words.

But it was here, in this type of situation, that he was at his best. He imagined himself, though he never told anyone, as some kind of hero from the comics he sometimes read or the TV shows he watched: He could take care of himself.

And of Stewart. He would take care of him, too. He was the rookie, Arnold the vet. That's the way it was.

Darkness came, and it became obvious that he and Stewart had been made. You couldn't be the Man in Fort Siberia for long and not take a burn. That was okay, Arnold thought. It was Luis Perez he was after.

More than a few times Arnold thought about Miss Susie and Miss Keefe. The old lady would wait for her dog . . . forever.

By eleven o'clock both Arnold and Stewart looked as if they had been in a steam bath all day. Perez hadn't showed. The street, of course, was still jumping.

From time to time, when energy permitted, Arnold and Stewart would talk cop talk, with Arnold playing the role of teacher. He loved it. He only wished that he could have done it at some other time.

By midnight, the action on the street had thinned a bit. Some of the women with babies had gone into the buildings, and so had a few of the older people. Time wore by, and soon it was three A.M.

Arnold considered pulling the stakeout. Both he and Stewart were on day tours; a few more hours and they wouldn't get any sleep at all. And a guy like Perez might easily stay out all night.

But Arnold recalled the words of a veteran detective who had been on many stakeouts: "It's the old airline pilot routine," he had said. "Hours and hours of boredom interrupted by moments of sheer terror."

Just because nothing was happening, it didn't mean nothing would happen.

At four-thirty they heard the throaty roar of a high-performance car—or an airplane. Then, in the rearview mirror, the black Trans Am. It was Perez.

There were a couple of parking spaces across the street from the house. As they had hoped, Perez started to park in one of them.

Arnold and Stewart freed the retention straps on their holsters and approached the car.

Arnold waited until he saw both of Perez's hands on the wheel before saying anything.

"Luis Perez?"

"Yeah?"

"Police. Get out of the car."

Perez, a wiry man with curly black hair and the flattish features of a boxer, seemed to hesitate, but then he got out of the car.

"Up against the car and spread 'em," Arnold said.

"What the fuck you hasslin' me, mon?"

"This is about a missing dog," Arnold said.

"I don't know nothin' about no fuckin' dog," Perez said, and started to walk away.

"Okay," Arnold said, "keep walkin'. We didn't arrest you, did we? You'll hear from your parole officer in the morning."

Perez stopped as if turned to stone. "What?"

"You heard me," Arnold said.

Perez came back. He looked up at Arnold. He was a defiant sort of guy. But he knew about parole.

"Up against the car and spread 'em."

Reluctantly, Perez assumed the position. Stewart searched him. Stewart nodded to Arnold.

"You want to take a ride with us, Perez?" Arnold said.

"Where?"

Arnold and Stewart took Perez back to Fort Siberia. The booking desk, near the front entrance, was, as usual, like a mini Grand Central Station, so Arnold, Stewart, and Perez went up the stairs without being noticed.

They took Perez into one of the small rooms in the back on the third floor. It was not the epitome of fine decor. There were three straight-backed wooden chairs flanking a wooden table which was scarred and stained. A fluorescent light with one tube constantly blinking lit the room.

Perez was seated on one side of the table and Arnold and Stewart on the other.

Arnold glowered at Perez. "Why did you steal the dog?" he asked.

"I didn't steal no fuckin' dog."

"This is our last warning," Arnold said. "Curse one more time and I'm going to lose my temper."

Perez's instinct was to say something, but he swallowed it.

"I'm also going to ask you one more time: Why did you steal the dog?" Arnold held up his hand. "Don't lie, or the meeting here is over and I call your PO. And I want to tell you, too, that we have a witness."

Luis Perez had been glibly lying since he was five. He was polished, expert. Instantly, he had a tightly woven narrative to unload on Arnold.

But the big man's eyes bored into him. Now was not the time.

"A guy hired me," he said.

"Who?"

"Some dude named Bailey. Luther Bailey."

"Where's he from?"

"Long Island, Huntington."

"How come he hired you?"

"I worked with him for him a week once."

"What does he do?"

"He owns a dog kennel—Silver Sunset Kennels."

Arnold tried not to, but he blinked.

"What's the address?" Stewart asked.

"Jericho Turnpike. 2356 West Jericho Turnpike."

"What happened to the dog?" Arnold asked.

Perez's eyes shifted. Arnold held up his meaty hand like a traffic cop.

"What happened?" Stewart said, almost growling. This was fun.

"Bailey. One night Bailey put him in a ring with one of those killer dogs."

"One?" Stewart said. "How many does he have?"

Perez had a look on his face like he had smelled something very bad. He was getting in deeper and deeper. He held up his own hand.

"Wait a minute," he said. "What the . . ." He caught himself. "What guarantees do I have that you won't burn me with my parole officer if I talk here like I am?"

Arnold's brow was furrowed. "Listen, Perez," he

said. "You don't need to talk anymore, and there are no guarantees of anything. We already got enough to send you back to do the rest of your bit. We decide if we're going to do that based on the way you talk."

"Fuckin' A," Stewart added.

"All right," Perez said. "What do you want to know?"

"Everything." Arnold said. "Tell us everything you know."

Yes, he thought, that was the best way. That way he wouldn't leave out any important questions.

Perez took a breath.

"I started working for Bailey a few months ago. Cleaning his kennels and shit . . . 'scuse me. Anyway, after a couple of weeks he asked me if I wanted to make some extra bread. I said yeah. He said I was to go around the city, or wherever I could, and collect dogs. He would pay me twenty-five dollars for every dog I brought to him, plus expenses, and he'd supply the van."

"Did he tell you what kind of dogs?" Arnold asked.

"Yeah. He gave me a list. German shepherds, Doberman pinschers, big poodles . . ."

"How many dogs we talkin' about?" Stewart asked.

"Thirty. Thirty dogs since I started collecting them a couple of weeks ago."

Arnold strained. There was . . . then Stewart asked the question he was struggling to form.

"You said he made this offer a few months ago."

"Yeah, that's right," Perez said. "I ain't lyin'. But he just wanted me to start collectin' 'em two weeks ago."

"Where'd you get them from?" Arnold asked.

Perez looked at him, silent for a moment. "All over. Loose dogs. Just loose dogs."

"Did you go into anybody's property?" Stewart asked.

"Yeah, well, if a dog was loose in a yard I took 'em."

"You remember where you took these dogs from?" Arnold asked. He felt like crushing Perez.

"Yeah," Perez said. "I could remember."

"How many of those killer dogs does he have?" Stewart asked. "More than one, right?"

"Ten."

Arnold blinked.

"Ten. How do you know so exactly?"

"I got 'em when they started coming in on the airlines. He gave me ten bucks a head. I had some trouble. They're mean fu . . . dogs."

"When did this start?"

"Just a few days ago. Some of the owners came with 'em."

Arnold felt as if a fist had invaded his lower bowel and squeezed. He looked at Stewart. The significance was not lost.

"Did he say anything about having a big fight soon?" Arnold asked.

"He don't tell me nothin'. I get the dogs, and he pays me. That's it."

"Okay," Arnold said. "That's it for now, unless you got questions, Ray."

Stewart shook his head.

"Can I go?" Perez asked.

"For now," Arnold said. "Though maybe I will just call your PO."

Perez looked at him.

"Don't say nothin' to this guy Bailey," Arnold said. "Just continue doing what you're doin'. But I don't want you to steal any more dogs. And," Arnold said, "I want you to make a list of who you stole the dogs from. We're going to return 'em."

"Some of them I just took off the street," Perez protested.

"How many?" Stewart asked.

"Five."

There was a silence.

"What do I say to Bailey if he asks me how come I'm not getting any more dogs?"

"Just tell him," Arnold said, "you can't find any."

"How long? He's a nasty fu . . . 'scuse me. Nasty."

"Very soon," Arnold said.

They took Perez back to Creston Avenue and dropped him off. Then Arnold drove Stewart to his home, an apartment on 242nd Street and Broadway.

"Thanks for your help, Ray," Arnold said.

"No problem, Arnold. Glad to do it," Stewart said. "How you going to handle this?"

"I don't know exactly yet," Arnold said. "But I got to do something pretty fast."

CHAPTER 40

Arnold called Haggerty at home the next morning at six-thirty. He apologized for calling so early.

"I'm grateful you called," Haggerty said.

Arnold explained what had happened.

"That's great," Haggerty said. "Congratulations. What are you going to do now?"

"I don't know," Arnold said, "but there's not going to be any fight. We're going to stop it right away."

"Good," Haggerty said. "I'm relieved."

Before he hung up, Haggerty told Arnold that the name Luther Bailey sounded familiar.

"I'll check it out," he said.

At breakfast, Arnold told Naomi what had happened—and apologized for not telling her the truth about his whereabouts.

"I knew that, Arnold," she said. "It's okay."

As he ate his four eggs and a protein concoction that defied description, Naomi watched him. Arnold was not happy.

"What's the matter, honey?" she said.

"I'm a little worried about how to handle this."

Translation, Naomi thought: very worried.

"Why?" she asked.

"Captain Bledsoe. I got to tell him about this, and I wonder what he's going to do. I want to go in there and arrest this guy Bailey. But he's so . . . he likes to be in

173

the papers so much . . . he might say something like
let's wait for the fight. That could be very risky."

"I don't think he'd do that," Naomi said. "He's a
publicity hound, but that would be taking too much of a
chance. What if the fight somehow took place?"

"Yeah," Arnold said. "Yeah. I want to make sure we
stop it."

"You will. Just go in and tell him and see what he
says."

"Yeah," Arnold said. "I'm worried about something
else."

"What's that?"

"Whether he'll be in. He's hardly ever in."

CHAPTER 41

Bledsoe was in.

"What do you want to see him for?" said Fletcher, his oily aide-de-camp, who sat outside the office.

"I got something that may be good for the precinct. Something about dogs."

"Just a minute," Fletcher said, going inside the office.

I'm learning, Arnold thought.

"Go on in," Fletcher said when he came out.

Arnold had nothing to be nervous about in seeing Bledsoe. He just was. He was that way with all authority figures.

Bledsoe, who resembled the actor Edward Asner, except with thicker eyebrows and a little more hair, said, "What have you got, Arnold?"

Arnold explained what he had. As he did, he could almost see Bledsoe warm up. Arnold became more enthusiastic and was able to give him the details more clearly.

Finally, Arnold was finished.

"Tell you what you do, Arnold," he said. "Get in touch with this little spic—Perez?—and get the list of owners from him. Then we'll raid this fucker with a few of the owners. Can you do that?"

"Yes, sir," Arnold said.

"You did good," Bledsoe said. Already he was thinking about the best way to handle this with the media. Timing was important. And so was satisfying the media.

175

You didn't want to give one network or paper preference or they'd have a hard-on for you, and somewhere down the road they could stick it to you.

Arnold smiled at Bledsoe before he left. Despite knowing or at least sensing how Bledsoe was, he liked to hear the compliments. Bledsoe was smiling too. He thought it ironic that this moron did him more good than 99 percent of the rest of the cops in Siberia.

While Arnold was in Bledsoe's office, Luis Perez was making a phone call to his uncle whose first name was also Luis: Luis Serrano, an attorney who operated out of storefront offices in the Tremont section of the Bronx and, in the words of one insurance company executive, "specialized in fucking insurance companies."

It took Perez a lot of change to tell him about his talk with Arnold and Stewart the night before, but Luis Serrano's analysis was pungent and to the point: "Fuck 'em, they don't have a fuckin' thing."

"What about the fucking witness?" Luis said.

"Fuck the witness. Just deny it. They got no fuckin' proof."

"Okay," Luis said.

"Yeah," Luis Serrano said. "Call this fuckin' guy Bailey and tell him to get rid of the dogs. Hide 'em or kill 'em or something."

"But I admitted stuff."

"You were pressured, okay? If they had something on you, why the fuck didn't they bust you?"

Perez felt relieved. Now there was no way they could hold a parole violation over his head. He was very glad that his uncle had gone to law school.

CHAPTER 42

At around five on the same day he saw Bledsoe, Arnold
Gertz took a run up to Creston Avenue, on the off
chance that Perez was there. He was surprised to see
the Trans Am parked in roughly the same spot it had
been the night before.

Maybe, Arnold thought, he had the white van. Maybe
he just left it parked there. He would see.

Arnold went down a short flight of concrete steps into
an alleyway that led to the super's apartment. He opened
the door, which led to the cellar, then rang the super's
bell.

A middle-aged woman with dark eyes and a troubled
look answered the door. *"Qué?"*

"Is Luis here?" Arnold said softly. "I'm with the
local precinct."

The woman's look seemed to grow more troubled.
She turned toward the interior of the apartment. "Luis.
Someone to see you."

It seemed like a long time until Luis Perez appeared.
The woman, who Arnold assumed was his mother, had
gone back into the apartment. Luis seemed different
from the night before. He was dressed, as then, all in
black, but he seemed to saunter when he walked. Arnold wondered why. Maybe he was on something.

"Yeah?" Perez said.

"I need that list of dogs you got."

"I don't know what you talkin' about," Perez said.

Arnold felt flustered. "The list of people . . . the dogs you stole. Where you stole them from. You were supposed to have it ready."

"I don't know what you're talkin' about," Perez said.

Arnold tensed. He did not want to stutter.

"If you don't give it to me I'll tell your parole officer."

"Hey, bro, you do what you want. My uncle, he a mouthpiece, and he tell me you ain't got shit."

And Perez closed the door in his face.

Arnold didn't know what to do. Perez had admitted he stole the dog to him and Stewart. And the old lady, Mrs. O'Rourke, had seen him.

But he could deny it all. It was Perez's word against theirs. Arnold called Stewart, and they decided that it would be difficult to prove anything against Perez. At the very least, they should have taped their interrogation of him.

He had gone too fast without thinking. Legally he was at a dead end.

"What are you going to do now, Arnold?" Stewart asked at the end of their conversation.

"I don't know," he said. "But something. I'm definitely going to do something."

CHAPTER 43

The next morning at about nine o'clock, Arnold Gertz and Captain Arthur Haggerty were in Arnold's car going east on the Long Island Expressway. Both men were relatively quiet, because each was alone with a single preoccupation: Whatever it took, they were going to stop Bailey from running a mixed convention, or any convention at all.

Arnold had discussed with Naomi what to do, and both had decided that it would be useless to talk with Bledsoe. A year earlier, when Arnold had botched a stakeout of some goat thieves, Bledsoe had offered no help or understanding at all. He had ripped into Arnold and reduced him, literally—though out of sight of everybody—to tears. Now, on this, he would be the same way. He would rip into Arnold and tell him what he might have done. All Arnold could do now was avoid Bledsoe as much as possible.

But that wasn't the important thing. The important thing was to stop the fight.

Haggerty had a good idea. Photograph the dogs, and then distribute their photos to the various humane organizations in the metropolitan area, including the ASPCA. If they could get the photos publicized, some owners were bound to come forward. Once they had that, they could put Bailey out of business—and in jail.

Bailey, of course, would likely object to Haggerty

taking the photos. Arnold hoped he would, and tried something.

Huntington was on the North Shore of Long Island. Unlike many suburban areas, it was not what land planners call "homogenized"—endless rows of tract houses set side by side on flat streets intersected by macadam paths. Huntington was flat in places, but it was also hilly and covered with trees and ponds, and residents had access to seven separate beaches. For a lot of people in the city, it was a place where they went on vacation.

The Silver Sunset Kennels was located in an area which was particularly dense with woods. The last part of their journey took them down a hard-packed dirt road, called Sweet Hollow Road, flanked by dense greenery and with only an occasional house.

It looked like the perfect place to dump a body, and, in fact, some eight years earlier the body of a young girl had been dumped there, and the perp—or perps—never found.

A wooden sign on a post said SILVER SUNSET KENNELS, and Arnold turned the car into a narrower dirt road.

The kennel was on the side of a hill. It was a large white block building, one story, set in the middle of a flat cleared area. The area around it was dense, low grass which gradually gave way to woods. It looked like a frontier settlement that had been hacked out of the wilderness.

Arnold parked the car on the right side of the building in front of a door that said OFFICE.

They went inside. It resembled Haggerty's office in the city. A small room with a counter and a door leading somewhere else.

There was a bell on the counter. Arnold rang it, waited thirty seconds, then rang it again.

No one answered.

"It's weird," Haggerty said. "Something's wrong."

"That no one's here?"

"No," Haggerty said, "and yes. There's no sound. Where are the dogs? This is a dog kennel. There should be constant barking."

Arnold and Haggerty went through a closed door adjacent to the office door.

It was dim, but they could see. There were perhaps forty interior penned-off runs leading, via openings in the wall, to outdoor runs.

No dogs.

With Arnold trailing, Haggerty walked slowly down the length of the building, examining the pens with great intensity.

"There were dogs here," Haggerty said. "Today."

They reached the end of the building. "A couple of dozen dogs, at least."

"Bailey moved them?"

"Somebody did."

Armold ground his teeth. He should have gone in and arrested Bailey right away. But on what?

The two men went outside.

They stood there a moment. Arnold had no idea what to do. He would have to think about it a long time. He was about to say something when Haggerty's hand came over quickly and touched his mouth, silencing him.

"Listen," he said with low urgency.

Arnold said nothing. He just stood listening to the sounds of the insects . . . and then he heard it: a dog barking in the distance.

"This way," Haggerty said, pointing to the woods to the right of the building.

They started trekking through the woods and noticed something. The brush had been trampled. At one point, Haggerty stopped and looked at droppings.

Occasionally, the barking stopped, then started again. Then it stopped completely when they were fairly close to the source, and a strange whirring mechanical sound could be heard.

They climbed a slight hill and peered through some foliage. There were at least twenty cages, side by side, and every other one was empty, leaving spaces between the dogs, which were all pit bulls. They were eating.

The rest of the scene was gruesome. There was a dead cat, tied by its neck, and a live chicken in a sort of net onion bag tied to a large wheel raised off the ground.

The mechanical sound was coming from this wheel turning, turned by a frenzied pit bull, running in circles after the chicken and cat.

A man watched. He was big, with a big belly, hair cut short, light eyes. His arms were covered with tattoos.

Arnold felt like killing him. He came out of the woods. "What are you doing?" he asked.

"What business is it of yours?"

Arnold showed his tin. "Police."

"This is my property," the man said. "Unless you got a warrant or legal paper you got no right here."

A warrant, Arnold thought. He could get a warrant. Technically, he was out of his jurisdiction. But he didn't care.

"Who owns these dogs?" Haggerty asked.

"None of your business," the man said.

Meanwhile, Arnold was looking at the pit bulls. They were all different colors and not very good-looking. They had immense jaws relative to their size. Fearful creatures.

He thought of Miss Susie.

"We know who you are," Arnold suddenly said. "You're Luther Bailey, and you've done a lot of cruel things to animals. Now you think you're going to have pit bull fights and have them fight other dogs. Well," Arnold said, "you better forget it if you know what's good for you."

"No warrant, off my property."

Arnold hesitated. He could hospitalize Bailey in thirty seconds. But there was no way Bledsoe would back him.

"I'm warning you," Arnold said. "We're going to be watching you. Don't try to have any dogfights. I don't need a warrant to watch you."

Bailey stared at him.

They left. The wheel was still being pulled by the frenzied pit bull.

CHAPTER 44

The veins in Piccolo's neck stood out like rope, and his face was the color of a tomato.

"What scumfuckers," he said to Spagnoli, sitting behind a massive oak desk. "What scumfuckers you have for help! How could they let this jig walk?"

It had been a long time since anyone had spoken to the Bronx County District Attorney this way. Like when he was seven.

"Everybody makes a mistake, Frank," he said.

"This was a whopper," Piccolo said. "A fucking whopper."

He pointed a finger at Spagnoli.

"You," he said, "you bear responsibility. You were making a speech while one of your fucking ace assistant DAs allowed that black fucker to walk out of here into the arms of shyster lawyers."

"It was a weekend. The assistant is new."

"Fuck him!" Piccolo said. "What do we do for a case now?"

"We'll convene a grand jury," Spagnoli said. "See if we can get an indictment."

Piccolo laughed, showing the gap in his teeth.

"That's a fucking joke. When this Ace comes in here—after the shysters are finished with him—he won't even be able to tell you his own name without advice of counsel. He's safe. Fishman's putting up big bucks for him. That fucker is safe too."

"We still have the tapes," Spagnoli said. "we can still try to squeeze him."

Piccolo's voice lowered.

"Fuck, you know how lawyers are. They'll claim entrapment or some other shit and trot out character witnesses for this guy and do all kinds of shit. They'll pull some shit. Let's face it; we lost him."

Spagnoli said nothing. Piccolo was probably right.

After he left Spagnoli, Piccolo met Edmunton in a bar under the el across the street from Yankee Stadium. Piccolo had suggested Edmunton not come with him to meet with Spagnoli because he knew he was going to blow his stack. He had been fuming since the night before when he learned that Ace, aka Winston Gaines, had been sprung on a low bail, asked for by an assistant DA. Piccolo had assumed that Spagnoli was going to ask for no bail.

"I don't want you to get in trouble if I do," Piccolo had said. "It's between me and Spagnoli."

Piccolo joined Edmunton at the long bar, which was, for the time—nine o'clock Monday morning—surprisingly crowded.

Piccolo ordered a double shot of Scotch for himself and Edmunton.

He told Edmunton what had happened.

"We lost him," Edmunton said.

"You got it," Piccolo said.

They sipped their drinks in silence, looking at the oversize pictures of the Yankees arrayed across the back of the bar above the whiskey bottles.

They finished the doubles and ordered two more.

Occasionally, Edmunton would glance at Piccolo. Edmunton knew Piccolo was hurting, but he knew something else: He would not give up so easily. Piccolo never talked about what he felt deep inside, but you could tell what he felt. And he did not like Ace driving people like Charley Murphy from their homes.

Piccolo looked down at the drink for what seemed like a long time, then lifted it and whacked it down in one gulp.

He turned to Edmunton. "I got an idea." He was smiling.

"Let's," he said, "let's have a talk with fucking Ace."

Edmunton whacked down his drink, and they left the bar.

CHAPTER 45

The next afternoon at around four-thirty, Piccolo and Edmunton sat in a battered brown van a block down the street from 2605 Bainbridge Avenue. It was raining hard, but they still had a clear view of the white Corvette that Ace owned.

They had been sitting on the house for two hours. The car had been there when they arrived. Ace, Piccolo thought, was having a busy day.

Today and yesterday, after they left the bar near the stadium, had been busy ones for Edmunton and Piccolo. When their business was finished, at around noon, Piccolo had said: "I worked hard before to answer questions on an exam, but this is the hardest I ever worked to get the questions ready."

Knowing what Piccolo planned, Edmunton had howled at that one.

Ace came out of the building, and before he had gotten into his car Piccolo had the van fired up and had started to move slowly down the block. Based on where Ace lived and assuming he was going home, Piccolo and Edmunton had figured out which way he would travel.

He followed just about the route they expected, though it was not that simple to keep up with him. He drove aggressively, weaving in and out of cars on the West Side Highway, heading downtown, a couple of times running red lights.

"The fuck has no regard for the law whatsoever," Piccolo said at one point.

"I know," Edmunton responded.

Ace lived in a brownstone in the West Seventies, near the Museum of Natural History. Piccolo knew this, but seeing Ace park his car and disappear into the house, a well-kept, high-rent unit that was considered the way to live in New York, frosted Piccolo. This black fuck was living in a brownstone, and Charley Murphy, and so many others, were with relatives or in one-room hovels.

They parked by a fire hydrant down the block and waited.

An hour later, just as it was getting dark, Ace emerged from the building.

He was dressed all in black: shirt, pants, and shoes.

He started to walk up the block. He went past the Corvette. Piccolo started up the van and moved very slowly down the block in the same direction.

When Ace turned at the corner, going south, Piccolo speeded up, and was in luck. The light changed just as he got to the corner. He stopped. Halfway down the block Ace was on the street. He was waiting to hail a cab.

The light changed, but Piccolo didn't move. He just hoped Ace didn't notice him sitting there.

He didn't. A cab came and Ace got in. It headed downtown. Piccolo followed.

At 57th Street, the cab pulled to a stop. It was a busy street, but Piccolo had no idea where Ace was going, and he didn't want to sit on him anymore.

"Let's go," he said to Edmunton.

Piccolo made a right against the light and zipped down 57th. He pulled to a stop near the curb about ten yards ahead of Ace and jumped out.

Ace saw him coming and stopped. He didn't know quite what to do.

"You can run," Piccolo said, smiling fiendishly, "but can you run faster than fifteen hundred feet a second? That's how fast a bullet"—he pulled open his sport jacket, showing the massive Magnum in its shoulder holster, which actually overlapped his belt—"from a .44 travels."

"You got nothin' on me!" Ace said. "I'm on bail. Speak to my attorneys."

"You don't get it, do you?" Piccolo said. "What I'm doing is not legal."

Ace blinked. The door to the van slid open.

"Get in the fucking van," Piccolo said.

A few passersby had slowed down, and one man had stopped.

"Keep moving," Piccolo said. "This is police business."

The people moved.

"Get in the fucking van," Piccolo said.

Ace's brow furrowed. He got in the van.

Piccolo shut the door behind him, then went into the back with Edmunton. Piccolo pulled the .44. Ace blinked, gulped; there were beads of perspiration on his forehead.

"Down on your belly," Piccolo said.

"I got clean clothes on."

"Good."

Ace, alternately glancing at Piccolo's face and the .44, got on his stomach. Edmunton grabbed his hands, pulled them behind his back, and cuffed him. Then he used some cord to tie his ankles together.

Ace farted.

"Do that again," Piccolo yelled, "and I'll blow your brains out."

Edmunton guffawed.

Edmunton came up front and got in the passenger's seat. Piccolo climbed into the driver's seat and pulled away.

They drove west in silence. As they did, Piccolo put the radio on and manipulated the knob until he reached an FM station playing Brahms.

"Da-da-da-da-de-da . . ." Piccolo sang along with the music in a high-pitched squeal. He glanced at Ace. All he could see was the top of his bushy head.

"How you doin', Ace?" Piccolo asked.

"Where you takin' me?"

"A surprise, Ace," Piccolo said. "A surprise."

Piccolo got on the West Side Highway and tooled north. The music enveloped them.

At Fordham Road, Piccolo pulled up on the shoulder of the road, put the hazards on, and went into the back of the van.

Wordlessly he took a roll of something from a compartment on the wall of the van and almost feverishly started to wrap it around Ace's head, over his eyes.

"What the fuck you doin'?" Ace whined.

"It's an Ace bandage," Piccolo said. "An Ace bandage for an Ace."

Ace tried to pull away. Piccolo reached over and pounded his ass with his fist.

"Ugh."

"Be good," Piccolo said.

When the bandage was completely around Ace's head Piccolo clipped it closed, then got back into the driver's seat and pulled the van back into traffic.

Almost immediately he exited at Fordham Road. He bounced along Fordham, which was riddled with construction holes and potholes.

At Jerome Avenue, he hung a left and was technically in Fort Siberia.

Then followed a series of lefts and rights. If Ace was trying to track the route in his head, he had his work cut out for him.

Soon, they were heading north up the Grand Concourse, the road that was once called the Fifth Avenue of the Bronx.

Throughout the journey, Piccolo hummed along to the music, and at one point he interrupted the mellow sounds with his best imitation of Crazy Eddie, the loud-mouthed electronics pitchman.

"Hey, Ace," he bellowed. "Following all this? It's really INSANE! isn't it?"

Edmunton laughed.

Gradually, though Ace had no way to tell, Piccolo worked his way west to Broadway, up near Manhattan College and past where their peerless leader, Bledsoe, resided.

A few minutes later they were in Westchester County,

in Yonkers, and going north. A few minutes more and they were at their destination: a run-down abandoned house in a neighborhood of similar houses.

Piccolo parked the van about mid-block, and then they manhandled Ace out of it onto the sidewalk and down concrete steps which led to the lowest floor of one of the houses. A sector car was unlikely to pass, Piccolo thought. A cop he knew on the Yonkers PD had told the car to stay away.

They went through the front door, which was open, and then Edmunton flicked on a flashlight and guided them through what once had been a living room; there was rubble and garbage everywhere and big holes in the wall and ceiling.

They went through another doorway. More steps down.

"Watch your step, Ace," Piccolo said.

Edmunton tittered.

They reached the bottom. It was the basement. It smelled. If you listened carefully you could hear things moving.

Using the flash, Edmunton led Ace over to a straight-back chair and sat him down. Piccolo used two sets of cuffs to secure his ankles to the chair legs.

Piccolo turned on a Coleman lamp as Edmunton unwound the Ace bandage.

Ace blinked as his eyes adjusted to the light. Then he looked left and right. Piccolo's caged pets flanked him. He inhaled sharply.

"So you're the dude," Piccolo said, "who likes to terrorize old people. Piss and shit on their clothes, steal their stuff, flood them out, drive them out into the street."

Piccolo paused. He lowered his head and said softly, "That's not nice, Ace."

Piccolo went over to the chair, knelt down in front of Ace, and roughly stripped his pants and underwear to his ankles.

Piccolo stood up and smiled at Edmunton.

"Hey, this guy is built like they say all niggers are built. It's going to make a nice meal."

Edmunton guffawed and Piccolo sniggered. Ace's eyes

were wide, glancing first at Piccolo, then Edmunton. He realized he was dealing with madmen.

"So," Piccolo said, stepping in front of Ace and rubbing his hands together enthusiastically, "what'll it be? Monitor, python, boa, or tokay gecko?"

Sweat trickled down Ace's face.

Piccolo put up his right hand, forefinger extended.

"Before you decide," he said, "let me explain each of my pets a little more completely to you than last time."

He stepped up to the monitor.

"The monitor," he said, "has very sharp teeth, and though you can't see it now, a long black tongue. It is a creature you got to keep away from your eyes. It'll go for your eyes as quick as look at you."

Piccolo laughed gutturally, joined by Edmunton.

He stepped over to the boa. Ace's eyes followed him. Ace was aware that the sweat was flowing freely down his back and off his forehead.

"This is a boa. Like I said earlier, I don't need to explain a boa. It is a constrictor; it will choke you to death, in case you don't know what that means.

"This is the python. Like the monitor, it is attracted to the eyes—the movement. So if per fucking chance it gets near your face, don't move your eyes. It'll be eating your eyes but you won't be able to see it, ho-ho."

He stepped over to the tokay gecko. He fairly swelled with pride.

"I told you about the tokay gecko," Piccolo continued. "About it having to be removed surgically if it bites. But did you also know that it can climb anything, including sheer glass. Did you know it has no eyelids and cleans its eyes with its tongue? With its tongue and your salami you wouldn't have to work!

"You got ten seconds to make up your mind," Piccolo said. "Mississippi ten, Mississippi nine, Mississippi eight, Mississippi seven, Mississippi six, Mississippi five, Mississippi four, Mississippi three, Mississippi—"

"Hey, man!" Ace said. "What the fuck's goin' on?"

"Time's up," Piccolo said. "I pick the tokay gecko for you. It likes kielbasa!"

Edmunton roared.

Piccolo went over to the cage holding the gecko. The gecko was motionless.

"Tokay gecko, forward!" Piccolo commanded. The lizard scuttled quickly forward. Before it reached the far end of the cage Piccolo said, "Gecko, tokay! Stop!" Then, "Gecko, tokay! Backward!"

The creature backed up until Piccolo ordered it to stop at its original position.

Piccolo looked down. He paused, his hand like a claw above the motionless lizard.

"I had to get it just right," he said, "or I'll be wearing it."

He slowly lowered his hand and then, in one quick movement, grabbed the creature by the back and picked it up. It turned its loathsomely ugly head with a desire to take off Piccolo's hand, but he had it just right.

"Thank God," Piccolo said gutturally.

He turned to Ace.

"Okay, Ace, we're going to leave now, but first Ed has to put a little something over your mouth."

Edmunton took out a small rubber ball and a piece of tape and approached Ace.

"Wait!" Ace said. "What do you want from me?"

"I want," Piccolo said, his voice charged with shaking emotion, "for this here gecko to eat your salami, you no-good motherfucker oppressor of old defenseless people."

He spurted the few steps to Ace and jammed the gecko against his thigh near his genitals. Ace yelped. Piccolo quickly drew the lizard away.

Edmunton approached with a ball and tape.

Edmunton hesitated. He stopped.

"Wait, Frank," he said. "Maybe he'll cooperate."

Ace turned and looked at Edmunton. Ace's head and upper torso were bathed with sweat. Large areas of his shirt were plastered to the hard muscularity of his body.

"What?" Ace said. "What you want?"

"We want," Piccolo said, "the guy you report to. And we want the names of other conspirators. We want the whole story, Ace."

Ace looked at Piccolo. He seemed on the edge.

"Look at it this way, Ace," Piccolo said. "If you give us—I mean the DA—the story, then you can probably take a walk. If you don't, you'll be tried anyway"—he pushed the gecko toward Ace—"after you get out of the fucking hospital."

As Piccolo talked, Ace kept his eyes on the gecko.

"All right," he said.

"One thing," Piccolo said. "If the DA asks why you're comin' in, just tell 'em you had a change of heart."

Ace said nothing, which Piccolo took to mean yes.

Suddenly, the room was filled with the sound of Piccolo's booming squeak:

"AND DON'T FUCKIN' DOUBLE-CROSS ME, UNLESS YOU WANT TO GO THROUGH LIFE WITHOUT YOUR WANG!"

Ace looked at him. He might have been thinking that the night had not turned out exactly the way he'd planned.

CHAPTER 46

Unlike his predecessor, who lived in Fort Lee, New Jersey, Anthony Spagnoli lived in the Bronx, in fact the Pelham Bay section, not too far from where Lawless lived. It was one of the sections of the Bronx that were still relatively safe. Of course, he had a bodyguard anyway and was licensed to carry a pistol.

He got the call from Wagner, an assistant DA, that Winston Gaines, aka "Ace," had had a change of heart. He wanted to talk about charges against him, and everything concerning the case. He was prepared to name names.

Spagnoli put Ace's turnaround on a level with Larry Flynt of *Hustler* magazine being canonized, but he understood fully when, in response to a question whether Gaines was accompanied by anyone, Warner said, "Frank Piccolo and his partner, Edmunton."

The first question that popped into Spagnoli's mind was whether Ace was ambulatory, but he didn't ask it.

He said he would be there right away. He was excited, because this would be like bringing the case back from the dead. But his sense of joy was tempered a bit by the knowledge that Ace had probably been coerced into his action. He would see when he got there.

He got to the Bronx County Courthouse about ten-thirty, and went as fast as his considerable bulk would carry him to his office on the third floor.

He went into the anteroom and found Piccolo, Edmunton, Wagner, Ace, and a stenographer.

Everyone was sphinxlike. Spagnoli did not see any marks on Ace, who seemed very quiet and contained, a far cry from the bellicose dude who had been bailed out the weekend before.

They all went into Spagnoli's office. Piccolo said, "Ace approached me. He feels bad about what he did, and wants to make amends. Ain't that right, Ace?"

Ace looked at Piccolo as one might regard a mad dog. "Yeah," he said, "I don't want to go to no trial neither. I figure maybe if I help you, you help me."

"Where's your attorney?" Spagnoli asked.

"I told him he don't need an attorney now," Piccolo said. "This is an informal kind of thing."

Spagnoli nodded. Holy shit, he thought.

"I can't make any promises," he told Ace, "but I'll see what I can do. It all depends on what you give me."

Spagnoli started to ask questions, and Ace started to answer them.

After an hour, Spagnoli sent out for sandwiches and coffee.

All told, he and Wagner alternately questioned Ace for two hours. It was quite a story.

Ace, and three other enforcers like him, got a $500 fee for every tenant they drove out of an apartment. Over the last six months, Ace had driven fifty-eight tenants out at that price. He didn't know how many the others got, but he thought it was probably less—they didn't work as hard as he did. There was also bread paid to people who helped drive the people out: some pimps, three or four prostitutes, six new superintendents, and a variety of others. There were seven buildings involved. To Ace's knowledge, five were completely empty—he had the addresses—and two—including 2605 Bainbridge—were almost empty.

Ace didn't know the full names of the other people who were hired to work the buildings. That, of course, was part of the plan: It was impossible to charge people with something if you didn't know their names.

Ace also admitted to two assaults in 2605, but none elsewhere.

A few times, particularly when he implicated himself in a heavy crime, like assault, he hesitated or shut down. It was then, Spagnoli discovered, that Piccolo was able to get him going again.

But it was confusing. When Ace hesitated the first time, Spagnoli thought Piccolo had said, "It's okay, Ace," but the second two times he said it, it sounded more like, "It's tokay, Ace."

Spagnoli had no idea what he meant.

Unknown to Ace, he had given Spagnoli not only a statement taken by a stenographer but a visual one as well: His presentation was videotaped using a camera hidden in the wall.

Ace also gave Spagnoli what he had been looking for: a link to Fishman. Ace said he reported to one David Bender, who, when he talked to Fishman—and Ace had only overheard him once—called himself Charley Rosen. It was Bender who paid Ace and all the others.

He was also the planner. He moved people into and out of apartments, assigned the various enforcers to their posts, and in general ran the show.

It was working out just the way Spagnoli hoped. If they could collar Bender and turn him, they could reach Fishman.

Bender also was in the Bronx. He had an apartment up on Bailey Avenue. Ace visited him there weekly.

Ace was freed, but warned not to contact any of the other conspirators.

The warning was strong.

"You have a chance," Spagnoli told him, "of getting off lighter than the others. But if you hump me I'll stick it to you. What you're facing here is a Class C felony—conspiracy—which carries seven to fifteen per count. You would have multiple counts. Get the picture?"

Ace got the picture.

After Ace left, Piccolo asked him whether he planned to arrest Bender next.

"No," Spagnoli said. "Not right away. Not until we can get together a team who can knock down as many of these guys as possible all at once."

"What's the difference," Piccolo said, "as long as we get to Fishface?"

"We get the other people, we can turn some of them. That will give us a stronger case against Bender. Ultimately the stronger our case against him, the better we can hang Fishman."

"It makes me nervous," Piccolo said, "thinking that Bender is our only show in town, and he's going to run free for a while. Maybe he'll find out we're on to him and take a powder."

"How?" Spagnoli said. "How's he going to find out? And I'm not talking about a long time. Day after tomorrow we go after him."

Piccolo said nothing. He didn't like it.

CHAPTER 47

Frankie Pinto's abiding advice to Barbara was that you had to "think like a dealer."

A dealer, she thought, might think that his phone was tapped. So when she called Frankie Pinto three days after she made the first buy, she did it from a public telephone a few blocks away.

"Hello?"

It was good to hear Frankie's voice. Very good.

"This is Barbara Russo, Frankie," she said. "How's it going?"

"Fine. How's with you?"

She explained about the Fuenteses' visit.

"You handled that beautiful," he said, "but remember it's just the first of who knows how many tests. Miguel Fuentes is a paranoid of the first order."

"Ricky's starting to move in already."

"You'll have to let your own instincts tell you how to handle that," Frankie said. "I'd say, though, go back to the business thing. That should hold him off."

"Okay," Barbara said, "what's next?"

"Make another buy."

"How much?"

"A quarter."

"Where will I get the money?"

"I'll send it with some flowers."

"What a nice idea."

Frankie laughed.

A computer voice cut in, asking for more money.
Barbara put it in.

"You calling from a booth," Frankie said. "Good
idea. I should of told you that. You don't want a phone
bill with the DEA number laying around."

"No," Barbara said. "How's Joe?"

"I haven't seen him."

"Oh."

"You're doing a good job, Barbara," Frankie said.

"Thank you."

Barbara almost called Joe late that night, but she
resisted. The more she called, the more he would worry
about her. She would wait until the end of the week. It
would be like a report she was making.

But she did do one thing. She took her engagement
ring out of its hiding place and slipped it on. She watched
the eleven o'clock news wearing it, gently touching the
diamond, running a finger along the gold of the ring.

She went to bed with it on, letting herself imagine, for
a moment, that Joe Lawless was beside her. Most of the
time she would live the part of a drug dealer, but sometimes she just had to be herself.

Late the next afternoon, the intercom buzzed while
Barbara was watching a game show. Someone had sent
her flowers, Roy said.

A few minutes later, her bell rang and she opened the
door. She tipped the delivery boy a dollar, and brought
the box inside.

She laughed when she took the top of the box off.

Frankie had sent her a dozen roses. He could have
sent her anything, but he had sent roses.

She opened the rather bulky envelope inside. It contained a wad of cash and a card that said, "From a
friend."

Barbara laughed. Then she thought of all the money
the DEA pumped into drug deals. Agents didn't even
need any special approval on amounts below ten thousand dollars, and she knew that informers—the Jimmy

Pollos of the world—could make more on one deal than most cops made in annual salary.

It was money, she thought, that could be used much better elsewhere.

She put the roses in a vase of water, then went back to the television. The show that was on was unbelievably stupid, something about winning scads of money for naming various celebrities. In a way, it scared Barbara. That such shows could exist just demonstrated how unthinking people were. And the people who kept these shows on the air for years were the people who elected presidents and lawmakers. They decided, in effect, matters of life and death, not only in America, but in other countries as well.

Scary—and sad.

Her mind wandered. Wandered, she thought, to where it should be: the Fuenteses.

It was going to be a very delicate operation getting Ricky to say anything. Miguel, she felt, was a lost cause. It was going to be an operation composed of a lot of things, but mostly one of her trying to alleviate any suspicions that she was the Man.

And composed, too, of dangling herself in front of Ricky Fuentes. Dangling, but not getting hooked.

Yes, she could do it. They might never give her any details on their drug operation, but on the Castelli hit, Ricky might. As the DEA guy, Fenwick, had said, the Fuenteses might be suspecting a setup on drugs, but they—or at least Ricky—would not see danger in talking about a homicide.

Maybe. She didn't really know what would happen. She'd just have to play it day by day.

At around four o'clock, she called the number that Ricky Fuentes had given her. The Chinese guy took a message to have Ricky call her. A half hour later, he did.

"Hey, baby," Ricky said. "This Ricky."

"How you doin'?"

"Okay. What can I do for you?"

"What's the story on doin' more business?"

"No problem."

"I thought there might be."

"That's my bro, baby. Serious guy."

"I almost said fuck it," Barbara said. "But I guess you got to do that."

"What you need?"

"More than last time."

"All right," Ricky said. "You come here. The restaurant. We take it from there."

"What time?"

"After nine."

"Okay," Barbara said.

"We can get a few drinks after?" Ricky said.

"I got something set up already," Barbara said.

There was a silence.

"See you after nine," Barbara said.

She hung up, and so did Ricky.

CHAPTER 48

Barbara figured ten o'clock was a good time to see the Fuenteses. It wasn't too much after nine, and it wasn't too early. It would give her time, theoretically, to do what she had "set up" after.

She was packing now, a Walther PPK with an eight shot clip. It wasn't the Fuenteses she was afraid of. She figured word would get out that she was a dealer, and make her a prime candidate for being ripped off. A rip-off artist would figure he had a better shot at ripping her off than a man, and he might try to do things to her, up to and including taking her life, that she would not allow.

She arrived at the restaurant at around ten-fifteen. It had been difficult getting a cab. The same Chinese maître d' who had met her when she was with Ricky greeted her at the door.

Smiling and nodding—and remembering her—he took her to the rear room, where Ricky let her in.

Miguel was sitting on a couch against one wall watching TV, a Spanish musical program of some sort. He looked like he was dressed to stay in for the night, Ricky, wearing something out of *Miami Vice*, looked like he was set to go out on the town.

"How you, Barbara?" Ricky said.

"I'm good. How's with you?"

"We doin' all right."

She accompanied Ricky to Miguel. He looked up at

her. Light glinted off his glasses. She could swear that somehow he knew she was a cop.

She slid her eyes away. If there was anything in them to give her away, she didn't want him to see.

She stood watching the TV. She could feel Ricky looking at her, his eyes going up and down her body. He stepped up to her. She could smell his cologne. It was sweet and heavy.

"You got the bread?"

"Sure," Barbara said, opening her pocketbook. She got the money out and handed it to him.

"Here's for the quarter plus the fifty I owed."

Ricky turned around and handed it to Miguel. He made no attempt to count it. Barbara was aware that he had been watching her closely since she came in.

Ricky left. She turned and watched the TV. Miguel's head was turned toward the TV, but she could still feel his eyes on her.

Ricky turned a few minutes later. He handed Barabra a tin.

"As good as the last batch? We liked the last batch."

"The best," Ricky said.

He looked at her. She had a weird image. Jeff, in the coffin, reflected in his eyes. She smiled. "See you," she said.

"When are we going to get together?" he said. She noticed a pulse in his neck. It was going rapidly.

"I don't know."

"I like you," he said.

Barbara said nothing. Then: "I'll see you again."

She walked out without saying good-bye to Miguel.

When she got home, Barbara took a long, hot bath, though she had showered that morning. You didn't need to be Freud, she thought, to understand what she was trying to do.

Later, in bed, she thought about calling Joe. She had vowed only to call him on weekends, but vows were meant to be modified.

She sat up, flicked on the light, dialed his home number.

It rang twenty-five times before she hung up. She turned off the light and lay back down. It had helped; just calling an empty house had helped.

CHAPTER 49

Barbara made two more buys from the Fuenteses during the next two weeks, the second an eight. Frankie Pinto had had to clear that buy with the DEA. Barbara got it for five thousand, after working the Fuenteses down from six.

At the end of each week she talked with Lawless. He had put the Castelli investigation in the drawer for now, and he and Benton were on new business.

The second time they talked—actually the third time since Barbara had gone undercover—Barbara let Lawless know more of what she was feeling.

"Joe," she said near the end of their conversation, "I really miss you. I mean really. I wasn't going to tell you that, but maybe it's better I did."

"You already told me without knowing it," he said. "You can't hide your feelings from me, Babalino. And I wouldn't want you to."

"How are you doing?"

"It only took me a few days to get over you."

Barbara laughed. "The great stone face is a humorist."

Lawless laughed.

"Christ, I love you," Barbara said.

"If you don't come back soon," Lawless said, "you're going to be putting me in a rather silly position."

"What's that?"

"I'd rather not say," Lawless said.. "Let's just say it involves a practice common in puberty."

Barbara laughed heartily. "You're in rare form."

"I think not having you around has driven me out of my mind."

Her conversation with Lawless only pointed up to Barbara just how far she had not come. All she was doing was seeing the Fuenteses every week, plunking down the taxpayers' money, and buying cocaine. She was getting nowhere. She had to do something to get inside, to make them trust her a little more.

The idea occurred to her just as she was turning off the light to go to bed. It made her turn the light back on and think about it.

CHAPTER 50

Barbara called Frankie Pinto the next day, and he suggested something he didn't have to twist her arm about—that they get together so she could detail her idea. They arranged to meet early evening in a bar in the Village.

She looked forward to the meeting all day. Not just because she would be seeing a friendly face, but because the idea might be a good one—she certainly thought it was—and might help end this thing quicker.

Frankie was sitting at a table in the back. Barbara laughed. He kind of shone in the dark. He was at his flamboyant coke-dealer best: purple satin shirt, lots of chains, yellowish skin-tight pants. She remembered something he said about dealers: "They put their money on the street in clothes and cars. They want people to know what they got."

Barbara wasn't exactly reserved of course. She wore a flashy red spangled dress, white pumps with spangles, scads of jewelry and makeup. Her bright red hair looked like a beehive.

She felt the urge to kiss Frankie before she sat down. She did.

"We're some pair," he said. "You look perfect."

"I'm sorry you said that," Barbara said, and they both laughed hard.

They ordered drinks, and then Barbara filled him in on what had occurred over the last few days.

"Nothing's changed," she said. "Status quo. That's why I hope we can make something else work."

She waited until the drinks came before she told him.

"The idea," Barbara said, "really came out of what you said: 'You got to think like a dealer.' "

Frankie nodded.

"Okay," she said, "Miguel is constantly suspicious of me—or anyone else—and though Ricky has his eyes on me, he's got to be alert to treachery too, right?"

Frankie nodded again.

"They know how the Man operates. He makes some buys, usually at lesser amounts, then comes in and makes the bust buy when there's weight involved, right?"

"You'd be surprised how many dealers don't know that," Frankie said. "But it's reasonable to say the Fuenteses do."

"Right. So in the three weeks I've been buying from them the amounts have gradually gone up. The last buy was an eight. They know I'm working to half a key or maybe a key or more."

"They should."

"My idea," Barbara said, "is not buy from them next week for a simple reason: Somebody broke into my apartment and ripped off the money. And who do you think I suspect?"

"The Fuenteses," Frankie said.

"That's right. A kind of reverse psychology."

"How you going to get this across without a direct accusation?"

"I don't know. Impromptu. Right, Frankie?"

He nodded.

"You got to be very careful here," he said. "You're dealing with machismo. They might be less inclined to get rough with you than a man, but they might not. You got to remember these guys killed a family."

Frankie saw something dark in Barbara's eyes.

"I couldn't forget that, Frankie. I'll never forget that."

There was a silence.

"I take it you approve," Barbara said.

"Yeah," he said. "What are you going to do about future buys?"

"Well," she said, "I'll play it by ear. Make believe I believe it wasn't them. Anything. I just want to put Miguel on the defensive now."

Frankie looked at her. "Okay," he said. "Let's say that you do this and they trust you. How you going to get close enough so you can talk about the Castelli hit?"

Barbara looked at Frankie, then slugged down her drink. "Let's get another," she said.

Frankie ordered two more drinks. Barbara waited until she sipped on hers before she continued.

"It's a two-part idea," she said.

Frankie nodded.

"I thought," she said, looking down into the top of her drink, which was a Bloody Mary, "that I'd encourage Ricky a little."

"You got to be careful there, too," Frankie said. "If you encourage too much and he goes at you and you turn him down you're into his macho thing again."

"It does scare me a little, but I think I can do it. Impromptu. We'll see." Barbara smiled.

"Okay," Frankie said. "Keep in touch."

They finished their drinks, and five minutes later Barbara left, threading her way through tables and people, her progress not unnoticed by some of the men. Frankie watched her too. It was difficult to believe, he thought, that she was a cop. She looked like a pros, or a coke dealer. And, he thought, as female as she was, she had something else in abundance—balls.

CHAPTER 51

The next Saturday Barbara showed up at La Hoy Restaurant at the usual time. Both Fuenteses were there. She sensed they were more relaxed; Miguel actually looked at her.

But she wasn't more relaxed.

"How much, baby?" Ricky said.

"A gram."

"A gram? How come?" Ricky said.

"I got fucking ripped off," she said. "Some mother-fucker broke into my apartment and got all my bucks."

"Oh."

"I can't understand it," she said. "I'm only in town a little while and already everybody knows I'm dealing and where I live and gets all my bucks. Motherfucker!"

She was looking at Ricky, but her eyes flicked to Miguel at the exact moment she said "motherfucker." It was as if she called him that. But he couldn't prove it—she hoped.

Her eyes went back to Ricky. "It had to be an inside job," she said.

"Jimmy Pollo?" Ricky said.

"He's gone."

There was silence for a moment.

"I'll get the stuff for you," Ricky said. She gave him the cash and he left.

They watched the TV in silence for half a minute. Then Miguel spoke.

"Hey, you want to find out who stole your money, you look for a small-timer. No one with a big operation is going to risk a burglary charge for what amounts to chicken feed. To him, I mean." He watched Barbara.

Barbara nodded, continued to watch the TV.

Ricky came back with the tin of coke. He handed it to her.

"Thanks," she said.

"No problem," Ricky said.

Barbara left.

At home, she thought about the effect she had had on Miguel. She sensed that she might have put him on the defensive a little. Otherwise, why would he say a "small-timer" did it? He didn't have to explain anything to her.

At around eleven o'clock, she went out on the patio and looked out over Queens. It was a very clear night and she could dimly perceive the Manhattan skyline. She could not hope to see the Bronx, but somewhere in it was her baby. Christ, she missed him. And, she knew, he missed her.

The phone rang, and she went back inside. It would be—it might be Joe.

It was Ricky Fuentes.

"Hey, Barbara," he said. "What you doin'?"

"Watching TV."

"You want a drink?"

Barbara hesitated.

"Yeah," she finally said. "I could use one."

"I pick you up in twenty minutes."

Immediately after she hung up, Barbara wondered about the wisdom of what she was doing. And whether she could handle it.

The guard announced Fuentes about fifteen minutes later.

Barbara wore the most conservative outfit she had. She didn't want to give Fuentes any messages—any more than she already had.

Fuentes was waiting in the lobby for her. She saw a glint of disappointment in his eyes. Good.

Barbara suggested a local bar, and they went there.

Fuentes ordered rum and Coke, Barbara white wine. Fuentes paid with a hundred he peeled off a roll of bills thick enough to choke a horse.

"You have no idea who took your bread, huh?"

"No," Barbara said.

"You find out," Ricky said, "you tell me. I'll get it back for you."

"You will?"

Fuentes smiled. "Sure. No problem. In fact," he continued, "I'll put the word out now. If anybody found it, they're to return it to me."

Barbara furrowed her brow, her eyes showed doubt.

"Just like that?" she said.

"Just like fuckin' that," Ricky said. "I don't think you know how big me and Miguel are. We're fuckin' big and getting bigger. We got dealers all the way up to fuckin' Riverdale."

"Doesn't the Mafia—"

"Fuck the Mafia," Ricky said. "They don't fuck with us. They know better."

Something grabbed Barbara's stomach and twisted it.

"Geez," she said, "I had no idea you were so big." She looked really impressed. She smiled a little. "How come you took on someone like me?"

"You came through a friend. I like you. I want to give you a start. Me and my brother, we started small."

Barbara nodded. And wanting to screw me, she thought, had nothing to do with it.

She thought suddenly of Jeff, and of the handsome kid with the grotesque hand. This image didn't hold her next statement down. It helped drag it up.

"I like you too," she said. She smiled.

Ricky Fuentes smiled, showing very white teeth.

"You married, you got a boyfriend?"

"No," Barbara said, "I had one."

"One what?"

"A boyfriend."

Fuentes looked at her drink, which was half full.

"Have another drink."

He beckoned to the middle-aged waitress who was serving them.

"I'm okay now," Barbara said. "You have one."

Fuentes looked at her and ordered another rum and Coke. He took a long gulp of it when it came. He looked at her, a half smile on his face.

"I got a surprise for you," he said.

Barbara smiled, though a little something crawled inside her. "What's that?"

"It's in the car."

She smiled more broadly. "What is it?"

Fuentes gulped the last of the rum and Coke, then peeled off a twenty-dollar bill and dropped it on the table.

"C'mon."

Barbara finished the wine. They got up and went outside. Barbara was alert as they went toward the car, which Fuentes had parked about ten yards down the block.

The street was relatively empty.

He opened the driver's side door, got in, and opened the passenger's door for Barbara.

She got in and he reached under his seat and took out a paper bag. He handed it to her.

"What's this?" she said.

"Half a key."

"Really?"

"You pay me after you sell it."

"I don't know how to thank you," Barbara said.

"It's okay. I like you," Fuentes said.

Barbara took the stuff, which was in a glassine bag, out of the paper bag. It looked like a small sack of flour. It was worth after cutting $200,000 on the street.

Fuentes pulled away. He drove fast and aggressively. She just hoped they wouldn't be stopped by a radio car.

They weren't. Twenty minutes later, Fuentes pulled the car into an underground garage not unlike the one in Barbara's house in Queens. The building, on East 57th Street, was even posher than hers.

"Where we going " she asked as they rode the elevator.

"My place," he said.

Just like that. What an arrogant fuck, she thought.

Fuentes' place was on the nineteenth floor of the building. It was straight out of a movie set. There was a big picture window with a view of the East River and lower Manhattan, and everything was white or a shade of white: white carpet, furniture, modernistic lamps. Against one wall was a bar made of some sort of white marble.

"What'll you have?" he said as he went behind the bar. "Wine?

"Okay."

He made himself a rum and Coke and poured Barbara a glass of white wine. As he did, Barbara examined the decor a little more closely. She noticed a couple of paintings on the walls: nudes, and two statues, also female nudes.

There was nothing warm in the room. She had a curious thought. Hadn't she learned in college that the novelist Flaubert used white as the symbol of death in *Madame Bovary*?

Barbara doubted that Fuentes had read Flaubert. He used the color instinctively.

He handed her the drink and stood close to her.

"You want to change into something more comfortable?" he said.

"I'm fine," she said, sipping the wine.

He walked over to the window. "Did you ever see a view like this?"

Barbara thought, Yeah, from Windows on the World. She shook her head.

"Not bad, huh, for a kid from the streets of Santo Domingo."

Christ, Barbara thought, Humphrey Bogart must be doing cartwheels in his grave.

"Yeah," she said. "Great."

"Come here," he said.

Barbara went there. She stood next to him.

"Right now," he said, "we got enough dough to buy plenty of that."

He slipped his arm over her shoulder. She did nothing to stop him.

"I like you," he said. "You stick with me you won't be sorry."

Barbara swallowed the rest of her drink.

"Want another?"

"Sure."

Fuentes went back to the bar and poured her another drink.

She drank half of it. "This will have to be a nightcap," she said.

"What?" Fuentes said, his eyes flashing. "What you mean?"

"I like you a lot, Ricky," Barbara said, "but I got some problems right now that are just there."

"What kind of problems?"

"Just problems," Barbara said. She wanted to keep it vague. Excuse herself but make no commitment of any kind.

"Okay," Ricky said, "we got time. Plenty of time."

Barbara told him that she would take a cab home.

Before she left he kissed her long on the mouth.

She went downstairs and started to walk up the block. She had held him at bay. She was getting closer to what she wanted. She had kissed a coke dealer who had killed babies.

Tears formed in her eyes, spilled down over her makeup.

There wasn't anything, she thought, that was going to make her feel clean tonight.

CHAPTER 52

The next day, Miguel and Ricky Fuentes sat in the living room of Ricky's apartment. They spoke in Spanish, as they almost always did when they were alone.

"Why'd you give it to her?" Miguel said.

"I think she's going to be a steady customer. I want to see her make it."

Miguel took off the dark sunglasses, revealing totally black eyes devoid off warmth.

"You expect me to believe that, brother? I know what you want. You're thinking with your *bicho*."

"Yeah," Ricky said. "I want that—and I'll get it. But I also want her as a steady customer."

"Sure," Miguel said. "You'd give every potential dealer half a key to get started, right?"

Ricky said nothing.

Miguel took out an unfiltered Dominican cigarette, lit it with a metal lighter, and inhaled deeply.

"No question," Miguel said, "she's a nice-looking woman. I'd like to poke her myself. But she worries me."

Ricky looked at him.

"Why? It seems to me she's okay. You think she's the Man."

"Not necessarily," Miguel said. "Maybe she's a stool pigeon. I don't know."

"No fucking way," Ricky said.

"No," Miguel said, taking two deep drags and hardly

letting any smoke out. "I'm not sure. What do you know about her, bro?"

"She came out of Jimmy Pollo."

"Don't you remember? We took everything of his. Can he be in love with us?"

Ricky shook his head.

"Also," Miguel continued, "she's very thin about her background. What else do you know about her?"

Ricky thought. He did not know much.

"I want to have her checked," Miguel said.

"By who?"

"McKenna."

"Everything under the table?"

"Of course," Miguel said. "He may be a *hijo de putana*, but he can do it under the table, and if he clears her, she's clear."

"Okay," Ricky said. "Meanwhile, business as usual."

"Hey, you want to fuck her," Miguel said, "be my guest. You can't go to jail for that."

They laughed.

Miguel called McKenna at three o'clock at his home, in the Bay Shore section of Brooklyn. Miguel knew if he wasn't there, he would be at the B Street Bar, close to the 11th Precinct.

He was at his house.

McKenna, a large, rumpled, gray-haired man in his late fifties, had a hangover, but he could still listen. He listened as Miguel spoke.

"Off the top of my head," McKenna said when Miguel had finished, "she sounds like the genuine article."

"I still want her checked."

"Okay," McKenna said. "The usual arrangement?"

"Plus two thousand if it turns up positive."

"Good. Talk to you."

Miguel hung up.

McKenna, he thought, had done very valuable work for them. It was from him he had heard that Larocca, who was getting more and more into their operation, was Johnny Padilla, a cop. If this *putana* was a cop, or a plant, this ex-cop would find out.

CHAPTER 53

On the Wednesday following her visit to the Fuenteses, Barbara called Frankie Pinto from a public booth on Queens Boulevard. She explained all that had occurred. He thought it very good.

"Now, next week," he said, "you go in there with bucks. You show 'em you keep your word. You're solid."

"What should I give 'em?"

"Ten grand," Frankie said, "with a promise of another ten the following week. Okay?"

"How am I going to get it?"

"You're going to be in Friday?"

"Yes."

"You're going to be receiving some more flowers," he said.

On Friday, Barbara received a dozen roses and an envelope containing $10,000 in fifty-dollar bills. She called Ricky at the restaurant. He wasn't there, but she left word that she would see him the next night. Miguel wasn't there either.

On Saturday, she got into one of her dealer-design dresses at about eight o'clock.

This one was all white, with drapes and spangles, and she had also bought white shoes. The fact that Ricky Fuentes liked white hadn't escaped her.

She was looking forward to a great night: getting all

gussied up to turn the ape on, and then having to figure a way to keep him off her. Great life, undercover.

She got to the restaurant at about nine o'clock. She immediately gave the money to Ricky.

"I'll have the rest next week," she told him.

Ricky nodded. He tossed the envelope to his brother, who was, as usual, on the couch watching TV.

"So now," Ricky said, "let's hit the town a little, huh?"

"Ready when you are."

They left, and Miguel immediately went to the phone hanging on the wall. He dialed a number.

A few seconds later, he said, in English:

"She's gone."

CHAPTER 54

The fact that there turned out to be no BCI report, and no mug shot, did nothing to alleviate the slight fluttering Frank Piccolo felt about leaving Bender, aka Charles Rosen, on the street. This Bender didn't have a record.

But that was the point, Piccolo thought. He wasn't Bender; he was someone else. He was an older guy, Ace had said. Had to be clever. If he somehow got the word before the DA's squad made the roundup raid, he would be gone into the night like a cockroach, and they would see him no more.

And Fishface would continue to operate.

"We got to make sure this guy don't take a powder," Piccolo told Edmunton shortly after the empty BCI report came back.

By early afternoon, Piccolo and Edmunton had come up with a plan.

At around two o'clock, an expensive-looking light brown van with darker brown accents pulled up in front of the building on Bailey Avenue where Bender was the managing agent.

Piccolo, alone in the driver's compartment, felt a terrible surge of anger when he saw it, similar to what he had felt when he saw where Ace lived.

It was a tall, tubelike building finished in rough cement with mirrored windows and small patios. It looked like a building transplanted from a science fiction movie.

Piccolo got out of the truck. He was wearing tight-fitting Jordache jeans, a Lacoste shirt, and Capezios, all

219

in shades of light blue. His hair had been cut and styled, and he wore aviator shades.

There was a doorman dressed like he was all set to head off on safari. Piccolo smiled, keeping his mouth closed to conceal the missing teeth.

"How you doin', my man?" Piccolo said to the doorman.

He nodded.

"Do you know where Mr. Bender is?"

"First floor, front. Suite 1A."

"Thanks."

Piccolo went through the glass doors, which opened electronically, like in a supermarket.

The interior had been designed by someone with a fetish about mirrors. Walls and ceilings were covered with them. Mirror tiles. They reflected Frank Piccolo hundreds of times.

He found Apartment 1A. There was a small sign: MANAGING AGENT. Piccolo rang the bell.

The man who answered the door looked like he had two separate identities, neither of which jelled. He was, Piccolo gathered, about sixty-five, with heavy features, a heavily lined face, and a bad toupee. He wore thick glasses. His clothing was modish, and he wore lots of chains around his neck. He was an old man trying to look young—which made him look older.

"Hi. You Mr. Bender?"

He nodded.

"My name is Rader, and I was interested in if you had any units for rent."

"Not right now," Bender said. "In a few months, maybe."

"Oh," Piccolo said, looking past Bender into the apartment. There was a young, shapely black girl in the distance, probably the living room. Bender was white. Piccolo guessed it wasn't the fuck's daughter.

"Thank you," Piccolo said.

Bender closed the door.

Piccolo exited the building, then went across the street and down the block to the van. He looked back before he got in. The doorman was inside the building. Piccolo got in the back with Edmunton, who had watched him enter and leave the building through one of the mirrored porthole windows.

Bender was watching, too, idly at first, just looking out one of his own mirrored front windows as Piccolo walked down the block and got into the van—but then his interest increased when he didn't see the exhaust pipe cough.

Why was he staying inside the van so long?

Just go in a van and stay there?

He watched for twenty minutes; he had been planning to have some fun with the schvartze, but the van was making him too nervous to do anything but watch.

Inside the van, Piccolo was feeling good. He radioed Spagnoli's investigative unit that he had Bender under surveillance, just to be on the safe side. He could tell that Wagner was miffed, but fuck 'em. Piccolo felt better.

Two hours later. Bender, aka Charles Rosen, left the building. He stopped for a moment, his back to the van, to talk with Pete, the doorman. But that wasn't his real purpose. His purpose was to find out what, if anything, was happening with the van.

"You okay? Mr. Bender?" the doorman asked.

He had seen Bender go pale after Bender had seen the back of the van open and a big guy get out.

"Yeah," he said. "I'm okay."

Bender started to walk in the direction away from the van. Whenever he could, he looked in a plate-glass window or sneaked a glance or otherwise checked to see if he was still being followed. He was.

He went back to his apartment—followed all the way—and immediately got on the phone. He reached two of the guys he had hired to clear out the apartments. He could not reach Chico or Ace.

He asked them the same question: Did they notice anything strange or different today? Did they get the feeling they were being followed?

They didn't. Bender let it go at that. It was probably just him. He thought about why it would be just him. The answer was simple: He was the head man, next to Fishman.

Bender started to fantasize what it would be like if things went wrong. The schvartzes in prison would have fun with him. Never mind that he was sixty-six. They would work him over.

He could not accept the idea of going to prison. No, that was one idea he could not accept.

Then he realized he was panicking. What could they have on him? Just what?

Plenty, he thought, if the others implicated him. And they would. They were just offal, the dregs of life. They would implicate him in a minute to save themselves.

He drank a couple of mixed drinks—two in less than fifteen minutes—but they didn't seem to help. He had to do something else.

He dialed the number he knew by heart.

It rang three times, then a lilting, male West Indian voice answered.

"Fishman residence."

"Yeah, this is Charley Rosen. Let me speak to Morris."

"Just a moment, please."

Charley waited nervously, sipping his third drink. Thirty seconds later, Morris Fishman came on the line.

"Yeah, Charley."

"Morris, we got a problem. I'm being watched by the cops."

"How do you know you're being watched?"

Rosen explained about the modishly dressed man and the van, and the guy following him.

"So, what's the problem? You're just being watched."

"Yeah, but I don't know what they're going to do next. Ace was arrested. . . ."

"They got nothing on Ace, or anyone else. Calm down."

Rosen was about to say something, but he was silent. Then: "So what should I do?"

"Just sit everything out. Go about your business. If they make a move, arrest you, don't say anything. I'll have you on the street in an hour. Okay?"

"Okay," Rosen said.

He hung up, and thought about Ace. If Ace talked it would be him, Rosen, who would be vulnerable. But Fishman would help him. He'd better.

CHAPTER 55

The key ingredient in the success of any police raid on multiple locations is timing. All of the people involved in the raid must be on the same clock and hit at the same time to prevent any of the alleged perps from warning one another.

Spagnoli had assembled his people, twenty in all, the night before. They had set their watches at 5:00 A.M. The raid was to be conducted at 6:05, just after dawn at seven separate locations. Arrest warrants had been prepared the day before.

Spagnoli had detailed two additional people to work with Edmunton and Piccolo. They came, in another van, around four in the morning.

There was no radio contact. At 6:05, they were to just go in.

Piccolo did not expect trouble from Bender. He looked like a wimp. But one never knew. Lee Harvey Oswald looked like a wimp; so did Arthur Bremer and scads of others.

Edmunton armed himself only with his service revolver. Piccolo had that, plus a sawed-off shotgun and, in its holster, the .44 Magnum.

At 6:05 they went in.

The four men got out of the van and headed toward the condo. For a moment, a man walking his dog thought that the four men, all brandishing their weapons, were after him, and he almost went along with the dog. But

they weren't. And he just stood there, like stone, only
his eyes following their progress.

Bender had had a sleepless night. His stomach ached,
and he had diarrhea. All told, he had slept perhaps two
hours in stretches of fifteen or twenty minutes each. He
kept checking the van, and when he spotted the additional van he immediately went to and spent a half hour
on the toilet.

Then he decided that the second van might not be for
him. But it did not help him sleep any better.

He was looking out the window and up the block at
the vans for the nth time when he saw the backs of both
open and men get out. Armed men.

He had planned what to do if something like this
happened, and he was glad that he had, because his
mind went sort of blank.

Quickly, he picked up the suitcase by the door and
went out into the lobby.

Pete, the doorman, was near the doors, sitting in a
chair, half asleep. He saw Bender. Bender smiled. "Don't
tell anyone where I've gone, okay?"

"Oh, sure, Mr. Bender."

He could take the elevator or stairs to the garage
level. He took the stairs.

A minute later, he was in his car, a gray Mercedes
hardtop. It only took him three tries to get the key in the
ignition.

Then he was roaring through the garage. He headed
toward the rear entrance/exit to the garage. They might
be watching the front entry, but not this one.

The door opened electronically, and he bounced onto
Hillside Avenue. There was no one there.

Something screaming inside him to go faster, Bender
aka Charley Rosen proceeded down Venture, waited for
a light, feeling sweat starting to trickle down his back,
then made a right turn—and was out of sight of the
building.

Piccolo, Edmunton, and the two men from the DA's
office burst into the lobby. For a moment, the doorman
didn't know what was going on. They simply went past
him to Bender's apartment.

Piccolo rang the bell. No answer.

Piccolo went back to the lobby. He showed his shield. "Is Bender in there?"

The doorman hesitated, but something in Piccolo's eyes told him not to. "No."

"When did he leave?"

"A while ago."

"How fucking long?"

"Five minutes."

"How'd he leave?"

"He went downstairs to the garage. The stairs."

"What kind of car?"

"Gray Mercedes hardtop. Brand new."

"I'll get an APB out," Edmunton said.

Piccolo looked at the doorman.

"It's a good thing you told the truth," he said.

Thirty seconds later Piccolo was in the driver's seat of the van. Edmunton was getting out an APB before Piccolo had started the vehicle. The DA's men were already rolling down the street.

Without the necessity of verbal communication, the DA's van went east and Piccolo headed west. Bender only had a five- or ten-minute head start. They had a shot at getting him.

Two hours later, Piccolo pulled the van to a stop on the Concourse about a block north of the courthouse.

He was quiet, and Edmunton knew it was better to leave him alone at these times. He was depressed because Bender had gotten away. And after Bender heard of the raid on the other headbreakers and sleazes he would probably stay under.

When Piccolo and Edmunton got to the third floor, the media were there in full force—TV, radio, print. It was the kind of story that readers and viewers would lap up.

Piccolo and Edmunton stood in the back as Spagnoli, who was using the hall outside his office as a forum, announced what had occurred.

Altogether, eleven people had been arrested on crimes ranging from assault to criminal trespass to conspiracy.

When questioned on how the DA had gotten a lead on the ring, Spagnoli was artfully evasive: "Just solid police work," he said. He also didn't go into specifics on who the ringleader was or that the only link to the evil force, which is the way Piccolo thought of him, had gotten away.

The interrogation of the prisoners took all day. Piccolo and Edmunton were part of it. It soon became clear that no one knew anyone beyond Bender. They all reported to him: He gave out the assignments, he paid the money, he told them exactly what to do.

Early in the evening, Spagnoli widened the APB to the tristate area, but so far, nothing resembling Bender or his car had been spotted.

Piccolo's best hope was the car. If Bender held on to that, he might be fairly easily recognized. Though Mercedes were now more common than they once were, they were still unusual enough that chances of spotting one were better than for the average car.

Unknown to Piccolo, however, Bender had increased the odds against his capture. At the very moment Piccolo was hoping that the car would be spotted, it was traveling down a winding, macadam path flanked by heavy trees in Laurel Hill, Long Island, an area where Mercedes and other expensive cars were the norm. It was an area whose inhabitants were among the richest, if not the richest, on Long Island. Homes valued at half a million dollars and up were common; many of the homes were worth several million.

Bender had been heading in this direction when he heard the news flash on the radio that a tenement terrorist gang had been swept up by a squad of detectives from the district attorney's office. He realized perfectly well that their net had failed to catch the biggest fish, and that was him. And that they wouldn't stop until they did. He had to take some very drastic evasive action.

CHAPTER 56

Bender's destination was the home of Morris Fishman, a realtor, insurance executive, market player, and thief who had been superbly successful in accumulating money. His home, though not as impressive as the embassy-sized white masonry monster that belonged to his Arab neighbor, was not exactly chopped liver either. Fishman had spent over a million dollars to have it built. Set in woods like the others, it had its own double tennis court and commanded a lovely view, more visible when the trees were bare in winter, of Long Island Sound. The house had cedar siding stained a lovely russet color. The trim was done in light gray. Inside everything was oak—oak floors, banisters, furniture. For a man who had employed the sleaziest ways of accumulating wealth, it was a model of good taste.

Bender pulled into the blacktop turnaround, unannounced, about six o'clock. Then he realized that his car would be visible, so he backed up, went farther down the dirt road that ran by the turnaround, made a left, and pulled in under the deck that was adjacent to the living room.

Morris Fishman had been looking out the window, perhaps expecting a visit from someone. He watched Bender pull in, then out. Bender was nervous. No question. The question was just how neverous.

Bender climbed the stairs to the patio level and went

to one of the three patio doors. Fishman saw him coming and opened the door.

Bender, sweating, felt coolness envelop him. Fishman
smiled and extended his hand.

"Hey, Charley," he said. "C'mon in the living room.
You look all tuckered out. Like an iced tea or something?"

Bender glanced at the white-coated schvartze who
had materialized out of nowhere. He was smiling.

"I'll have a drink," Bender said. If you listened closely
you could hear the slight yiddish accent picked up from
his childhood on Madison Street on the Lower East
Side. "Scotch on the rocks."

"Hey, Charley," Fishman said. "Take it easy. I know
what's on your mind. We'll work it out."

Fishman, a bearded dark-haired, dark-eyed man in his
early forties who was tan from tennis and tanning sa-
lons, came over and put a big muscular arm around
Bender. He led him to the living room, an airy, well-lit
place with a few well-placed floor plants, then to a
couch. Bender sat down, and Fishman sat opposite him
in an upholstered chair with an oak frame.

"What's the problem?" he said.

"You know. You heard on the radio."

"So what. They got nothing to connect us to anything."

Bender looked at him. He was about to say something
when the schvartze came with the Scotch, a napkin
underneath. Bender took it without acknowledgment.

"Ace named everybody. He had to," Bender said.
"How else would they get everyone?"

Fishman said, "So what? How does that effect us?"

Bender took a long pull on the Scotch. It was a stiff
one, and he was glad.

"Because," he said, "I narrowly escaped today."

"How?"

Bender explained about the vans. "They might have
picked up my trail by now. I don't know."

Fishman looked at his nails, then at Bender. "Okay,"
he said. "He probably did talk. It still doesn't hurt us.
All you got to do is deny everything."

Bender looked at him with wonderment. "Are you
fucking crazy?" he said. "What if they all testify that it

was me that paid them, me that told them to break in and turn over the apartments, me that told them to break fuckin' heads. That Spagnoli, he's a tough fucker. He'll make 'em talk.''

Fishman's eyebrows went up. "So, what do you want to do?''

"I thought about it," Bender said. "I can't do no time—that's for sure. I wouldn't want to even risk doing time. I think I should clear out. Get out before they get me.''

Fishman nodded. "How?''

Bender finished the last of the Scotch. The schvartze took the empty away.

"With help from you.''

"How much?''

Bender felt the Scotch. He was going to help. The only question was how much.

"Whatever you think is good.''

"What will you do?''

"Leave the country. Never come back. Or at least not until it's safe.''

"I don't know," Fishman said, "if it's the best way to go. You can still deny, and I have the best attorneys money can buy.''

"I don't think so," Bender said. "Too risky.''

"It's risky for me, too, isn't it? If they crack you it would lead to me.''

Bender shook his head. "The best solution is for me to clear out.''

"Would one hundred thousand be enough?''

"No way," Bender said. "I'd be gone for good.''

"How much, then?''

Bender took a long gulp on the Scotch, almost all of it.

"Half a mil.''

"That's a lot of money," Fishman said. He smiled, but his eyes were a little glazed over.

"Can you?''

Fishman looked at the finely polished floor. He looked up at Bender. "When do you want to get going?''

"As soon as you get me the money.''

"I don't have that kind of money here," Fishman said. "Anyway, I don't think you should try to get through customs with a lot of cash."

"Get me, say, four hundred seventy-five thousand in cashier's checks and the rest in cash."

"I could give you twenty-five grand in cash and have the rest deposited in your name or under a number in Switzerland."

"No," Bender said. "I like it this way."

The schvartze appeared again. This time he took the empty from Bender and handed him a drink from the tray.

The business settled, Bender relaxed. As he talked with Fishman about Fishman's wife and kids, who were away on vacation somewhere, he calculated his escape route. He would leave the Mercedes here for Fishman to dispose of. He would take public transportation to Philadelphia and buy his ticket there. He would go to Switzerland first, then think about what to do from there.

The schvartze cooked them a steak dinner, and shortly after the end of it—it was delicious—Bender was helped to bed. With the emotional exhaustion of the day, plus the drinking, he was asleep almost instantly.

He slept well, awaking only once, at about two o'clock, though he didn't know the time.

A dream awoke him. He thought something was pointing, cutting into his throat.

He awoke. Something was. He could not see him, but he could smell him. A sweet smell. It was the schvartze, hunched over him. Bender could feel his blood trickling down from his neck.

"What?" he said.

"Mr. Fishman say you leave tonight. Fifty thousand. Okay?"

"Yes," Bender said. "Yes. Very generous."

"Good."

CHAPTER 57

Arnold Gertz's plan for stopping the dogfights was worked out during the next day, and when he figured it out he thought it would work, and he could do it himself: He would simply make himself as visible as possible, and make sure Bailey knew it.

Five minutes after he thought of the plan, he called the Silver Sunset Kennels. He got Bailey.

"Mr. Bailey," Arnold said. "This is Gertz, the detective from the Fifty-third Precinct. I want you to know that me and my friends are going to be hanging around you until you start returning the dogs to the people who own them. There's not going to be any fights."

"I'm going to get my lawyer," Bailey said.

"Go ahead," Arnold said. "That's okay."

Bailey slammed the phone down.

Arnold did not know if Bailey could file any charges. Arnold didn't care. There would be no fights, and that was that.

A threat of another sort did come: from Captain Bledsoe. He stopped Arnold on his way out the day his open surveillance was to begin.

"Hey, Arnold," said Bledsoe, who was coming in. "Whatever happened to that dog case?"

"Oh, Arnold said, "we had some bad luck. The guy moved the dogs. We're trying to track them down."

Arnold could tell that Bledsoe had a few questions, but it was an awkward time to ask.

"Keep in touch," he said.

Arnold had breathed a sigh of relief.

Arnold felt that it would be wrong to ask Stewart to help him on this. It could get sticky. If it did, Stewart would be in it with him.

So Arnold chose to do it alone.

He realized that he had to keep Bailey guessing, and hope that if he tried anything, Arnold would be there.

On the first two days, he showed up at the dog kennel five separate times, variously camped across the street from the kennel's entrance. On the second day, he followed Bailey to, as it turned out, a local bar.

On the third day, he showed up at the kennel twice—once early in the morning and the other time around eleven P.M. Fortunately, the kennel was not very far from his home, so he could make an appearance and then leave.

Arnold sensed that his actions were making Bailey nervous. Hopefully, it would only be a short time before he gave up the idea of the convention. But Arnold also sensed that Bailey was a tough customer. He probably had a lot of money tied up in the convention, and it wasn't going to be that easy.

Still, Arnold felt that at least as long as he was around nothing would happen, and the dogs were safe.

On the morning of the fourth day, Arnold went onto the kennel grounds, back to where the pit bull cages were.

They were all still there. He had a fleeting thought of stealing them all, but that would only get him into big trouble. And what would he do with them?

He made an upsetting discovery while he was there. He counted twelve pit bulls, two more than before.

Arnold watched the entrance to the kennel for two hours, then went to get a bit to eat.

But he had no appetite. He was just thinking, worrying, getting angrier.

When he returned, he drove into the kennel. Bailey's pickup was there.

Arnold went into the office.

Bailey was there, behind the counter. When he saw it

was Arnold he tensed, Arnold thought, but then relaxed.
Arnold sensed something strange about his behavior but
couldn't put his finger on exactly what it was.

"You got two more dogs," Arnold said.

"It's a public kennel," Bailey said.

"You better give it up," Arnold said, "or you'll regret
it. I'm telling you."

Standing there, 270 pounds of chiseled immensity, Arnold Gertz was an imposing figure.

But Bailey was not rattled. He had a strange expression. A smirk, that was the word.

Then Bailey turned and went through the door to the
back.

Arnold went home at six. He figured he would go
back out at ten, and then deep in the A.M.

He parked the car in front of the house as usual and
was heading toward the gate when he saw Naomi coming down the path toward him. She held up her hand as
if to say: Stay there. He did. His pulse spurted. What
was wrong?

She came through the gate and looked up at him. Her
eyes were red.

"They took Misty," she said, her eyes filling with
tears. "They kidnapped Misty."

"Who?"

"I don't know. I came out above five o'clock and she
was gone. Then about a half hour ago I got a call. A
terrible man said, 'We got your pooch. Tell your cop
husband to mind his own business or your dog is going
into the pit.' "

She started to cry. Arnold held her. He felt like
crying himself. Then a blast furnace opened inside his
head.

"It's Bailey," he said. "It has to be him. He got my
address."

He released Naomi. She wiped her eyes.

"I'll get Misty back," he said, turning toward the car.

"Wait," Naomi said. "Please. He said Misty would
be let go in a few days if you mind your own business."

Arnold looked at her. "Naomi, if I don't do anything a lot of other dogs will die."

She shook her head. Tears ran down her face. "I don't care about other dogs. I just care about Misty. She's been our dog since Aaron and Jude were babies."

Arnold stood, immobile, like a huge tree being whacked by hatchets, incapable of self-defense.

"I've got to do something, honey," he said, tears forming in his eyes. "I can't let those dogs just die. I can't. Please."

"Oh, Arnold," she said. "Just wait. Think. Let's think of what we're going to do. Call the trainer. Call Haggerty. See what he suggests. If you go there now to that kennel, they'll . . . Please."

"All right," he said. "I'll call Haggerty."

They went inside the house. The twins were down in the basement. They had not yet noticed that their dog was missing. But they would.

Chapter 58

As Arnold had hoped—and expected—Haggerty, who worked twelve-hour days as a rule rather than an exception, was at his school when Arnold called. He told him he could be in Freeport in half an hour, and they arranged to meet in a local diner.

A half hour later, they were in the diner and Arnold fleshed out what he had told him on the phone.

"I don't know what to do," Arnold said. "If I wait, then all those other dogs may die. If I don't wait, I go after Bailey, then Misty could die. I just don't know what to do."

Arnold paused. He put his head down, shook it. When he looked up his eyes were filled with sadness.

"No," he said. "I know what to do. I have to try to save all the dogs. I just can't bear doing it."

"What were you thinking of doing?" Haggerty asked.

"Confronting Bailey. Collaring him. Maybe worse. I don't know. I'd have to see when I got there."

Haggerty looked at the table, then looked up. "I'll tell you what I think, Arnold, because I want us to know exactly what we may be up against. It . . . it . . . I don't think it matters what you do. I don't think Bailey intends to return Misty anyway. He's a slimy guy, and a vicious one. He doesn't want any kind of charges against him. Misty is the only proof against him."

"God, I hope you're wrong."

"I have no way of knowing I'm right. But that's the way I think we should go."

"What can we do?"

"Play along," Haggerty said. "Make it seem like we're going to do nothing. Try to find out when this convention is going to be."

"How?"

"Well, you'd get Misty back—when? In a few days? After tomorrow? Then maybe it's tomorrow. Maybe not. But when you call him, you should try to pin down exactly when you're getting her back. Then we'll have to assume the convention is the day before."

Arnold nodded. "And what do we do then?"

"I'm going to get on the horn," Haggerty said. "Just call everyone I know. Someone, somewhere, has to know exactly when that fight is scheduled to happen. And where."

Arnold nodded. He was so glad Haggerty was in this with him. It helped—a little.

"It's a long shot, isn't it?" Arnold asked.

Haggerty looked at him. "Let's call Bailey," he said.

A few minutes later, Arnold called Luther Bailey from a pay phone on the corner.

"I know you got my dog," Arnold said. "I'm not going to bother you. When is it going to be released?"

"I don't know what you're talkin' about. You worry too much."

He hung up.

CHAPTER 59

The day after he talked with Miguel Fuentes, the private investigator, McKenna, started to check Barbara Russo out. Like most PIs, he had friends in the right places, so he could do as thorough a job as the police would, perhaps better. He didn't worry about being hauled onto the carpet for using illegal methods to gain information.

A friend of his in Personnel at One Police Plaza ran her through BCI. Another friend on the Albany PD ran her through the Motor Vehicle Bureau. He also intended to run her through Social Security, but he wanted to wait until he got her number. Her name alone was not specific enough.

He also made a call to the Los Angeles Police Department and to a friend on the job there who had worked with McKenna for ten years before moving to California. Miguel Fuentes had told McKenna that Barbara said she had spent time in Los Angeles. McKenna thought they should have some record of her being there.

At around ten A.M. on the day after he started his probe, he visited the house where Barbara lived. It was a good time, because there was very little traffic in and out of the building.

McKenna approached the guard, Roy, who was in his usual position behind the counter. McKenna showed him a gold NYPD detective's shield.

"How you doin?" McKenna asked. "We're doing a little checking on someone in the building and wondered if you could help."

"I'll try," Roy said.

"Do you know Russo, the woman in 6D?"

Roy made believe he was thinking a moment. But he knew her. He sure did. Christ, those tits.

"The redhead. Barbara Russo?"

"Yeah," McKenna said, "that's her. Does she have many visitors?"

"Not that I see. But I'm not on nights."

"No boyfriends?"

Roy shook his head.

"She go out often?"

"Once a day."

"When?"

"Midday. I don't know about nights."

"You want to do me another favor," McKenna said, withdrawing a folded-up fifty-dollar bill from inside his coat pocket. Roy's eyes followed the bill for a moment.

McKenna handed it to him.

"I'm going to park across the street. If she comes out in the next couple of hours, you come out after her for a moment. That'll tell me what she looks like.

"Sure," Roy said. He smiled, showing dingy teeth. "Once you see her, you won't forget her," he said.

Barbara was still feeling the effects of her contact with Ricky Fuentes. She hadn't been raped, but she felt that she definitely had a better understanding of it.

Now she had a longing to do something innocent and pure. To visit a zoo, go to church and say a prayer, go to a movie. Visit Joe.

But she knew she couldn't. She had to live the life until the job was done.

Today she planned to buy another dealer-design dress. She had seen one in a shop in Manhattan that was perfect.

As she walked down the block adjacent to her building, she had a nice thought: When the job was over she would put all the stuff she had bought in a pile and burn it.

She crossed the street, glanced back at the building, and noticed that Roy had come out. She didn't give it a second thought.

She hailed a cab—drug dealers never walked anywhere—and headed into the city.

McKenna had positioned himself two blocks away
and down the block from her building and had photographed her with a 35mm camera equipped with a 400mm
lens. That night he developed and printed eight-by-ten
black-and-white pictures in the darkroom in the basement
of his home.

After drying the prints, he examined them.

She was, as they used to say, "some dish."

As a matter of course, McKenna would show the
picture to the Fuentes to make sure he had the right
subject. Once when he was a detective they had made a
mistake like that.

He looked at her face, which he had blown up.

She was beautiful. No question. More than that, though,
she looked slightly familiar.

Where had he seen her before?

He let associations kind of wash in on him. But he
could not come up with anything. The only word he
came up with was *famous*. She looked like someone famous. That probably was why she looked familiar.

The following day, McKenna got the reports.

The BCI was negative. If she had a sheet, it was
somewhere else.

She had nothing in Los Angeles, but one thing did turn
up: She had a California license that was due to expire in
January. It listed her address as 2605 Wilshire Boulevard.

His LA contact gave McKenna the Social Security
number, but McKenna's Social Security contact turned
out to be on vacation. He would have to check that out
next week.

McKenna decided not to follow her. If there had been
a hint of something amiss, he would have. But following
her involved at least two other people, and would have
to be done very carefully.

If she were a cop she might be able to smell a tail.
Cops, McKenna knew, were all paranoid.

But he still wanted to get closer to her, further inside
her life than he was. And he knew how to do it.

CHAPTER 60

McKenna was home when he received the call from Miguel Fuentes, and it only took him twenty minutes to get to Barbara's apartment. He could toss her place at leisure because Ricky would keep her out until at lesat twelve.

McKenna waited in Queens Boulevard, which was on the opposite side of the guard's station, for someone to come in or out of the underground garage which had an electronic door.

He didn't have to wait long. It was Saturday night, and many people were heading out for a night on the town. Anyway, he always thought it was a perfect day to toss a place. No one broke into your apartment on Saturday night.

Three minutes after he started waiting, the door lifted and a black BMW driven by a man who appeared to be in his forties exited. McKenna slipped into the garage before the door closed.

He waited another few minutes until someone drove into the garage—a couple—parked their car, and headed for a door which, he knew, led to the elevators. He joined them, a cherubic smile on his Irish face.

The night guard, watching the garage-level elevators via closed-circuit TV, would, McKenna hoped, assume he was with the couple. Which, in fact, the guard did.

He rode the elevator up. The couple got off at the fifth floor. He got off at the sixth, stepped into an empty hall, and found his way to apartment 6D.

He rang the bell a few times, and after a minute, when no one responded, he picked his way into the apartment fairly quickly. He closed and locked the door behind him.

He took off the light sport jacket he was wearing and hung it on the front doorknob. Then he commenced to toss the place.

He did the job slowly, methodically, a craftsman with long experience at his work. In the living room, in addition to turning the furniture practically inside out, he shook out the magazines lying casually on a glass coffee table, he checked under the bases of two heavy chrome lamps for signs the bottoms were removable, he examined the patio from inside the living room for signs of something hidden.

Frequently he used a penlight to peer down drains or into dark corners.

He went through all pockets and linings of the clothes Barbara had. She didn't have that many, he thought, but he thought also that they had a certain glittery flavor favored by pimps, proses, drug dealers, and the like.

It took him forty minutes to work almost all the way through the apartment, though it was only three rooms. And, overweight as he was, he was sweating freely at the end of that time.

As he went, he formed an opinion of Barbara. She looked like the real thing.

He was almost finished when he found the ring taped to the back of a bureau beneath a lip, so that no one could see it just by looking down between the bureau and the wall.

Very carefully, noting its position—as he did whenever he moved something in a search—he pulled the bureau away from the wall six inches, then went down on his haunches, carefully peeled the tape back, and picked the ring off.

He stood up and looked at it.

A diamond engagement ring, medium-sized.

A couple of thoughts occurred to him. For one thing, she could be hiding it against a burglary. For another, she might be engaged and was trying to hide it. But why? McKenna had no idea.

Then, as he looked at it, grasped between thumb and forefinger, the light playing off its facets, he had another thought that set off a tiny alarm bell in him: The ring was simply out of keeping with her apartment and the rest of her possessions. It was not a cheap ring. It didn't have that certain glitzy feel that all the other things did.

He could go no further with the idea. He did not really know what it meant. He would tell Fuentes about it.

Carefully, he retaped the ring in the same position it had been in and then moved the bureau back to its original position.

Five minutes later, after rinsing his sweaty face in the bathroom, McKenna left the apartment.

As the evening wore on with Ricky Fuentes, Barbara found herself smiling a lot to cover up what she was feeling inside. She was worried. All night he had been coming on very strong, and she knew that tonight he was going to try to bed her. How could she turn him away?

At around one o'clock, just after he had told her a story about how he had four girlfriends when he was an eleven-year-old in Santo Domingo, Barbara excused herself. If she was going to spring something, she thought, she had better take the initiative.

They were in a disco, the Maximum.

Barbara went to the ladies' room and stayed in one of the stalls a long time. She knew that what she was about to do would set their relationship on an inevitable course. Still, tonight was tonight—you had to survive one day at a time—and she would think about the next time before she got into it.

She left the bathroom and returned to the table. As she approached him, and saw the smile plastered on his arrogant little face, she knew that she would enjoy what she was about to tell him.

She sat down, a morose look on her face. "Can you take me home, Ricky?"

"How come?"

"I just got my fucking period."

The smile disappeared. "Yeah? So what?"

"I don't have fun when I'm this way."

Ricky looked at her. For maybe the first time since she had been dealing with him she got the feeling that she was looking directly into his soul. And it was scary. This was the guy who could shoot babies in the head.

The face suddenly smiled. "Hey," he said, "you don't know what you're missing."

At home, Barbara stood by the terrace and looked at the lights of Manhattan. A deep sense of loneliness gripped her. Maybe Joe was right. Maybe she wasn't cut out for this. You were either tense or angry or sad or lonely—or you felt dirty.

She went into the bedroom and sat on her bed.

She couldn't call him when she was like this. It would only upset him.

She undressed and took a long, hot shower. Joe was on her mind, and then Jeff. The good things that had happened in her life.

She wished one of them were here now. She felt so frail and weak. So vulnerable. She wondered, at one point, just how long she could keep the charade up, play along with this little psychopath. Not too long. Two minutes, she thought, ha-ha.

It was time for her security blanket.

She went back into the bedroom, put on a nightgown, and went over to the dresser. She knelt down to grab the ring and felt a sudden cold gripping sensation.

The bureau had been moved. She knew it because, though the front legs were in proper position on the carpet as they always were, the bureau had been pulled forward; Barbara could see the slight marks on the wood flooring not covered with carpet.

Quickly, feeling a sense of urgency, she checked the drawers, the closets—everything—and five minutes later, a light sweat on her face, she was sitting on the bed wondering just what it meant. It was not, she decided, the kind of thing she was going to wonder about alone.

CHAPTER 61

Barbara called Frankie Pinto at his home in Kings Park, Long Island, the next morning at about seven o'clock, and told him what she had discovered.

"I think we should get together on this," he said. "I'm going to tell Joe, too."

They set a meeting for early that afternoon at Roach's Bar, which was across the street from the Mineola, Long Island, railroad station.

"You have to assume you're being followed," Frankie said.

"Okay," Barbara said.

Barbara left for the meeting at around twelve o'clock. She wanted to give herself at least an hour to shake anyone who might be tailing her.

She left by the front entrance, grabbed a cab, and had it drive normally to Penn station in Manhattan. She exited the cab in the crush of trafic on Eighth Avenue, then spent twenty minutes wandering around Penn Station in a cicuitous way.

When she stepped on the train she was sure she wasn't being followed.

The train was a little late, and Barbara entered the bar about ten minutes after two.

It was narrow, a typical neighborhood place, with a mahogany bar—a drinker's bar.

There were only a few people at the bar itself, but

there was an area in the back with tables covered with red-and-white checked cloths.

Frankie and Joe Lawless were sitting at one of the tables.

It had been four weeks now since she had seen him, and the sight of his weathered face with those beautiful blue eyes made her go all hollow and fluttery inside, and then she felt filled up with warmth. So good. It was just so good to be with people who cared about her.

As carried away as she was, she could tell Lawless was taken aback too.

"Hi, Frankie," she said, and then went around and kissed Lawless on the mouth for a long time.

"And how are you?" she asked.

"I'm fine."

Barbara sat down next to Lawless. Frankie went to the bar to get her a glass of wine. While he was gone Barbara said, "Take me away with you!"

"Tell me about it," Lawless said.

Frankie returned with the drink. He was drinking Perrier, Lawless light beer.

Frankie sipped the Perrier. "Do you," he said, getting right into it, "have any idea who moved the bureau?"

Barbara shook her head.

"And nothing else was disturbed?"

"Not that I could tell."

They drank in silence a moment.

"Has their attitude toward you changed lately?" Frankie asked.

"No," Barbara said. "Miguel is paranoid—though probably less so than before I faked the rip-off—and Ricky is . . . Ricky."

Frankie nodded.

"I don't like it," he said after a while. "It seems to be beyond normal paranoia. Maybe not, but my instincts tell me to watch out."

Barbara took a deep breath.

Lawless looked at Frankie, his eyes flat. "What do you think we should do? Close it down?"

Frankie's eyes had been on Lawless. They flicked to Barbara.

"That's up to Barbara and what chance she thinks she has of getting an admission this early in the game. And, of course, whether you think it's worth the risk, if any. I mean, if they suspect you bad, you'd be going into a hornet's nest."

"I'm not going to ask either of you what you think," she said. "I think this should be my decision.

"To be flat-out honest," she continued, "I'm ready to close it down. This Ricky is coming on real strong, and I'll tell you truly, I'm leading him on and then fighting him off. It's making me feel like . . . Christ . . . a bar rag. And I'll tell you, I don't know how long you could keep this guy off without him trying to take matters into his own hands."

Frankie looked at her. He nodded.

"But I think it's worth trying to get an admission the next time I see him. If I went in there and I smelled something bad, I'd get out."

"It could get hairy," Frankie said.

"It could, but we're assuming they have a very definite idea I'm undercover. They may not. Probably don't. I don't know. I'd like to try."

Frankie nodded. Lawless looked at her. He said nothing.

"The question," Frankie said, "is how. Transmitter or recorder?"

"I'm for the recorder," Barbara said. "It goes with me wherever he goes. We'll just have to hide it well."

"Inside the leg is best," Frankie said. "I'll give you the name of a female UC who'll give you the details."

Barbara nodded.

"Of course," Frankie continued "the best place to record, is where there's no background sound, like TV, radio, records."

"I'll try to get him to my place, though if they suspect me that may not be easy. In fact, he may not even want to go anywhere with me."

Lawless said, "How would you get an admission from him? If he suspects you, he won't say anything. Even if he doesn't it would be hard."

"Yeah," Barbara said, "but I have an idea which is based on his machismo and might work."

She explained it to them briefly.

"I think it's got a good shot," Frankie said.

Lawless nodded.

They finished their drinks and Frankie got another round.

"What we got to work out now," he said, "is what you do if and when you get the admission."

"Basically," Barbara said, "what I was thinking was to get the hell away from him as soon as I could."

"You got it." Frankie smiled.

Later, after they worked out the details, Frankie took a train east toward Kings Park and Lawless and Barbara drove to Queens in his car.

They didn't talk much. Just being with each other was enough. Or maybe it went further than that. Maybe they were afraid to talk, afraid to let go until this thing was over. They were like soldiers in a trench, waiting for dawn and the attack. They didn't dare think of the past, or of the future. The best way to stay alive was to think only of the moment.

Lawless drove her to within five blocks of her house, then kissed her good-bye and let her out.

She came around to the driver's side window and kissed him good-bye.

"I'll be all right," she said.

Lawless nodded. Something screamed inside him to tell her: Don't go.

"Okay," he said.

Then she turned and was gone. It was almost dark, and as she walked she became more and more difficult to see. Then she stopped, turned and waved good-bye, and vanished in the darkness.

Just like Frankie Pinto did that night. A street animal. Christ, he hoped so.

CHAPTER 62

Frank Piccolo looked down into the courtyard of the building he lived in. It had been ten days since Bender had escaped. There had been no progress in the DA's office. They would be able, Spagnoli said, to indict and convict everyone they arrested, but there was no way to Fishman. Bender was the bridge, and he was gone.

Piccolo turned from the window and went back into the center of the living room. Edmunton was staring at the TV.

"Ed," he said. "Got to tell you something."

Edmunton looked at him.

"Fishman ain't going to walk away from this."

"What have you got, Frank?"

"An idea: that Fishman ain't going to walk."

For a moment, Edmunton didn't know what Piccolo meant. Then he did. Just that: Piccolo had decided that Fishman would not walk from the charges. He was going down.

"I'm going to do something," Piccolo said, "that could get kind of risky, see? And I just wanted to tell you I understand why you wouldn't go with me."

"What's at risk?"

"Your job. What I'm going to do could flush it."

Edmunton felt a tightness in his stomach. To him, as to most cops, the job was everything, an anchor to safety, security, a sense of just who he was.

On the other hand, there was Piccolo. If one thing in

the world of a policeman went higher than the Job, it was his partner. Partners were everything.

"Whatever you do, Frank," Edmunton said, "count me in."

Piccolo nodded. Edmunton thought there was actually a hint of softness in his eyes.

Piccolo told him his plan on the way out to Long Island. It was simple: He was going to ask Fishman something. That was the beginning. Then they would see.

It was a beautiful day, and as they tooled down the narrow wooded sun-dappled road that led to Fishman's house, Piccolo looked over at Edmunton and smiled. "Christ, all the beautiful homes in here. I wonder how many of them are owned by thieves."

Edmunton felt Piccolo's downcast mood lifting. He was going to enjoy this. Edmunton imagined Fishman wouldn't.

Piccolo drove into the turnaround. There was a Porsche, a Mercedes 1500 SL, and a sleek black Jaguar.

He went up to the door and rang the bell. Half a minute later, the door opened and the West Indian butler appeared.

"Yes?"

"We're here to see Mr. Fishhead. Tell him we're here." Piccolo showed his shield.

The West Indian went away, and thirty seconds later Fishman appeared.

"Yes?" He looked pissed off.

"My name is Frank Piccolo. Perhaps you've heard of me. Anyway, I'm here to offer you a deal."

"A deal? On what?"

"On the crimes you have been committing against the elderly of the city."

Did they find Bender? Fishman thought.

"What evidence do you have?" he asked.

"The best," Piccolo said. "We know you're guilty."

Fishman would have laughed full out, but he suppressed it, only half smiling. The little man had a strange glitter in his eyes.

"You know the way out," Fishman said.

"The deal is this," Piccolo said. "I'll talk to Spagnoli in return for your confession."

Fishman started to close the door.

"You made me mad," Piccolo said. "Very mad."

Fifteen seconds later, Fishman watched Piccolo driving his Trans Am out of the turnaround and up the hill so fast that the car fishtailed. The rear wheels spewed rocks.

Fishman did not like it. He felt as if he had been in the presence of something sick.

CHAPTER 63

Haggerty decided to make the calls from his home in Saddle River, New Jersey, rather than from his office. It would be more comfortable, and he would have a place to flop if he had to wait for someone to call back.

Traffic of the George Washington Bridge to Jersey was light, and as he drove he had an unusual feeling, brought on, maybe, by just crossing the bridge, or by the dark look of the Hudson beneath a sky filled with clouds.

He was remembering something: how it was a long, long time ago, when he was maybe ten years old and first realized how much he loved dogs.

That's all it was then, a love of the animal. It was later, he thought, that he became what he became: one of the top dog trainers in America, an actor, a kennel owner, a featured speaker, someone who hobnobbed with the wealthy and famous and had been on a hundred talk shows.

But then it was just him and the dogs. He used to bring them home—just pick up strays—and keep them in an unused garage to hide them from his parents, who had a private house then on Sedgwick Avenue. He remembered that his father had come back there once and found him with nine stray dogs and had said that he had to get rid of them. Haggerty had thought: If they go, I'm going with them.

His father must have seen that in his eyes, because he let him keep the dogs.

Now the years of being noted dog trainer Captain Arthur Haggerty had been stripped away, and it was like he was young again. He felt that same love for the dogs, unfettered and unfiltered by time, and he knew that somehow he had to save them. And sweet Jesus Christ, somehow he would.

He sat down at his desk, took out all the reference and phone books he had, and started calling.

He tried to be logical, calling people who would most likely have an insight into where a convention would be held, but he found himself also calling people other people recommended.

But he also called vets, and police, and other dog trainers, and officials, and dog kennel owners, and guys he knew in various towns who worked on newspapers.

Incredibly, he realized, he went right by lunchtime without eating anything, and his supper consisted of an American cheese sandwich on white bread and a Coke. On other days, that would have been a warm-up for the appetizer.

He didn't eat because he was full. Deep inside was a clock, and it was going, and every time he thought of it he would think of the pit bull fights he had seen on film, and it would spur him on.

And spurring him on, too, was the knowledge that someone, somewhere in America, knew where this fight was being held. All he had to do was find out.

He had two phones, and he left the number of one for calling back on, but by four o'clock in the morning, Eastern Standard Time, no one had.

At five, he set his alarm clock for seven and lay down on the couch. He realized he was very tired when he felt himself drift off to sleep seconds after he had lain down.

At seven, the alarm went off. Or he thought it was the alarm. He awoke blearily and looked at the clock on a table near the couch. Only six-thirty. It was the phone.

He got up, went over to his desk, and picked up on the ninth ring.

"Captain Haggerty speaking." Or, he thought, trying to speak.

"Hello," a female voice said. "My name is Dr. Maureen Ralston. I'm calling from San Angelo, Texas. You left a message with my answering service about the mixed convention."

"Yeah," Haggerty said, instantly awake.

"Well, there was a writer here who I know was working on a story about mixed conventions."

"Really?"

"Yes. He had been all over the country. I thought he might be able to help you. I remember him saying they had one in Austin."

"What's his name?"

"Benno Schmidt." He worked for a German magazine called *Der Spiegel*.

Haggerty got more awake. He had spent a lot of time in Germany and knew all about *Der Spiegel*. It was one of their top publications, on a par with *Time* in America. A writer with *Der Spiegel* would be as tenacious a reporter as you could find.

Haggerty thanked Dr. Ralston, put the phone down, and had a brief memory of his days heading the K-9 Corps in Germany. He remembered how excited he had been as a young man to go to a country that had produced such great working dogs as the boxer, shepherd, and Doberman pinscher . . . and eating currywurst on a brisk autumn day, and the girls . . . God, the girls in Germany. Berlin, that's where he had been, at McNair barracks, and . . .

It was no time for reminiscences now, he thought.

He calculated. It was around twenty to seven. Germany, Berlin was eight hours ahead. If Benno Schmidt was in, he could catch him. He picked up the phone and called the overseas operator. While he waited to be connected, he glanced at the one window in the den. There was daylight outside. If this was the day of the convention, and he had to assume it was . . . he cut the thoughts off.

"Der Spiegel," came the voice across the Atlantic, sounding, not surprisingly, very far away.

In German, Haggarty asked, "Is Herr Schmidt there? Benno Schmidt."

There was a pause. Maybe he's in. Please.

He was.

Haggery identified himself. He assumed Schmidt could speak English, but he knew that speaking someone's native tongue would help him knock down a barrier fast—and he needed that now.

"I'm sorry for speaking gutter German, but that's what I learned when I was there."

"When was that?" Schmidt asked.

Haggerty explained his nine-and-a-half-year hitch in the army. His time in the K-9 corps. Every word was a plea.

"What can I do for you?" Schmidt said.

"We got a problem in New York," Haggerty said, getting the sense that he was understating it badly, and he detailed what had happened. "Now," he concluded, "we think it's going to be held tonight. I've got to know where it is so we can stop it. A vet—a Dr. Ralston in San Angelo, Texas—gave me your name. She said you were doing an article on mixed conventions. I thought maybe you would have a lead, the name of someone who might give me an idea of where it might be."

Haggerty felt the ensuing silence in his belly, the sound of staticky, distant surf. Schmidt knew nothing.

"There is a guy," Schmidt said suddenly, "who might help. His name is Ryan. John Ryan. He used to fight pit bulls, but there was a tragedy that turned him away from them."

"What was that?"

"His youngest boy was mauled to death by a pit bull, and his wife had a hand amputated after trying to save the boy."

"My God."

"Ryan never told anyone what the event did to him. The good old boys that fight the pit bulls think he's still one of them. Ryan wants it that way. It's the way he can do the most good, he says. He gave me tremendous inside information. We got to photograph two mixed conventions, and the story is coming out in our January issue. It's called 'Bloodlust.' "

"Where does he live?"

"A little town in New Hampshire. Center Sandwich."

"Do you have his number?"

"He doesn't have a phone. He lives alone on a farm—he and his wife got divorced. He's a logger and handyman up there."

"Is there any way to reach him?"

"You've got to go to his house, or wherever he might be working. But there's no guarantee he'll talk. It took me four months before he trusted me. But this guy has the contacts, and I think he could help you."

"Well," Haggerty said, "I've got to give it a try."

"I'd like you to contact me after it's all over. Maybe I could do a follow-up."

"Yeah," Haggerty said. And he thought, I hope it has a happy ending.

Haggerty reached Arnold at home. He told him what had happened.

"If I find out where it is, what should I do?" Haggerty asked.

"Just call me here. I'll get some guys together. We'll go out and stop it right away."

"That's great," Haggerty said. "I'm on my way."

"God bless you," Arnold said.

"Good-bye."

Haggerty didn't pack any clothes and didn't shave. He just took a quick shower and left the house, hailed a cab, and told it to head to Newark Airport.

As the cab sped through the streets, the rain that had been threatening all day started to come down. A half hour later Haggerty was sitting in the rear of a 727 climbing through rainy skies toward Boston.

CHAPTER 64

Haggerty was in luck. At Logan Airport in Boston he made a good connection, and half an hour later was on a small plane heading toward Laconia, New Hampshire. A half hour after that the plane landed in Laconia, a flat, lazy, spread-out town surrounded by some of the most beautiful mountains and lakes in America. The weather was clear and because it had been cold for several days there was already color on the countryside. Haggerty couldn't help but remember—now it seemed so appropriate—a cartoon he had seen once where one ghoulish character standing in front of a resplendent autumn scene says to the other: "I love the fall. Everything dies."

He rented a car and was soon driving north on the black roller-coaster roads of New Hampshire.

At another time, he would have appreciated the vast beauty of the mountains. But now they made him feel small, a dot on the universe, and somehow seemed to diminish his chances. That, in turn, only made him more determined to succeed.

He found the town of Center Sandwich and got directions to Middle Road. Ten minutes later, he was on a bumpy dirt road that went through a virtual tunnel of trees, the road only occasionally dappled with sunlight and only occasionally breaking into a clearing on one or the other side where there would be a house.

The clock he was running against seemed to have taken up permanent residence in his stomach, and it

didn't help that it took him twenty minutes before he
found the still narrower, heavily rutted dirt road that led
to Ryan's house.

Ryan was not home, or at least it looked that way.
The house, a white Colonial like most of the other
homes in the vicinity, was set in a cleared area with
spaces for parking vehicles in the front. No one was
there.

He parked in front of the house. He got out, and went
to the front door, and rapped sharply.

C'mon, he thought, be in.

He knocked again.

There was no answer.

He peered in one of the windows. He was looking into
the kitchen. It seemed neat and clean, and there were
definite signs that someone lived there.

Haggerty went back to the car and stood by it.

What now? he thought. What do I do now? All I can
do, he thought, is wait. Wait—and pray that he comes
home.

He inhaled sharply. It was about three o'clock.

At three-thirty, gloom started to settle over Haggerty.
The guy will probably be gone all day, he thought, and
then, being single, why would he come home? He might
have a girlfriend, or go out to eat, or, depending on what
was happening in his life, drink. Who knew?

I need a miracle, Haggerty thought. To get this thing
done I need a goddamn miracle.

The day, which had been bright, now darkened quickly,
matching his mood. Then the wind came hard through
the trees and kicked up swirls of dust. Haggerty felt a
drop of rain on his bald dome, and then more, and he
had to get into the car.

The rain came down with a kind of demented sav-
agery, the like of which he had never seen, he thought,
in his life.

And then he realized: Maybe this was the miracle. If
Ryan was in the woods, this would drive him out, and
maybe, home. And then . . .

Fifteen minutes later, the rainfall had slackened from
demented to merely intense, and Haggerty could see

little out the windows, which were opaque with sheets of water.

But, Jesus, he heard.

From behind him came the throaty growl of a truck. Haggerty got out of the car. Within fifteen seconds he was drenched, but there it was: a big truck, its hopper filled with cords of wood.

A medium-sized man wearing jeans, a khaki rain slicker, and a baseball cap got out of the cab and jumped down.

"Are you John Ryan?" Haggerty yelled above the rain.

The man nodded. He eyed Haggerty.

"Benno Schmidt sent me here," Haggerty said. "I have to talk with you."

"C'mon inside."

They went inside. Haggerty followed Ryan into the kitchen. The table and chairs and other things had a feeling of having been salvaged from somewhere.

"I know you don't know me," Haggerty said, "but I need your help badly, though I don't even know if you can help."

"I know you," Ryan said. "I've seen you on TV."

"Good," Haggerty said. "Then I think you know I care about dogs."

Ryan nodded.

Haggerty explained the situation. Finally, he said, "You're the only hope I've got."

"I heard of Bailey," Ryan said. "A real bad actor."

He paused.

"I'll try to help," he said. "Let me think about it a minute."

He went over to the window and looked out. The sun was out again and in the distance behind Ryan, Haggerty could see the outline of a mountain. Which, he thought, was approximately what he and Arnold had to climb.

Ryan turned. "We'll have to get to a phone. We'll go to Moultonboro."

They stopped at a bank and, Haggerty insisting, got thirty dollars in change. Then they went to a glass-enclosed phone booth near a gas station in Moultonboro, a very small town on Route 25 about five miles from Ryan's home.

Ryan kept the door open as he dialed the number.

Someone answered. The transformation in Ryan was nothing short of amazing. He was effervescent down-home charm itself.

"Hey, Dave," Ryan said. "How you doin'?" Pause. "Good. I'm on my way to New York. I heard they're having a mixed down there that I want to catch. You know where it's goin' to be?"

"Oh," Ryan said after another pause. "I'll try him."

Ryan made three more calls—which finally led to a dead end, of sorts.

"No one knows," he said, coming out of the booth. "The last guy suggested I call Ray Fallon. He fights dogs all the time and lives in the New York area. I did. He's not in. I got his old lady. She said he wouldn't be back till later—I could call later."

"Oh," Haggerty said. "There's nothing else we can do, huh?"

"No, that's about it."

Haggerty called Arnold and told him to stand by. They might not have much of a shot, but whatever it was, they'd try for it.

Ryan called the New York number at seven. Fallon was not in. They were running out of time.

At around eight-thirty, the sun went down.

Ryan went into the booth. He didn't say it, but Haggerty got the feeling that this could be it. He had to learn something now, or not at all.

Haggerty watched Ryan. His face, illuminated by the interior light of the booth, was a study in emptiness. Then it brightened.

"Hey, Ray," Ryan said. "How you doin'? You tryin' to avoid me? Ha-ha."

Pause.

"Yeah, I'm on my way into New York and I heard they was having a mixed. You know where it is?" Haggerty had stopped breathing.

Ryan's eyes flicked to Haggerty.

"Oh, yeah, I think I can still make it. Uh-huh. Let me write this down."

"I see," he continued. "Friends Farms, Plainview Road, Woodbury, Long Island."

He repeated it.

"Hey, Ray, thanks. I'll see you there, I hope, 'Bye."

"He was on his way to the fights and he came back for something. His wife didn't tell him I called. You got the address?"

Haggerty nodded.

"The fights should be starting right now. At dark. In a barn. It's supposed to be the biggest ever held."

Haggerty was on his way into the booth—or as far into it as he could get. He looked at Ryan, and for the first time he saw the terrible sadness in the man's eyes.

"Can you stop it?" Ryan asked.

"I don't know," Haggerty said. "But we do have a shot. I can never thank you enough for that."

Haggerty dialed Arnold's number.

Arnold picked up the phone before the first ring had finished.

"We got the address. The fights are to be held at a place called Friends Farms, Plainview Road, in Woodbury. Got it?"

"Yeah."

"They're scheduled to start now, Arnold, right now. At dark."

"I'm on my way out the door."

"Go!" Haggerty yelled. "Go!"

Then he hung up, and he and Ryan stood in the blackness of the New Hampshire night. Haggerty looked up. The sky was full of stars. Please, he silently said. Please.

CHAPTER 65

One minute after Haggerty called, Arnold, Stewart, and the other two cops were powering east toward Woodbury.

For a moment, as he had come out the door, Arnold had thought about calling the Nassau County Police. Technically, he should have. Woodbury was theirs. But there was no time for that. He figured that if everything went perfectly, they could be in the barn within forty-five minutes. In that time, he knew, some dogs would be hurt, and perhaps die. But he could stop a lot. And he hoped to God he could save Misty.

Chapter 66

The morning sun, filtered by high trees, dappled Morris Fishman's house and glinted off the sleek black Jaguar parked in the turnaround, its shiny surface still beaded with morning dew. Birds chirped; small animals scurried in the surrounding woods; to the east you could see a piece of Long Island Sound twinkling in sunlight.

It was a peaceful, tranquil scene.

And then, quite suddenly, the tranquility was shattered by the sound of three cars pulling down the dirt road leading to Fishman's property, and then coming to a screeching halt in the turnaround, one of them clipping the Jaguar as it did.

Men dressed in work clothes poured out of the cars like clowns from a circus car. Without exception they carried tools, both power and hand: bayonet saws, circular saws, drills, prybars, sledges and regular hammers, drills, ladders, stud finders—they looked like they could stock a small hardware store.

They were led to the door by Frank Piccolo, who was wearing green coveralls and a yellow hard hat and had a bayonet saw in one hand.

Morris Fishman, asleep upstairs with his wife, Renata, opened his eyes when he heard the cars screeching to a halt.

"What was that?" said Renata, jolted from her sleep.

"I don't know."

As Fishman got out of bed he could hear the car doors

slamming. As quickly as he could he went to a window that overlooked the turnaround. He looked down on a horde of people clustered near the front door.

Alarmed, he headed down the sweeping stairway, expecting to hear a rap on the door. He almost stopped in shock as he heard the morning stillness absolutely shattered by the angry snarl of a power tool. Then he saw it: A saw blade was chewing through the door down near the lock. He watched, mesmerized, as a section was cut out, and dropped with a clatter to the floor. A hand reached in and turned the latch, and the door burst open.

The skinny cop, Piccolo, was the man with the saw, and he came into the house, followed by the others, as if Fishman, wasn't there.

The men went quickly and with great purpose to various jobs. Fishman watched Piccolo. He went past the foyer into the living room, where he immediately started to cut through the Sheetrock on the wall closest to the front of the house.

Fishman, his eyes bugging from his head, half staggered to Piccolo.

"What the fuck are you doing?" he cried.

Piccolo turned to him. He smiled broadly, showing missing teeth. Already his dark hair was white with plaster, and, underneath his eyebrows flecked with white, Fishman saw the glazed dark eyes of a madman.

"Remodeling," Piccolo said.

Fishman started for the phone. From every room there seemed to emerge a bedlam of drilling, sawing, prying, ripping, bending, groaning. It was a madhouse filled with madmen.

He dialed the local police and got them right away.

"This is Morris Fishman! Come quickly! They're tearing my house apart!"

He hung up. Upstairs, his wife started to scream. He bolted up the stairs, past busy-as-a-bee workmen in the hall, and into the bedroom. Renata was in the corner. She screamed again. One of the people was in the process of removing the last piece of Sheetrock from one of the walls.

The Laurel Hollow police arrived within five minutes. They entered the house with hands on guns.

As soon as he saw them Piccolo yelled, "Stop!"

The machine noises stopped as if Piccolo had flipped a switch.

Piccolo went up to one of the cops and handed him a piece of paper.

He looked at it.

"What is it?" Fishman yelled.

"A search warrant," the cop said, "for the presence of controlled substances."

"What? That's ridiculous!"

"It's legal, though."

Fishman tried to stop them, but the Laurel Hollow cops left.

"Back to work," Piccolo screamed, and the machines sprang to life.

A half hour later, Piccolo yelled, "Stop!" again. The interior of the house had been, in a word, trashed. All rooms had Sheetrock and ceiling material stripped to the studs and beams. It would take a week just to clean up the mess.

Fishman was standing outside when Piccolo emerged from the house. Slowly, the men started to get into their cars.

"You can't get away with this," Fishman screamed at Piccolo.

Piccolo, his face white with plaster, looked at him, dropped his chin to his neck, and glared up malevolently.

"Listen to me, and listen carefully, you no-good cocksucker of a scumbag asswipe of a shitface humphead shiteating turdball motherfucker. If you don't cop a plea with Spagnoli on the tenant thing, the next time I search your dump I will find the H. You know where? Up your wife's twat!"

Fishman felt the blood drain from his face. He looked over at his wife. Looked over and down. She had fainted.

CHAPTER 67

On Saturday night at around nine o'clock, Barbara Babalino entered the La Hoy Restaurant. The Nagra was strapped to the inside of her left thigh and was going.

She was dressed to focus attention on herself, wearing a tight white dress with slits up the outside and showing a vast expanse of cleavage.

The Fuenteses were in the back of the restaurant as usual. Barbara was half surprised that she couldn't detect any increased suspiciousness. Ricky greeted her like a long-lost buddy, and Miguel actually turned from the television and said hello.

For a moment, she felt a chill. Were they setting her up? No, she decided, they weren't.

She read nothing suspicious in Miguel's face. In Ricky's she read lust.

She opened her pocketbook, aware that the PPK Walther was at the bottom, and took out an envelope.

"Here's the rest of the bread I owe plus ten for another quarter."

Ricky took the money and gave it to Miguel.

"Okay," Ricky said, "I get it for you later. Let's go."

They exited the building and got into the Corvette. Ricky glanced at her as they settled in. Her skirt rode halfway up her thighs, and she kept her left hand on top of her leg, just in case he tried for a nice friendly feel: The Nagra wouldn't thrill him.

"Where we going?" Barbara asked as he pulled out into light traffic.

"My place," he said. "Okay?"

"Sure," Barbara said. "That's fine."

Lawless and Frankie Pinto were in a pickup truck, loaded with barrels, down and across the street. They gave the Corvette a little head start, then followed.

CHAPTER 68

McKenna ate at seven o'clock Saturday night, late for him when he was home. That was because his wife was in Freehold, New Jersey, visiting her sister.

After supper, he went into the living room to watch the Yankee game. He flicked on the TV and went back and spread his bulk over a couch. A show about some Australian animal was on. He would have to wait for the game.

He watched and heard the special without interest or enjoyment. The thing was bothering him again.

Where had he seen this Barbara Russo before?

He had thought, when he gave the report to Miguel, that he was confusing her with someone else. Now, though, he had come to believe that he had seen her before.

Where?

He should have gone to the library while it was open. But now it wasn't, and it would be closed on Sundays for the rest of the summer.

He didn't really want to wait until Monday.

He thought of his son, Terence. He was a stockbroker, but he read a lot of magazines and newspapers. Maybe he had seen her somewhere.

He called him. McKenna thought he might not be in. He had been divorced twice, and he liked the girls. And it was Saturday night.

He was in.

267

"Hey, Tim," he said. "I was wondering if you have any old magazines or newspapers around. I'm trying to make a woman. I think I seen her before."

"I got plenty, but not much time. I'm going out."

"I'll be right over," McKenna said.

He left the house, taking half a dozen eight-by-ten blowups of Barbara Russo.

Fifteen minutes later, McKenna was standing in the modernistically decorated apartment of his son, Terence.

"The magazines are in the closets. So are the papers. Are those the pictures?"

McKenna handed Terence the envelope, and he took them out. He spread them across the couch in the living room.

McKenna had been a cop for fifteen years. As he watched Terence he became aware that Terence was familiar with her to some degree.

Finally he looked up at McKenna.

"I know her," Terence said. "The hair is different. It was black and then blond. Now it's red. But, shit, man, I could never forget those jugs."

"Who is she?"

"That cop," Terence McKenna said, "who got knocked off the force for posing in the nude. Knocked off, and then let back on."

It took McKenna and his son twenty minutes, but they finally found the year-old story of Barbara Russo in one of the afternoon newspapers. There was no mistaking her, McKenna thought. Her real name was Barbara Babalino.

McKenna waited until he got on the street to make the call. Miguel was in.

"I got to see you right away," McKenna said.

"Come on over."

CHAPTER 69

Arnold made it from Freeport to Plainview Road in Woodbury in thirty-five minutes, very fast time indeed. Fortunately, he did not get stopped by the cops who might have gotten alarmed by a car full of men with shotguns.

Jericho Turnpike, most of which was a gruesomely ugly pastiche of neon and gas stations and fast-food places, changed its character near Plainview Road. It became wooded and desolate. Long Island had once been mostly farm country, and this area had remained relatively unscathed.

Arnold turned the car into Plainview Road. It was poorly lit, flanked by farmland or large sweeping grassy areas. The occasional light in the fields accented the sense of desolation.

How, he thought, was he going to find Friends Farms? He had no number. There were no names on anything. There—

There it was. A sign: FRIENDS FARMS, hanging up on a post at the end of a narrow dirt road. He turned up it. He decided to keep his lights on.

No one said anything, but the sounds of the shotgun safetys being released spoke eloquently of what the men were thinking.

It was very dark. There appeared to be a house, but no barn. Then the road took a curve and the barn hove into view, a mansard-roofed building bulking blackly against the night.

It was totally dark, and for a moment Arnold thought the fights had been switched to somewhere else or they had the wrong night or . . .

There was a sliver of light coming from between the doors.

Arnold followed the road around.

Where were the cars? If this was the place, where were the cars?

The answer was on the other side of the barn. There was a virtual sea of cars. Arnold saw one kill its lights. A man got out and with the help of a flashlight made his way to a rear door in the barn.

"Ray," Arnold said to Stewart, "why don't you come with me. Leo too. Roy, will you notify the Nassau police, then come in?"

"Okay," Leo said.

"Let's go," Arnold said.

They got out of the car and started toward the barn.

The detective stopped just outside the door. There was a window, and, although something had been hung over it, through a gap Arnold could still see inside.

It was packed with people, crowded around what had to be the ring. There were lights on poles illuminating the ring; thick smoke tumbled in the light. Behind the poles there were cages and cages filled with dogs of all kinds: pit bulls and shepherds, Dobermans and whatever. Ready for the slaughter.

Something primeval filled Arnold until he was almost quaking with rage.

"Let's go in."

Arnold took the door down with a grinding crunch, and the two detectives followed him in.

Faces turned.

"Everybody freeze. Police!"

Everybody froze.

Arnold's eyes scanned the crowd. He saw Bailey glaring at him. Cautiously, shotguns forward, the cops fanned out. In the distance, Arnold heard the sound of a siren.

Where are you, Misty? Where are you?

Then, suddenly, two of the three lights went out and the barn was plunged into dimness. People started to scurry.

"Freeze!" Arnold screamed.

Some did, but some didn't. Some ran toward the door on the opposite side.

Then Arnold saw Misty. Bailey had her under his arm and was going out through a single door in the far corner of the barn.

Arnold made an animal sound and took off after him, roaring through the crowd, knocking people over like they were bowling pins.

CHAPTER 70

Frankie Pinto and Joe Lawless followed Ricky Fuentes to his apartment building. They watched the car disappear into an underground garage, then parked down the street and watched the building.

"After tonight," Frankie said, "it's over. You get her back."

"How does your wife stand this?" Lawless asked.

"Which one?" Frankie said. "The first one didn't."

"I never knew you were married before."

"Oh, yeah," Frankie said. "It wasn't so great for either of us."

Upstairs, Ricky and Barbara entered his apartment. There was a table set up by the patio door. It was covered with a white tablecloth, and there was a magnum of champagne on ice near it.

"I'm going to have dinner sent up later," he said. "How you like it?"

"Great."

"Drink?"

"Sure," Barbara said. "Tonight I feel like drinking."

"Good. So do I."

Ricky made himself a rum and coke and Barbara a Bloody Mary.

They sipped the drinks by the bar.

Ricky fixed her with a dark look. "So how you feeling tonight?" he said.

272

"I'm fine," Barbara said. "No problem at all."

Ricky Fuentes smiled. "Good," he said. "We going to have a good time tonight."

Barbara nodded. On the way over, she had worked out how she could possibly get the admission. Tell him that she was being harassed by the Mafia. Tell him she had threatened them with the Fuenteses, but that the Mafia—she was going to invent some name—were not bothered. In fact, the guy told Barbara that the Fuenteses were all talk.

If Ricky had enough booze in him he might refer to the Castelli killings as a machismo thing. She could only hope. If not, she would try to work it out some other way.

If it became obvious that she could not get the admission, she would just concentrate on getting out. She knew that tonight was her last night with him, one way or another.

In their surveillance vehicle, Frankie and Lawless watched the street and the building entrance. They did not say much. There wasn't much to say.

One of the streetlights was out, so Frankie almost missed it: a large black Cadillac going into the underground garage.

Lawless could feel him stiffen even before he spoke.

"Hey," he said, "that was Miguel Fuentes' car."

"Yeah."

"What's he doing here?"

Now Lawless regretted that Barbara didn't have a transmitter on.

"I'm not too thrilled with this," Frankie said.

"Shall we go in?"

"No, let's hold it for a bit. Maybe he just dropped by for a minute."

Lawless watched the building. A steel fist had started to close around his insides.

CHAPTER 71

It struck Arnold as odd. Crazy. The one thing that he and Naomi had always tried to do was to cut down on Misty's barking. Now, when he wanted her to bark with all his heart and soul, there was silence.

It was very dark as Arnold made his way through a field with some sort of high plant in it—almost up to his waist. He would never find her. He wished he had a flashlight. He was always forgetting something.

His mind fought against an idea: Maybe Bailey had killed her, maybe—

A bark. Just one. To his left. He stormed that way, and then Bailey stood up, Misty under one arm, his other arm crooked around her neck.

"Take one more step," Bailey said, "and I break her fucking neck."

All his life Arnold Gertz had been tongue-tied at important times. But not now. Not here. Something primitive was actuated, something as basic as defending your cave.

"Let her go," he said, cocking the hammer on the shotgun, "or I'll pull the trigger. You're not getting away, and if she dies, you die with her."

The words spoke to something in Bailey. He let Misty down. She ran over to Arnold, now barking crazily. Arnold advanced, and with his left hand, because he didn't want to kill Bailey, he chopped him to the ground like a dead tree with a single blow.

He picked Misty up. She licked him on the cheeks furiously. His eyes misted.

Stewart ran up.

"The Nassau cops are here. They made a big collar. And there's no real damage. One pit bull was hurt, but we interrupted that. None of the other breeds was hurt."

Arnold nodded. He had to find a phone. To call Naomi.

CHAPTER 72

Miguel Fuentes entered the apartment of his brother Ricky.

He said hello to Barbara, smiling warmly, then to Ricky. Barbara had never seen him so outgoing and friendly.

And she knew in an instant that she was in mortal danger. She sensed it. He was setting her up.

She smiled. Her pocketbook with the Walther PPK was on the couch. She had to get to it.

If there had been a scintilla of doubt, it was confirmed when Miguel started to speak to Ricky—in Spanish. Barbara did not speak Spanish, but she spoke Italian well enough to pick up the drift.

Miguel smiled his way through it all.

"Hey, bro," Miguel said. "Sorry to bother you. But this *putana*, she's a cop. Undercover."

Ricky's brow furrowed slightly. "Sure?"

"Absolutely. McKenna found out. He wasn't wrong about Padilla, and he's not wrong about her."

Barbara stepped close to the couch, seemingly lolling along. But her heart was hammering; Christ, she hoped nothing showed on her face.

"What are you going to do?"

"Let's find out if she's got anything on."

Barbara was only a few feet from the couch. It was now or never. She took a quick nonchalant stride toward it, but Ricky picked up on it, and just as she went for the pocketbook he grabbed her by the hair, pulled her back, and punched her in the head. She saw stars and flopped to the floor on her back.

Ricky produced a wicked gravity knife, flicked it open, and then quickly cut her dress off.

They found the Nagra taped inside her left thigh.

Miguel was relieved.

"It's just a recorder," he said.

Ricky straddled Barbara and slapped her in the face, steadily increasing his rhythm until his brother had to pull him off.

"What we going to do?"

"Ice her," Miguel said. "We got to give a warning."

"But first," Ricky said, "I'm going to fuck her. Okay?"

"Sure. It isn't any fun fucking her when she's dead."

Barbara was strangely calm. It was weird. Calm and afraid at the same time. Stupidly, she thought, I'm an incurable optimist: I'm not dead yet.

CHAPTER 73

On the street, Lawless and Frankie watched the house. It had been about five minutes since Miguel Fuentes had gone into the garage.

Lawless looked up. The Fuentes apartment was nineteen stories up. Lawless could see the balcony.

He looked at the entrance, then at Frankie.

Frankie was blinking, his face expressionless. "I don't like it," he said.

"Neither do I," Lawless said.

They got out of the car and trotted across the street and went through a pair of glass outer doors to a kind of foyer. A doorman came up to the inside door. Lawless showed his shield. The doorman opened the door.

"You have an intercom?" he said.

"No."

Lawless went past him. He did not want anyone calling up ahead of him.

The elevator was waiting on the lobby floor. They got in and it rose.

Ricky Fuentes had taken Barbara into a bedroom. Miguel waited in the living room.

Barbara was naked except for her bra and panties. There was a red welt on her leg where Ricky had pulled off the recorder.

"So you a cop, huh?" Ricky said. "Make believe you like me, huh? You a smart bitch. But not that smart, huh?"

He stripped off his pants, folded them neatly, and put them across a dresser.

She had no chance, Barbara thought. There were two against her. Her gun was in the living room, and Miguel was there. Ricky had a knife.

Joe and Frankie were downstairs. They would have no idea what was going on. She was dead.

She knew, of course, thinking that, that she would not die without a fight. That could never be. For herself, for Jeff, for Joe, for everyone. She would not die like that.

She whimpered, put her face in her hands, took a short, slow step toward Ricky Fuentes, and then kicked him in the balls, her high heel practically entering the scrotal cavity.

He went down without a sound, and she took three quick steps, closed the bedroom door, and jammed a nearby chair under the doorknob.

Outside, Miguel had no inkling of what was going on until he saw the door being closed—by Barbara.

He pulled his 9mm and rushed over. But it was too late. The door was shut.

Inside, Barbara frisked Ricky, who was in the process of vomiting. There was no gun. She picked up the knife. She heard Miguel at the door. She did not know what to do next.

Then she did what came naturally: She started to scream, and as loud as she could.

Miguel pounded against the door. He couldn't use his gun, but if he could just get inside . . .

Lawless and Frankie had tried the front door to the Fuentes apartment: It was locked. All they had heard inside was talking.

They did not want to try to get in directly. Things might go wrong.

Then Lawless had an idea. From the street, the balcony of the adjoining apartment appeared to be pretty close. He could get onto there, jump across, and enter through the terrace doors.

They rang the bell. A young man answered. They showed their shields and entered.

"Why don't you go into another room," Lawless said.

The young man, wide-eyed, disappeared.

They opened the terrace doors. It was like a signal. Then they heard the pounding, and then, suddenly, Barbara's screaming.

"Let me go, Joe," Frankie said.

"No," Lawless said. There was no time for explanation.

On the terrace, he saw that the two terraces were not as close as he had thought. But it was only a detail. He pulled his gun, got up on the railing, and leaped across, nineteen stories of air beneath him. He landed on the balcony and did not pause: He shouldered his way through.

Miguel Fuentes had succeeded in getting the door open about six inches.

He raised the gun toward Lawless, but by the time he almost got it up he had three slugs in him. The last went through the right ventricle of his heart.

Lawless, aware of Frankie behind him, rushed to the door.

Barbara had stopped screaming.

"Barbara, it's me."

It took her a minute or so to get the door open. Lawless entered. Ricky Fuentes was still on the floor, holding his testicles, which had swollen to the size of oranges.

Barbara, still dressed in bra and panties and high heels, looked at Lawless. Her face was raw.

She smiled. "No more fucking undercover for me," she said.

And then she started to cry, and Lawless went up to her and put his arms around her. She cried in great heaving sobs, and Lawless felt tears run down his own face.

CHAPTER 74

Spagnoli was not really surprised when Fishman came forward to cop a plea. It was that or Piccolo. It was a clear choice.

They worked out a deal where Fishman would not do any time, but would pay upward of $2 million in fines. He would also make restitution and rerent apartments, where possible, to people who had been driven out.

Piccolo didn't like it.

"This fuck should do a bit," he said. "Give me more time with him and he'll look forward to the fuckin' electric chair."

After a while, though, he calmed down, particularly when he saw that Fishman was not happy with the sentence.

"Well," Piccolo said philosophically to Edmunton one day after the plea was worked out, "at least it will warn away some of these other humps. But the next time we're not going to be so lenient."

It worked out for Arnold Gertz.

The Nassau County PD was glad to make the collars—forty-four in all. It warmed the hearts of the Nassau brass because it warmed the hearts of animal lovers everywhere.

The NCPD neglected to mention that Arnold was off base in Woodbury. They explained it as a joint operation.

Bledsoe was furious with Arnold for not letting him in

on the raid, but he grew less angry when Arnold again got public praise for his work.

For his part, Arnold knew that Misty's barking would never bother him again.

The tape was recovered intact. Frankie Pinto got it, and began the job of hunting down the ''McKenna'' mentioned.

The slapping around that Ricky Fuentes had given to Barbara did not cause any problems or leave any marks. Fuentes, however, ended up in the prison ward at Bellevue. Word was that whoever had injured him could look forward to a long career as a field-goal kicker.

Inside, though, was another story. She and Lawless talked about it, and gradually she started to feel the overpowering sense of being soiled go away.

Then, one day, three weeks after the shootout had occurred, Barbara made a request of Lawless, and he understood. She wanted to go to the zoo.

''My folks took me there when I was a kid,'' she explained, ''and it has a big appeal for me now.''

They went to the Bronx Zoo on a Thursday morning and spent four hours there.

At one point, a short while before they left, they were down by the sea lion pond. Barbara saw a couple of young kids, a boy and girl, near the fence. She went over to them. Lawless followed, but stood back.

''Having a good time?'' she asked.

''Oh, yeah,'' the little boy said. ''The seals are funny.''

''And shiny,'' added the little girl.

''Yes,'' Barbara said. ''You have a good time.''

Then she turned toward Lawless. He had never seen her so beautiful. Her dark eyes were moist.

She came up to him, took his hand, and squeezed it. ''I'll be all right,'' she said. ''I'm going to be fine.''

Lawless's heart swelled with love.